I0554068

It was bad enough that Finn's mentor was missing, but now the government was accusing Finn...

Even Agent Finch, the driver, seemed rattled. He eased off the accelerator and held the wheel steady with both hands for the first time since leaving the nation's capital.

"The facts that we have, Doctor, are sparse. The chair of the physics department went to his office and discovered the final exam printed and ready for presentation, with no trace of the professor. After searching Hayhurst's office, he searched his lab and your lab, Professor McGee. Hayhurst was not there, but machinery was left on and unattended. Worse, there was blood spattered on some of the equipment and on the wall and ceiling of the opposite end of the room. Forensics is investigating now, and their conclusions are pending, but there is no question that Professor Hayhurst is missing. With the additional evidence pointing to some foul play and no corpse, we have concluded that the professor is lost or abducted. Central Intelligence asked us to bring you there for assistance after interrogating you. Initially, you were suspect in this matter. Now that seems to me less likely."

Finn was genuinely disturbed by Finch's summary. "Why," he asked, "would I have been considered suspect at all?"

Becker barged into the conversation. "Easy call, McGee. You are an expert on the Greek scientist Archimedes, right?"

"Yes."

"Didn't Archimedes write a treatise on spirals?

"Yes," Finn said anxiously. "But what does that have to do with implicating me?"

"The blood spatter on the wall, Doc, was in the shape of a spiral."

Driven by the need to discover Truth, Dr. Finn McGee uncovers a secret, hidden in Time, that catapulted the Roman Empire to find Archimedes. Hunted by the government, haunted by his past, and driven by passion, Finn must risk all and travel back through the vortex of Time to encounter mankind's greatest mystery.

KUDOS for *Archimedes' Claw*

A solid first novel; hooks one from the initial paragraph. Mystically transports the reader in time to the past, present, and future while stretching imagination limits. Fast-paced twists and turns abound in this ultimate passionate journey of love. Smooth prose descriptions provide an additional special gift for the booklover. Delicately combines history, science, and ethics in a mixing bowl of intrigue with exquisite results. An enchanting read. ~ *Robert Manniello, columnist and freelance journalist*, Orange County Register/Capistrano Valley News

In Archimedes' Claw by Theodore Morrison Homa, Finn McGee is a scientist who discovers time travel almost by accident. Of course this is a very important discovery and Big Brother Government wants to use it as a weapon. The story encompasses at lot of different and complex situations, everything from life in ancient, war-torn Syracuse, Jesus's crucifixion and resurrection, to man's first time on the moon. The plot is strong, the story well-thought out and well written. The author did his homework and the Archimedes' Claw has a solid ring of truth. ~ *Taylor Jones, Reviewer*

There's a lot to like about Archimedes' Claw, from its authentic portrayal of ancient cultures as well as modern-day government corruption. The book has a strong plot with numerous twists and turns that keep you both guessing and on the edge of your seat. The story is very complex and complicated. This is a book you will want to read more than once in order to catch things you missed the first time. ~ *Regan Murphy, Reviewer*

ACKNOWLEDGEMENTS

Special thanks to Robert Manniello MD for his patient assistance and technical advice.

Special thanks to my special New Order Franciscan friar for his innumerable contributions to the content and the cover design.

Special thanks to Natalie Gargano M.A. Ed and Henry V. Bender Ph.D. for historical oversight and Latin translations.

Special thanks to Kathy my committed proof reader

ARCHIMEDES' CLAW

Time Traveler's Edition

Theodore Morrison Homa, MD

A Black Opal Books Publication

GENRE: SCIENCE FICTION/TIME TRAVEL/PARANORMAL THRILL-
ER

This is a work of fiction. Names, places, characters and incidents are either
the product of the author's imagination or are used fictitiously, and any re-
semblance to any actual persons, living or dead, businesses, organizations,
events or locales is entirely coincidental. All trademarks, service marks,
registered trademarks, and registered service marks are the property of their
respective owners and are used herein for identification purposes only. The
publisher does not have any control over or assume any responsibility for
author or third-party websites or their contents.

ARCHIMEDES' CLAW ~ Time Traveler's Edition
Copyright © 2011 by Theodore Morrison Homa, MD
Cover Design by Rev. Patrick Magee F.L.H. F.
All cover art copyright © 2014
All Rights Reserved
Print ISBN: 978-1-626941-76-2

First Publication: SEPTEMBER 2014

All rights reserved under the International and Pan-American Copyright
Conventions. No part of this book may be reproduced or transmitted in any
form or by any means, electronic or mechanical, including photocopying,
recording, or by any information storage and retrieval system, without permission in writing from the publisher.

**WARNING: The unauthorized reproduction or distribution of this cop-
yrighted work is illegal. Criminal copyright infringement, including
infringement without monetary gain, is investigated by the FBI and is
punishable by up to 5 years in federal prison and a fine of $250,000.**

ABOUT THE PRINT VERSION: If you purchased a print version of this
book without a cover, you should be aware that the book is stolen property.
It was reported as "unsold and destroyed" to the publisher, and neither the
author nor the publisher has received any payment for this "stripped book."

IF YOU FIND AN EBOOK OR PRINT VERSION OF THIS BOOK BE-
ING SOLD OR SHARED ILLEGALLY, PLEASE REPORT IT TO:
lpn@blackopalbooks.com

Published by Black Opal Books **http://www.blackopalbooks.com**

DEDICATION

This book is dedicated to mulligan, which is the name you use when you achieve a less than desirable first golf shot. With mulligan, you get to have another chance to hit the ball, believing that the first shot didn't count at all.

CONTENTS

IMPORTANT DETAILS

Artemis Festival ~ in the Greek calendar, the date of the Artemis festival would be September sixth in the modern calendar.

First Cohort ~ the largest cohort in a legion, consisting of 800 infantry soldiers

Greek Calendar ~ the Greek Calendar begins with its new year on the first full moon after the vernal equinox

Legion ~ a military unit consisting of a minimum of 4,800 infantry soldiers.

Primus Pilus ~ commander of the first cohort.

Sestarces ~ the unit of currency used by the Romans

The Gathering Song ~ Based on Veni, Veni, Emmanuel-Alonso, adapted by Tony Alonso.

The Statue of Liberty – the statue is made of a sheathing of pure copper, hung on a framework of steel, with the exception of the flame of the torch, which is coated in gold leaf (originally made of copper and later altered to hold glass panes). It stands atop a rectangular stonework pedestal with a foundation in the shape of an irregular eleven-pointed star. The statue is 151 ft. (46 m) tall, but with the pedestal and foundation, it is 305 ft. (93 m) tall. (Wikipedia)

Author's Note

Deciding to write this story as a novel crystallized in my mind on a cool night in August on Cape Cod. My friend Henry, professor of humanities at The Hill School in Pennsylvania, had just lifted his glass in toasting my sixty-fourth birthday. True to his nature, he chose not to let the moment lay without some dramatic pontification of his most recent opinion as to origins of this or that clue usually found in some classical manuscript or work of art. The theme for the night was centered on the right lower corner of the famous Raphael painting titled *The School of Athens*. Henry explained the power of concentration demonstrated by Archimedes as he focused on geometric symbols drawn on slate, even as he was about to be murdered within minutes.

Such a classical moment, I thought, could not be wasted or hidden in a museum. I found myself compelled to research the historical meaning of such an event, and dissatisfied with available history written on the subject, I decided to write my own. Thus, this novel generated in my mind. It is what I prefer to have been the truth behind Archimedes' murder and mysteries. The historical facts are real, but the fantasy behind them is my creation. To those of you who helped me write this, and you know who you are, I am grateful for your patient input and sharing so that I could construct my characters. Except for Archimedes and Marcellus, none of the characters in this book are real. The others are my creations, using bits and pieces of observations and experiences.

PROLOGUE

212 BC, fourth day of the third month of the Greek calendar, Syracuse:

Timber cracked in the light of the hot sun as it moved slowly into the southwestern sky. Ripping noises cried from the sails as they tore away from the support lines under the entire weight of the ship as it was tossed onto its side. A large metallic claw pulled tightly against the side of the ship as it went over, one metal spike piercing the armor and the tunic of the Roman soldier standing watch on the deck. Now the soldier was affixed to the deck, his tunic oozing red, making the slippery wood even slipperier as he exsanguinated. The horror was instantaneously real. The remaining soldiers and sailors screamed out warnings before their breathing was stopped by the inrushing water that would end most of their lives within minutes. The sky was now to the left and the sea climbing to where up used to be. The salt air turned to salt water, and all was cold, wet, silent, and bloody.

A wooden barrel brushed by a drowning soldier's flailing arms. Philip hugged it to his body reflexively. Many ships burst into flames from concentrated rays of sunshine, marking the harbor with the sight of choking black smoke and the stench of burning flesh. He remembered those sailors leaving the ships in smaller craft, seeking refuge in the remains of the Roman fleet. He remembered the rage and helplessness, the faces of his dying comrades, the face of his beloved brother, also a Roman soldier, dying from the wound in his chest, which gaped apart as blood poured from his very heart. More scenes of horror became a streaming vision from which he felt more removed. He endured bravely each infinite moment of his anticipated death. Visions came of large hooks traveling through the sky from the shore, trailing heavy brown chains and grabbing the ships almost out of the water and onto their sides. With magic weapons, the Greek forces kept the mighty Roman fleet and army in check as the long siege of Syracuse was waged at the order of the great commander Marcus Claudius Marcellus.

Philip thought of the wage he earned. Twelve thousand sesterces a year made for a decent living, but it was a hard life being a legionnaire loyal to Marcellus. He reflected on Marcellus's order to capture the one they called the natural philosopher, who invented the dark weapons, the magician who was responsible. Philip wondered why Marcellus wanted the man alive.

As he was pushed deeper into the cold sea, the desperate pain of breathing faded, and consciousness ebbed from the body of the soldier. Life floated out of him like the tide, slowly, deliberately. Now tranquility rose from desperation, and Philip could see the hot sun of the last day he lived. There were flames coming as if from soundless lightning, scorching stretched sails into blazing fires. As his consciousness faded to black, he thought of only one thing: vengeance—then nothing.

ഇരുഇ

Philip became aware of lying in shallow salty water. Coughing and choking and burning pain in his lungs were a modest distraction from the shivering body that lay on the cold, wet, rocky shore. He explored his body with his free arm, the one not hooked to the wooden barrel by his cloak. Each movement was slow and rigid from pain and the uncontrollable shivering of his muscles. Bladder painfully distended, he relieved himself in spite of his garments and momentarily felt the warmth of the urine replacing the frigid sea. Working to free the coat and his right arm from the barrel warmed him as well, and slowly he realized he could pull himself up onto the rocks and out of the water.

It was dark, and the moonless sky filled with bright stars gave him only a glimpse of his resting place. Lying at the base of a great wall, he found himself on a narrow path of rocks, well-worn from the sandaled feet of fishermen and merchants who had traded on the shores of the Syracuse harbor in safer times. Looking around, he spotted a manger freshly filled with straw but abandoned before it could be fed to an ass. Drawing his cold body up with painful effort, he used his hands to rake straw out of the manger, spreading it on the ground by the wall. Taking off his wet garments, he draped them over the top of the manger and down the sides to dry. Wearing only his sandals and clinging to his sword, Philip climbed naked into the straw. Under the manger, he used his sandals for a headrest and kept one hand on the weapon. Bending himself into the position of a newborn baby sleeping at his mother's side, he covered himself with as much straw as possible. Using the city wall and the manger strewn with wet clothes for shelter, with straw for a blanket, Philip thought about sleep. He wished for the company of a stray dog to lie with him and share its warmth. Thirst and hunger would have to wait until morning. The Ro-

man legion had taught him to deal with that. The legionnaire known as Philip closed his eyes for the second time
that night, with the same passion for vengeance, but this
time knowing he would live to extract it from the magician.

೧∽೧

Fifth day of the third month of the Greek calendar:

The stink of rotting fish awakened him. Irritated,
abraded skin itched and tormented him. The buzzing of
flies deafened him as he lay under the straw on wet, slimy
stones. Peering out through the straw and the cloak he
had hung from the manger, he saw the cautious begin-
nings of day in the life of fishermen beleaguered by the
siege of the Roman navy. Warily, they brought their nets
from their morning catch to the merchants who also, with
great caution and under the ever-watchful eye of Roman
sailors, began to conduct the business of the day carefully. Appearing fearful and ready to break into a run at the
first sign of a threat from the anchored Roman fleet, the
merchants and the fishermen began to barter.

Philip was tempted to return to the safety of the
nearby ships. He glanced quickly at the nearest vessel,
and a wistful hope for safety rose in his spirit. In a single
beat of his heart, it was crushed with the desire for revenge. He watched with great patience as he endured his
hiding place, surveying the path along the harbor's edge
and the city wall for opportunity. The chance to escape
unnoticed into the city toyed with his soul. He lay and
waited, thirst and hunger put at bay by fear and instinct,
with the help of the foul stench from the fishermen's nets.
He was weak but not dangerously so. He could afford to
wait for the moment he knew would come.

The gods were with him, for an idea formed in his head. A cart full of straw drawn by asses approached his manger-hut. The driver walked by the cart, whipping the animals to take each step. As it came closer, the purpose was obvious. It was bringing a load of straw for the manger, and it stopped next to it, obscuring his presence. The load of straw was lifted with a pole and pushed into the wooden frame above Philip's head. He dared to move slowly at first, and then realizing that the cart was meant to haul away fish for a merchant, he tossed his clothes and sword up into the truck, pushing his naked body after them. Pressing his body into the bottom of the cart, he hoped not to be discovered. Two muscle-bound half-naked fishermen hoisted the contents of their net on top, concealing him under a load of writhing fresh fish. The cart began to move with its new cargo toward an unknown destination, hopefully to a place where he could find temporary safety before finishing his gruesome plan.

By the time the truckload of fish came to a stop, he had retreated into his memories. Philip was suddenly aware of the sound of water being drawn up into buckets. Then, as the merchant poured the water on top of the load of fish, it found its way to his bare skin and chilled him once more. The cart wobbled along the rough road for another hour or more before it turned abruptly off the cobblestone and onto a dirt path headed away from the walls of the city. He could hear in the distance the sounds of a market and knew that soon he would be discovered. He prepared mentally for the fight that would likely follow and considered his chances of escape.

Just then, the cart upended and spilled the fish and the naked man out on a grassy lawn in the middle of a crowd of shoppers from the city of Syracuse. Hysterical laughter broke out as the shoppers stared at the man who made no effort to cover himself, fearing that the crowd would recognize the tunic and cloak of a Roman soldier if he did. He was naked but free, and the laughs and torments of the teasing crowd soon turned into more serious thoughts about buying food for their families. He casually rolled his tunic into a bulky loincloth and joined other workers in the loading of fish and fruits and vegetables on the tables under nearby tents. Impersonating a native of the island was an easy transition for him, and he thanked the gods again for his deliverance to anonymity.

From the market where he worked all day without being questioned, he studied the land. Wildflowers were in bloom, characteristic of early autumn in Carthage. In the distant hills were the pink, gray, and green branches of groves of almond trees laden with fruit. The city itself was fortified with stone walls to a height of forty feet, and wooden doors or gates to the city were placed periodically. Merchants and soldiers came and went as if the Roman army and navy were hundreds of miles away and not menacingly close in the harbor. He saw tall towers with shining, reflecting objects that caught the sun's light and scattered it. He believed these were the magician's tools used to set fire to the ships of the fleet the previous day. High on the walls were complex catapults with many wheels, axles, ropes, and counterweights. Fastened to the tops were branchless, bark-less trees bent in bow-like fashion, with taught ropes holding them in place, as if anchoring them to the ground. Atop were large iron claw-shaped anchors ready for the next attack on the Roman ships.

He slipped away from the market without trouble and walked down a well-worn path to the nearest gate to the city. He carried a bundle of fish and fruit in his cloak, which he'd fashioned into a sack, and he had hidden his sword in it as well. There was only one guard at the gate, having a heated discussion with a merchant whose cart was blocking the entrance, its wheel having broken. A slave was working feverishly to repair the wheel so that the cart could be moved. Philip took advantage of the distraction and slipped by the broken cart, entering through the gate of Syracuse.

Once inside the gate, the spectacle of the preparations for the feast of Artemis was ubiquitous. Women were working in large groups, sewing together banners for display. Children were parading and practicing dances, miming hunters tracking game for the feast. Men gathered into large groups and moved wooden platforms from stables behind a smith's shop. Even the dogs were excited, running about looking for scraps of food and playing tug the rope with their masters. Few sentries were posted at the walls, apparently more interested in the preparations for the feast than the defense of the city.

He moved about the city easily, accepted as belonging there, and began to wander in the direction of the governor's palace, where the sorcerer named Archimedes had been sheltered. This was the place where the so-called philosopher of nature worked his magic and invented his marvelous machines. Marcellus wanted Archimedes as his own sorcerer—to make more marvelous machines for the use of the Roman army. Obsessed with revenge against Archimedes for atrocities and the death of his brother, Philip, an unknown legionnaire, would have his way. Marcellus demanded loyalty for generous wages but no amount of money could sway a man from avenging his brother's death, especially a death without the dignity of confronting one's opponent face-to-face as men in battle did. This was not battle. This was not dignified. This use of black magic could not go unpunished. Marcellus would still get the machines Archimedes made. It was not as if killing Archimedes would prevent the Roman army from having the weapons that held them back for so long in the siege of Syracuse. Yes, Archimedes would die, and he, the unknown legionnaire, would do the killing this time. He knew the gods wanted him to act on this compulsion. It was their desire as well!

Hunger and thirst overcame him finally. He stopped at a public fountain and drank of fresh water. He consumed fruit that he had stolen at the market and hidden in his cloak, which he'd disguised as a sack. He ate one of the fish in the sack by ripping it apart with his teeth and chewing the raw meat off the flank below the gills. He thought he looked like a bear he had seen in the north, eating raw fish by a stream. Passersby gave him a wide berth.

The sun was hot in the autumn afternoon, and those in warm tunics were shedding them for bare skin as they continued their industry in the city. Philip spotted a public bath and cautiously entered, as he had no coin to give. There was currently no caretaker. He was probably also busy preparing for the feast of Artemis. Philip scrubbed his body with soap made of mastic leaves and soaked for a long time in the tepid water of the bath. He took the time to rinse his tunic and cloak and wrung them dry, placing them in the hot sun on rocks arranged for that purpose.

When his body was refreshed and his clothes dry enough to wear, he donned the tunic as a loincloth again—putting the cloak-sack over his shoulder and hiding the sword—and set out to scout the palace of the governor. Once there, he easily learned the location of Archimedes' rooms by watching a group of scholars come and go from a portico on the east side of the palace. He saw them through the open shutters of the east wing and understood this to be the sanctuary of the magician.

Philip lay quietly in the branches of a tree, spying on the old man while he worked. He was fascinated by what he saw. Small models of the larger catapults, many prisms of crystal and mirrors with gears, and pages of parchment were scattered about the magician's den, and there in the center of the room, a slate on the floor had symbols written on it. Archimedes was sitting on the floor, staring at the symbols as if hypnotized by them. Long white hair lay randomly on his narrow shoulders and seemed to flow into a curly white beard that was stained with streaks of yellow. Furrows lined his brow from the tops of his eyes to the shiny bald crown of his head. His eyes were dark, and he peered at the symbols with a permanent squint.

Philip held his breath as he watched the man rise to his sandaled feet with the use of a walking stick. Archimedes was an old man with crooked hands and arthritic joints. He limped toward the window of the enclave. Philip noted that the color of Archimedes' skin matched the pallor of his white cloak that hung irregularly to his knob-like knees. This indeed was the guilty magician. Philip turned red with rage at the vision and suppressed his urge to leap from his perch to murder him on the spot.

With tempered disgust, Philip resisted his passions. The preparations for the feast of Artemis had given him insight into even greater revenge. He must leave the city and get a message to the Roman army about the vulnerability of Syracuse for the next night and day. He slipped down from the tree and away from the palace, turning toward the gate through which he had entered. It was late afternoon now, and the evening twilight would be a good time to arrange for his escape and reentry to the walled city.

Making his way through the crowded streets and amid revelers getting an early start on the holiday, he surveyed again the area near the gate he planned to use to depart the city. Next to the gate was a public well. Caretakers had temporarily abandoned it, and the rope and bucket lay across the stone table that was its top. He considered the utility of the well, thinking it a good place to hide until dark. He approached and, picking up the bucket and rope, tested the depth. He leaned in after the bucket as if to reach it, and in one motion, he was inside the well, clinging to stones and roots on the well wall. He let the bucket hang by the rope and waited. The blue sky above changed rapidly to pink and soon was dark. No one had come for water. He reached for the rope and shimmied up to the top, and again, in one motion, was over the wall and back on his feet.

Night had fallen, and parties had begun in some houses. Sentries were visible on the city wall, but they seemed preoccupied with the music and activity emanating from nearby dwellings. He walked slowly to the gate. It was locked by a small log wedged in the door to prevent inward movement. He pushed the log away with his foot and the gate opened. He slipped out without looking to see if it was safe, squatting down immediately when a merchant and his slaves brought their cart by the door. He pretended to clean a net lying on the market's edge, and when they passed without noticing him, he got up and took his sword out of his cloak, wedging it into the jamb of the gate to hold it closed.

He quickly departed in the direction he knew the Roman encampment to be, and as he gained distance from the city wall, he stopped to rearrange his clothing. The tunic made into his loincloth became a tunic again, and he covered himself with the cloak that had substituted for a sack. With a quick glance to determine his bearings, he broke into a slow run and continued up a steep hill, through groves of almond trees, for several miles, and then came down the easterly side of the hill, undetected. He came upon the temporary quarters of a Roman legion. The displayed tents and banners indicated that the commander Marcus Marcellus was directly in command of this legion, even if he wasn't present.

Philip approached the sentry with hands outstretched to his side. His dress was common to a Roman soldier, but he knew their security would not assume him to be friendly until they had interrogated him to their satisfaction. The interrogation began immediately as Philip explained himself and his past twenty-four hours. The sentry and other soldiers relaxed and took him up the chain of command to a centurion named Cornelius, a lesser commander than the great Marcus Marcellus. The centurion listened patiently to Philip as he laid before him his plan to enter the city of Syracuse.

Cornelius's chiseled face, at first stern and unyielding, clearly annoyed with the interruption from this unknown legionnaire, grew brighter as he listened.

"Soldier," he called out to a tall legionnaire waiting silently by the tent door. Barely taking his eyes off Philip, Cornelius ordered, "Prepare the men to move out on my command."

"Yes, sir," the soldier said. Philip saw in the way the tall man leaped to obey that Cornelius was a powerful leader, and he breathed deeply as the man turned to leave. His plan would soon come to fruition. Coming here had not been a mistake.

"And, soldier," Cornelius added, "send our fastest runner to my tent immediately."

Cornelius hurriedly prepared a note seeking Marcus Marcellus's final authorization. Philip was given the reward of a hearty meal and a comfortable place to sleep for his loyal effort.

As he lay down in his quarters for the night, he felt the anger and the passion grow within. He would be ready before dawn to show the legion the gate, pull out his sword, and essentially remove the arch stone to the impenetrable wall of Syracuse.

⟡⟡⟡

Dreams were inescapable to a restless warrior filled with extreme passions. So it was with Philip as he saw in his dreams the recurring horror of his brother's bloody death. So certain was death, the ultimate trap. In this life, there was no escape—even with magic! He had visions of Octavia Proba, the green-eyed beauty with golden locks, whose face drove him mad with love, and at whose words his heart of stone would melt. So far away was she now than when she became his brother's wife. Philip coveted her, yet he kept his distance and loved her silently. He loved her children as if they were his, never marrying but choosing a life as a professional soldier to one as a stone layer, as his brother had been before he was conscripted. He remembered his vow to the woman he would always love and never possess. Philip had promised he would look after his brother and bring him back to her safely. Oh, the disgrace he felt in failing to keep his vow to his beloved. He imagined the pain in her face, her tears, and her disgust with him. He shivered at the finality of failure, the completeness of death, and woke up cold and scared for the first time since his ship went down.

⟡⟡⟡

The sixth day of the third month of the Greek calendar, Kharisteria, the feast of the goddess Artemis:

Kharisteria meant "thanksgiving," and thanksgiving it was for the Roman cohort, as Philip pulled his sword from the gate he had locked and led them into the unsuspecting city. With a loud command from Cornelius the Primus Pilus, the first cohort charged the walls, climbing the ladders from within. At most, a dozen sentries stood guard. Legionnaires approached them with catlike stealth. Some of the sentries were silenced with sharp, swift blades across their throats; some succumbed, having been thrown off the parapet so swiftly that the surprise silenced their screams; and two sentries were garroted simultaneously, their muffled grunts and the gargling in their throats adding to the noises of the celebration. The carefully planned attack was choreographed into a dance of swift, bloody slaughter. Philip, held back by the commander, was deemed too valuable for his knowledge of the city to risk in man-to-man combat. He watched with pride the Roman killing machine in one of its finest moments.

The eight hundred men moved as one to disarm the city's guardians and to secure the quarters of the Syracusans, who gaped at them with sleepy disbelief on this solemn morning of the feast of Artemis. No one noticed Philip move away from the first cohort and toward the apartment of Archimedes. The first cohort moved on to the main gate and opened it to allow the remaining four thousand men of Commander Marcellus's legion to enter the city. As the legion entered, they were let loose to loot and despoil the victims of their assault. The rule of victory was simple. The rewards for their sacrifice were the riches and the women and slaves of the vanquished, which would be shared among them. There was one exception to the general rule, proclaimed by Commander Marcus Marcellus himself.

Marcellus ordered, "The life of natural philosopher Archimedes should be spared, and his tools and his possessions brought with him to the commander, to be taken back to Rome."

❧❧❧

Philip was now deep into his treason as he ran to the quarters of the sorcerer. He would get there first and convict him of his brother's death before slaying him. He knew he must be lucky to kill Archimedes and stay alive himself.

He saw the palace ahead of him as he ran. Sweating now to keep ahead of the looting legionaries, he pressed even harder. Surprise overtook him as he entered the sorcerer's enclave. There were students there, and the old man was stooped over the same drawing he had been studying the day before.

Archimedes was indifferent to Philip's presence, and this rude interruption did not even cause him to look up from his symbols. His head bent, he spoke to his students, and they, alarmed by the presence of a Roman soldier with a drawn sword, began to withdraw from their teacher. Philip wielded his sword and lunged menacingly toward the magician.

"Who are you, old man?" screamed Philip, his sword suspended over Archimedes' head. The man remained as if in a trance, peering down at the slate with the symbols for a triangle and a sphere intertwined. Philip became impatient and demanded, "Are you Archimedes?"

Apparently too much absorbed in sorting out his problem, Archimedes made no response. The indifference provoked Philip's wrath even more, and his blood boiled as the old man finally, slowly, acknowledged his presence.

Archimedes showed no fear as he turned his bearded face toward Philip. Covering the slate with his hands, he said merely, "I beg you—do not disturb this!"

Philip had counted on his being fearful. In his quest for revenge, he had pictured the old man whimpering and begging for mercy. He interpreted this indifference as passive-aggressive defiance of Roman authority. Giving not a second thought to his intended act, Philip thrust his sword through the old man's torso, at the same time ripping it upward to be certain of the result. Blood leaked from the wound in spurts. Archimedes' dark eyes showed surprise as he slumped forward onto the ground. Red blood soaked his cloak and yellow-white beard. Archimedes' body, missing the slate by inches, lay prone on the ground, his eyes open and staring blankly. Blood mixed with the dust on the floor. There was an instant flash of something glittering, and a metal triangle fell from Archimedes' hand. Shouts and screams followed.

Philip, transfixed in the crescendo of noise building in the crowd, studied the dead sorcerer and spoke softly to the spirit of his dead brother. "You have been avenged." The smell of human blood filled the room.

At the sound of more Roman soldiers approaching, Philip feared for his safety and turned to escape. His eyes met those of a soldier with an outstretched lance. In his paranoid rush to depart, he ran by chance into the spear of that same legionnaire, extinguishing his own life.

೮ഗ೮ഗ

In the morning sun, Roman sentries stood on the parapets of the Syracuse wall. Cool wind refreshed them as they watched over the vanquished city of Syracuse. Hushed silence, following the conquest, lent to the layer of apprehension in the conquering army as they awaited their leader's triumphant entrance into the city walls. Marcus Marcellus, the great commander, walked in solemn respect of the warriors who had served him in a pompous parade through the entrance of the city. Commander Cornelius marched out to meet Marcellus in the tradition well known to the Roman conquerors. With his stone-like face, Cornelius paused and raised his right hand in firm salute to Marcus, and then he leaned forward and whispered in his ear.

Even the breeze seemed to stop as Marcellus wailed in lament. The magnificent Archimedes had been slain by a treasonous legionnaire. Marcus took the sword of the slain legionnaire from the left hand of Cornelius and thrust it into the ground with a curse. Weakness was never to be displayed for more than political effect by a Roman general, and Marcellus, understanding his duty, knelt for a moment and then rose to his feet, raising his hand in salute to his faithful warriors.

Marcus declared to all present that the natural philosopher would be given the honor of being buried as a Roman citizen. He chose the location and arranged later for a special marker on Archimedes' tombstone. The symbols Archimedes mused over just before his death would mark his gravestone. Nothing ever afflicted Marcus Marcellus—and as fate would have it, perhaps the whole world—as much as the death of Archimedes.

CHAPTER 1

The Translation

Frank Hayhurst was a tall, thin, well-groomed, prematurely gray-haired Ivy League type, who wore a monogrammed starched white lab coat. His pale, unblemished complexion told of long hours indoors protected from sunlight working in his subbasement lab. He usually spent his time peering over his horn-rimmed bifocals as he delivered long, dry but brilliant analyses of his current science projects to his staff—who were quite literally his subjects in an academic feudal system. He had mastered them like servants during his long career. On a late spring day in his basement offices of the Syracuse University Physics Department, he abruptly called out for his protégé. "Finn, you're going to jump for joy when you see this."

Finn McGee darted out of his lab and into the older man's private office, eagerly waiting for what promised to be good news. Since returning to academia after a brief but fruitful medical career, which seemed like ages ago, Finn had worked alongside Hayhurst, and he enjoyed sharing moments of discovery with the department head. "Frank, you called me?" Finn queried as the smiling professor reached out toward him over his compulsively neat desk and handed him a large manila envelope heavily laden with folded letters and brochures.

"You made it, Finn. You are the nominee!" Hayhurst said with honest praise for his handpicked colleague.

Finn cracked a smile that split his dimples—making him, for a moment, look like a much younger man, almost passable as one of his students—as he read the enclosed letter. Raising his hand in the gesture of a high five at his mentor and doing a half bow in appreciation, he gave the appearance of a squire just knighted saluting his king.

Finn suddenly turned gravely serious. "Frank, I don't think I have time to pack and write a speech. Are you coming with me? Maybe you could help me with the formalities of writing something to tell the crowd?"

"Just tell them who you are, Finn, and enjoy the glory. Speech writing is for politicians. We are scientists. I'm sure you can get along without me on this trip. I have some pressing affairs coming up. You will have to go alone."

Finn was tough enough to go alone, and he knew it. He was actually relieved that Hayhurst was not coming to steal his thunder. He would also welcome the quiet time on the drive to Washington, DC. His mind wandered as he walked back into his own office to plan the trip.

He gazed at the replica of the translation he had fashioned. Framed in gold leaf on black wood and surrounded by shades of crimson matting, the parchment copy hung proudly on his office wall and was accompanied by the original photo. The writing was a duplicate of an ancient artifact he had discovered—and a pivotal moment in his academic pursuits. He stared at it for a long time and remembered.

 especso

"Why?" was the only question Finn ever seemed to ask in school. His father taught him the value of hard work. He learned to love by his mother's example, and he learned faith from his parish priest, who spent years as a close counselor when his mother died of breast cancer. After his wife's death, Finn's father was never able to rise above his own melancholy, and Finn was left alone.

In school, he was the scourge of the end-of-class bell. Always the kid with his hand in the air asking questions, he grew intellectually and became a medical doctor with a passion for understanding the causes of all things.

More than one person witnessed Finn solving the Rubik's Cube within five minutes of first holding the puzzle in his hand. An embellishment to the story, possibly added by later colleagues, was that he spent most of that five minutes studying the position of the squares and very little time moving them about until they found their way into perfect alignment in his hands.

Finn would preach that, as the major scientists throughout history had believed, there was indeed a Universal Theory or a Grand Design that just about tied all knowledge into some ultra-human, probably divine, equation. He believed and acted upon the belief that mankind was given the means to learn about the physical world in order to learn what was beyond the palpable and obvious order of existence.

Exploring first an excellent career in medicine, Finn was driven to look beyond the mysteries of human life, and he turned himself over to the abstract world of math and physics. There he was, pulled, as if by a rope, deeper into the understanding of the physical world than most men have gone in history. He'd once thought it was all within his grasp.

At least, that's what he believed, until he found a scroll written in ancient Greek in an ancient monastery ruin. His very presence at that archeological site was for the purpose of further exploration of the world of invention and geometry, authored by the famous Greek natural philosopher Archimedes.

Wanting to possess the scroll and learn from it, he used his Nikon camera, which he was never without, to photograph each page, meticulously arranging the lighting for legibility.

⌁⌁⌁

Finn smiled again at the reverie as he broke from his trance. The urgency of getting organized seemed overwhelming. He sat at his desk and began to make a list. Lists were his special way of organizing stressful problems. He jotted a few notes to remind himself what message he wanted to deliver at the award ceremony. Claire's photo was on the corner of his desk. She forever smiled back from that isolated moment, frozen in time. He would never forget her. He had shared his life, work, and obsessions with the love of his life, even though he regretted not giving her more time.

Time is a thief, he thought, sinking back into memories of the scroll.

⌁⌁⌁

Finn had spent countless hours learning ancient Greek in order to facilitate the correct translation of the words. He'd learned that the words had been written there by the scribe, who wrote at the behest of a Roman general who had witnessed the inventions of Archimedes.

Months ran into years, when the translation lent itself

to the scrutiny of many students in attempts at deciphering a key passage. Finn remembered the day as if it were yesterday, the day the meaning of the words was unveiled.

After triple-checking, he ran down the hallway of the college language department to ask another scholar for some help, compelled to make certain he reveled in discovery.

The passage that grabbed Finn and connected him by a strong link to the past, back to the Second Punic War, read in translation:

> *Boulders flew over the city wall and fell like hail, striking death upon the Roman legions and sinking many ships. The missiles moved at great speeds, with no obvious source of propulsion. The Romans had known about Archimedes' war machines but had never expected magic!*

Finn knew when he read it that it had nothing to do with magic.

CHAPTER 2

The School of Athens

National Academy of Sciences, June 2010, Washington, DC:

Multiple SUVs in standard government black with darkened windows suddenly surrounded the National Academy of Sciences building in silence, awaiting further orders. Radio chatter between vehicles consisted of men verifying their positions and reporting their areas secure. Then came the general's command: "I have verification. Our target is inside the building. Don't make a scene when you apprehend him. This is a matter of top-secret priority."

❧❧❧

Indoors, the ceremony was under way. Applause filled the room as the chairwoman of the National Academy of Sciences announced the evening's speaker and guest master of ceremonies, classical Greek historian Dr. Orestes Arcunalotis.

"Dr. Arcunalotis," the chairwoman continued, "has

the exclusive honor tonight to introduce the winner of the John J. Carty Award for the Advancement of Science. This year the award is targeted for achievement in the field of physics." Turning to shake hands with the honored guest, she delivered to him the gavel, murmurs of applause again rippling through the sea of more than fifteen hundred in attendance.

Dr. Arcunalotis held up the business end of the small wooden mallet, and without a rap, the room quieted. Dressed in a gray wool suit with white shirt and red bow tie, he stood at the podium with a boyish crop of jet-black hair tossed carelessly down on his brow. Grinning from ear to ear, leaving barely any room for his deep dimples, he peered down through his spectacles, over his black bushy mustache, at his scattered notes. Pausing to soak in the adulation of the audience, he looked at them over his reading glasses, waved the gavel again, and said with self-assurance, "My friends all call me Orestes." Laughter warmed the amphitheater, and he began to speak impeccable English with a British accent acquired at Cambridge.

"I have been chosen to present a prestigious award to an outstanding scientist. He is a man of a multitude of achievements, a true renaissance man. His curriculum vitae reads like a university catalogue: undergraduate degrees; BS in biochemistry and simultaneously a BA in classical history with minors in Greek and Latin from Fordham University, magna cum laude; doctor of medicine from Saint Louis University School of Medicine; postgraduate clinical training at Northwestern University, followed by board certification in internal medicine. That was just the beginning. His mind wandered to his favorite passions, and he was enrolled in the University of Syracuse, where four years of critical study earned him a PhD in the physics of alternate geometry and a doctorate in mathematics by acclimation for his self-developed skill in advanced theoretical math and physics. This illustrious career was then capped by his nomination to the new Albert Einstein chair in the Department of Theoretical Physics at the University of Syracuse, where he has endeavored for the past several years to advance the fields of natural science. Our honoree shares an obsession with me, and I would like to introduce him by sharing with you its historical roots. Be patient with me as I turn down the lights and project my only slide on the screen.

"Ladies and gentlemen," Dr. Arcunalotis said a moment later, beaming as the slide appeared on the screen behind him, "I show you a slide of the fresco painted on one wall in the Stanze di Raffaello. This room, devoted to paintings by Raphael, is located in the Palace of the Vatican. The fresco was completed five hundred years ago, in 1510 AD. Known to the world as *The School of Athens* since the seventeenth century, when it was given that name in a tourist guidebook, the original title given to this and other frescos in the same room in the museum was *Causarum Cognitio*, meaning *Knowledge of Causes*. They represented a blending of the knowledge passed down from the Greek civilization with the fundamental philosophy and theology of the Roman Christian era. Furthermore, the fact that Raphael painted this fresco is considered evidence that he was highly educated, and that the awareness of Greek science and philosophy was well known during the High Renaissance period."

Arcunalotis pointed his laser at the slide, indicating the central figures. "Scholars have given us to believe that these two walking in a peripatetic manner through the Lyceum are Plato and Aristotle. More controversial, but consistent with my studies and beliefs, the figure in the right lower corner of the fresco is Archimedes. Some scholars claim that he is portrayed with the face of Euclid, but the fact that he is represented bending over a slate with geometric symbols inscribed on it is consistent with that which we know about Archimedes' death. For Archimedes to be portrayed in this fresco elevates the importance of his work and contributions to Greek science."

"We know that Archimedes' grave marker is decorated with these very symbols." Arcunalotis sipped water from a glass on the podium while searching his notes. "Aggh-ha," he muttered in not-so-perfect English to himself. "Yes, here it is." Looking up from his notes at the audience, he declared in perfect Cambridge English, "Alfred North Whitehead wrote that in *An Introduction to Mathematics*."

Regaining control of the podium, he continued. "The death of Archimedes by the hands of a Roman soldier is symbolical of a world change of the first magnitude: the Greeks, with their love of abstract science, were superseded in the leadership of the European world by the practical Romans. In one of his novels, Lord Beaconsfield—Benjamin Disraeli—has defined a practical man as a man who practices the errors of his forefathers. The Romans were a great race, but they were cursed with sterility, which waits upon practicality. They did not improve upon the knowledge of their forefathers, and all their advances were confined to the minor technical details of engineering. The Romans were not dreamers enough to arrive at new points of view. Their understanding of the world could not give them a more fundamental control over the forces of nature. No Roman lost his life because he was absorbed in the contemplation of a mathematical diagram."

Once more, Arcunalotis paused for effect. He morphed his face into the image of academic authority and, twirling his mustache with the laser pen, surveyed the reaction of the crowd. When he was confident of their attention, he executed his final point flawlessly.

"The reaction of Commander Marcus Marcellus to the death of Archimedes was utter grief at the loss of opportunity. Marcellus may have been the exception to the practical Roman because he actually saw what the physicist Archimedes was able to accomplish just in the construction of 'machines' to prevent the conquering of Syracuse. He was so much affected that he chose to give Archimedes the funeral of a Roman citizen and ordered placed on the marker for his tomb the symbols represented in this fresco.

"When I ponder the wonders that Archimedes may have understood about nature, it brings to mind another famous quotation from Archimedes himself: 'If I have somewhere to stand, I will move the whole earth.'

"This background information brings me to my purpose tonight. I wish to introduce to you the one scientist who shares my personal curiosity about Archimedes. Though his perspective is on the science Archimedes understood but our world has never learned, and mine is about the man himself, and his place in Greek civilization, we pull at the same threads of hidden knowledge. Without further delay, ladies and gentlemen, I introduce to you the nominee for the Albert Einstein chair at the University of Syracuse and the winner of the 2010 John J. Carty Award for Advancement in Science Dr. Finbar J. McGee!"

Curtains parted, and the sandy-haired physicist stepped into the light and gaze of the applauding crowd. Grasping the hand of Dr. Acunalotis in exuberant gratitude, he engaged in personal conversation. Concluding this private dialogue, he turned to the audience, grinning with a broad smile, and leaned into the microphone at the podium. "My friends all call me Finn," was his self-introduction. The crowd predictably cheered and laughed at his personal declaration, finally settling into anticipatory silence until his speech commenced.

Precisely arranging his notes in a perfect stack, taking measure of them one last time, he held up a shiny metal triangle the size of his hand. He waved it ceremoniously about the podium, reflecting the bright lights from its surface to the watching eyes of his audience, and spoke.

"Ladies and gentleman, I accept your nomination and award with humility and purpose." Laying the triangle down on his notes, he unbuttoned his blue suit coat and loosened his tie. "Ever since I was a boy in grammar school, I played with mathematics and geometry as though they were my toys. I filled my life with geometric symbols and pondered the abstract notions of the world. As my education advanced, so did my curiosity. Finding little solace in working simple problems, I looked diligently for tougher and even unsolved problems. Not content with just the science, I broadened my research into the historical roots of mathematics and physics. For this, I needed additional skills in language rather than science. After stumbling across an incomplete biography of Archimedes of Syracuse, my curiosity did evolve into obsession."

Finn knew he had hypnotized the audience. He enjoyed their attention and knew Hayhurst had been right. All he needed to do was be himself. He found his own pace and soaked in their adulation. When the moment was right for drama, his eyes danced as he focused on the crowd and delivered his message.

"I studied his methods and his inventions with relentless abandon, and I never wanted to do anything more than solve the puzzles he pondered himself. I discovered so many amazing and even terrifying principles.

"Modern military establishments have spent billions of dollars in failed attempts at reproducing the weapons engineered by Archimedes just for the defense of Syracuse. His contributions to geometry, for instance, greatly aided the development of ballistics. He led scientists down pathways of discovery in applied physics and even into the realm of space exploration. He devised methods that resulted in his being named the 'father of integral calculus.' He is responsible for the logical measurement of the circle and the establishment of pi. He demonstrated principles of mechanics that use a small force to move a great weight.

"In my quest, I discovered a way to approach the physical world using what I believe are rules about the forces of nature, which Archimedes knew but never recorded for history. It was during my intense research that I became completely consumed by physics and chose to delve more deeply into it, forsaking my career in medicine."

Finn was now strutting about the podium, microphone in hand. His swagger told a story of confidence. Deciding to be a bit playful, he said, "It is sheer coincidence that I am now working at the University of Syracuse on projects related to some of my discoveries. I want to assure you that my obsession did not involve the Syracuse name. It is just a fine and arguably superb coincidence.

"Some of you may have wondered about this silver triangle." He held it up, displaying it so that it caught the light, and moved it above the podium with his hand in a semicircular motion. "This is a permanent reminder of the path I've chosen. It is reminiscent of the angle that was part of the puzzle Archimedes mused over just prior to his unfortunate death. It is a gift from my beloved wife to memorialize the beginning of our family, and she gave it to me just before her unexpected death. A symbol to me of the search for a grand design for which many scientists have devoted and even sacrificed their lives, I keep it with me wherever I travel. In the years to come, I plan to live up to the John J. Carty Award for the Advancement of Science, which you have bestowed upon me this evening. Thank you again for your confidence."

With that conclusion, Finn buttoned his suit coat, tightened his tie, placed his notes and the triangle under his arm with military precision, and marched off the stage with a brisk pace and a smile on his freckled face. Applause followed him down a hallway to an exit where his car was waiting for the long ride home to Syracuse, New York. He thought about the chair ceremony, which was next on the university calendar. He would endure it alone, just as he had these past several years. No one would know that his work was only one of his passions.

He thought of his dead wife, Claire. How she would have enjoyed this moment. How he missed her. How, without her, he was uncovering secrets of the forces of nature that would astound the world.

She would never be there to share his success, therefore, it seemed hollow. He could not go back and change the past. Man was just not quite able to perform that kind of miracle.

No, that seemed to be a divine rule that never would be broken. He must look forward, and he must continue, if for no other reason but her—and God, of course.

His reverie was quickly broken as he approached his BMW in the parking lot. Three men in black suits waving badges stopped him and, after few words of explanation, ordered, "Come with us now, Dr. McGee. There's been an accident in your lab!"

McGee felt shock at the news and then apprehension as they put their badges away and flashed their holsters.

Two men helped Finn into a black SUV. The third took the keys to the BMW and followed the black SUV out of the parking lot, into traffic, and eventually north onto I-95.

CHAPTER 3

Interrogation

Flashing lights and speeding erratically through traffic, the SUV tore at the open road with ferocity, matching the urgency of the questions being exchanged inside the vehicle. Finn was strapped in tightly in the right front seat. The agents seemed menacing, and they were both armed. The driver focused on the road, intent on speed, and seeming to enjoy the power of the enhanced V-8 engine as it whined through each turn and acceleration. Multitasking seemed to be his strong suit as he worked the interrogation from the driver's seat. "How long have you known Frank Hayhurst, Dr. McGee?" was the first of a volley of questions. "When did you see him last? Was it at the lab? What did you do yesterday before leaving for DC?"

The questions flew almost faster than the SUV. Finn closed his eyes as if trying to withdraw from the barrage and the view of the hectic pace on the highway. Heart racing with fear, he sensed a malicious intent in the interrogators. Agent Becker, sitting on the forward edge of the rear seat, leaning into the space between Finn and Agent Finch, lacked the finesse even to allow the professor a moment to collect himself. Shaking Finn's shoulder rather violently, he announced that there was no time for stalling. "Answer the questions now," he commanded.

Questions raced through Finn's mind. *Why is the FBI here at all? How did the government get involved in the research being done at the lab? Why are they asking about Hayhurst? Is he missing or injured?* They had said there was an accident in the lab when they took him away. It all went so fast that he hadn't really examined their badges—only had a quick glance. Were they really government agents? Opening his eyes to survey his surroundings, he understood that it would be a long ride. At this speed, there was no hope of escape. He demanded, "What the hell is going on?" Finn asked some of his own questions in rapid succession.

Turning his gaze away from the road, the driver, Agent Finch, stared at Finn. Even more anxious now with the speedometer reading one hundred miles per hour, Finn countered his gaze with a steel glance from his dark blue eyes and calmly requested that the driver keep his eyes on the road and he would be glad to cooperate with their questions.

"I'm glad you understand the seriousness of this, Dr. McGee," Agent Finch said slowly. Before Finch could ask another question, McGee responded.

"I will cooperate, as it appears I must, but please tell me what happened to Hayhurst."

"He's missing," Finch said. "Or he's lost."

Finn stiffened as he listened. The implication of Finch's statement momentarily confused him.

"There was some kind of accident, and we're investigating," Becker interjected. "At this point, little makes sense. We were told to pick you up and bring you to the University of Syracuse, where we have established temporary offices to proceed with this inquiry. You are cleared for top secret status as of now. Any facts that you learn here are not to be divulged to anyone without the same clearance. Now tell us what you know about Professor Hayhurst—and how you have come to work with him?"

"Hayhurst was my mentor. I was one of three graduate students who set their career goals on partnering with him after achieving doctorate status. He was fussy, compulsive to a point. He even measured his students on the habits they brought into the lab. No paper could be out of place, no scrap note left to clutter a desktop. To him, perfection was the golden rule. He often said that one careless mistake or leak of information could cost a career or a life. It wasn't enough to be neat and scrupulous. At the same moment, he asked for daring, inspiration, and insight. He never let us rest. I guess that I had the most stamina and imagination. I know I had the highest IQ and bravado to make him believe I also had nerves of steel, which I don't. Could you please keep your eyes on the road? And by the way, why are we not flying to Syracuse? I would have enjoyed avoiding this nerve-racking thrill ride."

Finch turned his eyes from the road again as if to emphasize control and informed Finn, "No one must know that we have you now!"

Alarm coursed through Finn's veins, making his limbs tingle and his muscles tense. He didn't much like the implication of "we have you now," much less the fact that his current whereabouts were a secret. But, he reasoned, he hadn't done anything wrong. Fixing his captors with a cool glare, he continued. "Hayhurst learned his technique of selecting a protégée from his mentor. After he chose me, he confided that piece of business and said I should remember it when the time was right for me to pass the torch. And by the way, I'm surprised that you didn't know that I had just been cleared for top secret status. My research demands that clearance level. I suppose it's one of the perks of receiving a government grant."

Becker again: "So tell us, Doctor, what is it exactly that you and Hayhurst were doing with your grant? My primary resources advise me it had something to do with finding a new way to transport mass. Am I correct?"

"Yes, you are correct, in essence," Finn responded, "but we were not close to any solution even last week, when I saw Hayhurst for the last time. We were experimenting with the concept of superfluids and developing ways to develop the extreme low temperatures required to keep the superfluid stable. Superfluid technology was developed in the quest for antigravity propulsion systems. The US government gave us the grant to pursue variants on the primitive antigravity science they have possessed for years. The interesting fact is that we seemed to have stumbled onto an unexpected twist: we have been able to lift small crystals of pure elements for several days at a time. In our last attempt, Hayhurst was playing with different frequencies used to propel the superfluid engine and simultaneously fluctuated the temperature module. The strangest thing happened. The crystal we were using disappeared. Had we not been observing it, we would have assumed that it had been stolen."

"Why is that?" Becker interrupted.

"Because our crystal was pure carbon—in other words, a diamond!" Finn replied, conveying the same sense of surprise he'd felt when he watched the diamond disappear in the lab. He paused and then inquired, "What is it that makes you think Hayhurst is missing or, to repeat your sinister suggestion, lost?"

There was a sudden sound of squealing brakes, and the SUV swerved as if unstable. Finch wrestled with the steering wheel, moving it frantically back and forth. Finn held his breath as the vehicle went up on two wheels and almost careened over. At the last millisecond, the SUV stayed upright and stabilized, continuing forward at breakneck speed. Finn exploded with rage, hurling curses at the two agents.

Even Agent Finch, the driver, seemed rattled. He eased off the accelerator and held the wheel steady with both hands for the first time since leaving the nation's capital. His tenor softened, Finch turned to speak, this time keeping one eye on the road.

"The facts that we have, Doctor, are sparse. Hayhurst's particle physics class complained to the department office that he missed his last lecture and failed to give their appointed final exam. The chair of the physics department went to his office and discovered the final exam printed and ready for presentation, with no trace of the professor. After searching Hayhurst's office, he searched his lab and your lab, Professor McGee. Hayhurst was not there, but machinery was left on and unattended. Worse, there was blood spattered on some of the equipment and on the wall and ceiling at the opposite end of the room. Forensics is investigating now, and their conclusions are pending, but there is no question that Professor Hayhurst is missing. With the additional evidence pointing to some foul play and no corpse, we have concluded that the professor is lost or abducted. Central Intelligence asked us to bring you there for assistance after interrogating you. Initially, you were suspect in this matter. Now that seems to me less likely."

Finn was genuinely disturbed by Finch's summary. "Why," he asked, "would I have been considered suspect at all?"

Becker barged into the conversation. "Easy call, McGee. You are an expert on the Greek scientist Archimedes, right?"

"Yes."

"Didn't Archimedes write a treatise on spirals?

"Yes."

"Isn't your current research an attempt to reproduce some of the lost physics of Archimedes, the knowledge he had about moving heavy objects as if by magic?

"Yes," Finn said anxiously. "But what does that have to do with implicating me?"

"The blood spatter on the wall, Doc, was in the shape of a spiral."

CHAPTER 4

Room 0045

*June 2010, University of Syracuse, the Physics Building,
Dr. Hayhurst's subbasement lab:*

Riding in silence for the remainder of the three-hundred-mile trip gave Finn a chance to rest. Long days were a part of his life in the academic research world. Nothing except the high drama of a major discovery could equal this day so far. *Adams Street Exit – 1 Mile*, the green-and-white interstate sign announced. Finch hit the turn signal to the right and drove in the exit lane, flashers off now and in no great hurry.

Dusk loomed in the eastern sky, and the last edge of the red sun slid below the horizon in the west as they drove along Adams Street toward University Hill, the familiar neighborhood that Finn once called home. The University of Syracuse was built upon a hill three hundred feet above the rest of the city. Old redbrick buildings stood out in the skyline in the light of the day, but twilight had its own way of making bright color fade to a blend of gray. So it was as they drove past the northern edge of the campus and through Walnut Park. After a left turn going north on Walnut Avenue, they drove three blocks to East Genesee Street and westward, then to the 2600 block of Genesee Street to the professor's home.

Finn noticed several black government cars parked strategically around his Victorian estate. He mused that it could no longer be secret that he was in the company of government agents.

Finch broke the long silence. "We will guard you tonight. Your car will be delivered in another two hours. Please don't attempt to leave without one of our agents accompanying you."

"Am I under arrest, Agent Finch?" Finn snapped.

"No, Dr. McGee, consider it protective custody. We'll come for you at eight in the morning."

Finn got out of the SUV and walked up to his front door. Turning the key, he entered the solitude of his home. Flipping on the light switch, the living room illuminated, and he lit the gas fire, responding to the unseasonably cool June night. He went to the bathroom and washed his face as if to remove the grit of this stressful day permanently. That done, he poured himself a large, perfect martini on the rocks. He sprawled on the loveseat in front of the fire and sipped it slowly on an empty stomach, feeling the gin rush to his brain. As he stared at the fire, he thought about the day to come, and he spoke to no one when he said, "Claire, if you could only be with me now."

Hours later, he slept fitfully. The mystery of the lab accident, the award ceremony, the dread of tomorrow with investigations in the lab, the coming chair ceremony in Hendricks Chapel, and the permanent absence of Claire were the storms in his dreams.

He awakened in a sweat at six in the morning. With the sound of the alarm clock, reality floated into his mind. He stumbled out of bed to his feet and worked off the morning stiffness in his legs with a cautious trip downstairs to the kitchen, where he filled and set the automatic coffeemaker. Taking off his sweat-soaked shirt, he tossed it into the laundry room before briskly heading back upstairs to the master bathroom. Brewing coffee scented the air as he finished his hot shower. Tension all but gone, he sipped black coffee, nibbled at dry toast, and read the *Post-Standard*, a futile quest to find information about the lab accident in the morning news.

At precisely 8:00 a.m., Becker and Finch knocked on his door. Finn followed the agents out to the SUV, and they rode to the physics building. As they arrived, Becker's cell phone chirped, and he answered it with his usual abruptness.

"Yeah, yeah, yeah," he said. "I'll inform them." He ended the call. "It gets more interesting by the hour," he said, poking his head forward between Finn and Finch. "The DNA is a match to Hayhurst."

Finn visibly stiffened. Becker saw the reaction and reassured him. "Don't worry, Doc. You're not a suspect, but we believe you have the key to this puzzle."

Tensing with concern, Finn tried to put his mind around their suggestion as they turned left from Adams Street and headed down Crouse Avenue. Driving through the hairpin turn, they screeched to a halt in the staff parking space in front of a long red brick and concrete building.

Entering the physics building by the door facing Hendricks Chapel, they proceeded to the first stairwell and descended two flights into the gloomy subbasement corridor.

They were two floors below ground level. Fluorescent lights reflected in the clear sealed concrete floors.

The walls were concrete block with medium gray paint. At the very end was a guard dressed much like

Agents Finch and Becker, and to their right was the entrance to a suite of offices and a lab.

All the rooms in the dreary subbasement were assigned numbers beginning with "00." The number on the door to the lab was simply 0045. No names were posted to indicate the occupants, but Finn approached it with the ease of familiarity and opened the door for the others. Inside were an array of yellow tape and two uniformed women with *FORENSIC* displayed in orange capital letters on the backs of their jackets. Devices known only to Finn and his mentor posed in the office lights within the square quarantined by the tape. However, they were slightly out of position, not in the ordinary arrangement engineered by Finn, which had him questioning, "Who moved them and why?"

Voices raised questions all at once. Then Finn raised his hand like a cop directing traffic. All stopped.

"I was told you found these machines running," Finn said in a questioning tone as he took inventory. "How did you stop them?"

A brunette woman, whose name tag read *Jones*, offered, "We pulled the fuse on the circuit right after we found the scene. I thought it wise not to let them run. Radiation, you know. You can't be too sure." And then, "They all stopped at once. We were lucky not to lose the lights."

"Did you touch them?" Finn said, beginning his own interrogation. "They're not as they were!"

"No one moved them," Jones said with assurance. "But we did brush them for prints and check them for particulate and blood spatter."

"And because of DNA, we know the blood spatter was Hayhurst's," Becker said. "The prints were yours, Doctor, and the fresher prints where Hayhurst's. There was also some hair and particulate matter common to others found in your private office and Hayhurst's office. One other set of prints may have been left by your new lab assistant, but I don't have that ID yet."

Finch interrupted with a question. "Dr. McGee, can you give us any explanation how the lab door could have been locked from the inside? The department chairman said the double lock can only be set from inside the office. How could he have gotten out?"

"Maybe he was mistaken?" Finn queried, almost wistfully. "I cannot conceive of a reason for Hayhurst to lock himself in the lab. No one disturbs us down here unless invited. At any rate, there's no other exit." He paused. "These devices are aligned differently now than when we were using them." Assuming it was his role to explain, he then started, "This one in particular, pointing—"

Finch stopped him. "Dr. McGee, the time for a demonstration and explanation of each machine must be delayed until our physicist from the Pentagon arrives. Please take some more time to examine every aspect of this room and let us know if anything else is out of the ordinary."

Finn obeyed, focusing on the room itself. Glancing at the suspended ceiling, he noted the pure white two-by-four-foot inserts. Far in the corner was a brownish-maroon smear covering two panels and the upper part of the beige walls. Blood, no doubt, based on all he had learned. Although the space was windowless, as would be expected of a subbasement lab, bright light still reflected off the surface of celery-white tiles. The suspended fluorescent lights were functional and bright and, at a cursory glance, not affected by the spatter. One glass panel was shattered on the blond wood cabinets. Ebony Corian countertops were fitted on lower cabinets in matching blond wood and custom designed into the walls. All the drawers where closed and the papers on top neatly arranged. Corkboard and slate panels filled the walls on the opposite end. These were covered with diagrams and equations, meaningless to the untrained eye. Central to the room were devices held in place by easels and struts that gave the impression of an old-fashioned erector set enlarged to extremes. All of these devices were wired into a large box covered in black housing, which sat on the beige tiled floor. From the back of the box, a fat gray cable disappeared into the plaster wall below the electric control panel that wore the Cutler-Hammer trademark on the latch.

Mounted on the wall near the center of the room were twenty-four clocks, each reflecting the time and date for a given meridian. The two large clocks were set at Eastern Standard Time and Greenwich Mean Time. Five hours separated the two times. Below and to the left of the Greenwich Mean Time clock was another blood spatter in the shape of a perfect Archimedes' spiral. More blood could be seen on the floor near the opposite wall, and spots covered the easel holding up the device he would soon have to explain.

Almost at the same moment Finn concluded his inspection, Major General Gunter marched into the room wearing his uniform. Bright florescent light reflected off the medals on his chest. His military head cover under his left arm was decorated with gold laurel. His hair was shaven so close that it was difficult to see the gray. The general smiled and offered his right hand to Finn in a friendly gesture. Before Finn could ask, Gunter immediately dismissed the idea that there would be a Pentagon physicist coming anytime soon.

CHAPTER 5

McGee's Analysis

The general's demeanor was overly patronizing. A sense of caution left Finn fidgeting in his own skin. Answers were expected, and they had to pass the general's scrutiny.

Finn reached into his pocket and removed his silver triangle. He placed it on the black countertop.

From another pocket, he produced a small laser pointer.

"Hold on," General Gunter said, cutting Finn off before he could get going. He objected to the presence of the forensics team and temporarily dismissed them for security reasons.

Once the forensics team had left, Finn turned to the group and began to speak to them as if they were students. "To put what I see here in some sort of orderly perspective, I'll have to start from the beginning of my research. Without that background, I am sure none of you will believe I am of sound mind."

The small group gathered around Finn as he brought them up to speed on his career. As the tallest, Finch stood in the back and surveyed the crime scene as he listened.

"When I first became interested in physics, I was fascinated by some of the great abstract thinkers and their contributions to man's knowledge of the universe. Efforts to understand nature over millennia have brought us to where we are today, yet we have so much more to learn. Scientific method applied repeatedly by Newton, for instance, gave us the basic understanding of the forces at work in gravity, but never told us what gravity was. The study of physical chemistry and the effects of individual elements and how they combine led us to truth and understanding of the existence of atoms and electrons and neutrons.

Einstein theorized the relationship between matter and energy, and we learned to split the atom and use its trapped energy. From there, we learned the secrets of fusion, the understanding of fusion power, and how stars work. Extrapolating that, man went on to develop theories of particle physics, finding and proving the existence of ever-smaller subunits of matter and the energies that link matter together like glue. Without seeing one, Hawking postulated and proved the existence of a black hole and an event horizon."

The general shifted his weight and looked bored as he glanced at his BlackBerry.

Finn smiled, silently asking himself, *Am I actually explaining this to a military general and expecting him to understand?*

Walking to a whiteboard, Finn started to list the points he was trying to make. He thought a visual would help keep everyone focused. He waited until he had the group's attention once more, thinking that he might spend an eternity in here explaining this.

"From there, we are all searching for the fabric of space itself and its link to time—and on and on. No one has yet to offer a universal solution that ties everything up in one single package. It seems that the more we discover, the more there is to discover." Finn emphasized his point by encompassing the list on the whiteboard with a large freehand circle.

He nervously picked up the silver triangle and played with it absentmindedly as he continued. "All these scientists have left behind volumes of details describing their work and their theories. However, there is one, and perhaps the greatest of these, whose contributions to science were not all recovered for posterity."

He wrote a name on the bottom of the list in large block letters: *ARCHIMEDES*.

"Known for his great achievements, and also because of a war, he left little, if anything, behind on record about the intricacies of fending off the most powerful army of his time for almost three years. He, with the use of science, repelled and kept at a distance the Roman navy and army. History tells us that Archimedes was a 'famous maker of war engines,' and when Marcellus was once attacking Syracuse by land and sea, it is said that he drew up some merchant vessels out of the harbor, actually lifted them up against the walls of Syracuse, and then smashed them into a heap of timber, causing them to sink to the bottom, crews and all.

When Marcellus had withdrawn his ships more than a bow's length, 'the old man gave all the Syracusans power to lift stones, large enough to load a wagon, and hurl them one after the other to sink the ships.' This I learned from an ancient book called *Book of Histories*, written in Greek by Tretzes. Furthermore, on the subject of the same war, this book reveals that the great Archimedes constructed a hexagonal mirror, and at intervals proportionate to the size of the mirror, he arranged smaller mirrors with four edges.

These were moved by links and by a type of hinge.

The effect was the concentration of the sun's beams. By using this device, he was able to turn Roman ships to ashes, burning them down to the waterline.

"It was clear to me when I read the original Greek documents that the knowledge Archimedes had at that time included an understanding of certain natural forces that had remained a secret all these centuries. I committed my career in physics to learning the secrets Archimedes left behind. Because of my efforts and my interest in the recovery of that specific scientific knowledge, Dr. Frank Hayhurst recruited me. We both theorized what it was that Archimedes had. We have done something extraordinary with that discovery."

General Gunter raised his hand in desperation and commanded, "Stop."

Finn stared at him indifferently with his piercing blue eyes. "But, General, are you completely disinterested in what we discovered?"

Gunter grumbled something about checking everyone's security clearance before continuing. A small argument ensued between Agent Becker and General Gunter, after which Finch made a cell phone call and got his commanding officer on the phone with General Gunter. Finn shuddered at the thought that Big Brother was now watching over his research—and that from now on, he would have to suffer with the micromanaging bureaucrats from Washington, DC, meddling into his every move. Finn cherished his freedom and his privacy with equal gusto.

Gunter addressed Finn again, with the air of a commanding general. He ordered him to continue his explanation, adding, "Get to the facts of the matter, Professor, and knock off the history lesson."

Finn reached for the laser pointer and pocketed his silver triangle. Then he responded, "In a nutshell, General, I believe we have engineered an antigravity device."

"How in the world…" The general's question tapered away into stunned silence.

Finn continued. "All the possible explanations for Archimedes' feats have been attempted by experiment, using the technology that historians tell us he had available. It was believed that catapults were the cause of the massive flying boulders that sank the Roman ships. Catapults have limits in this regard and require massive effort to be loaded and drawn down to the release position."

He took the time to draw a simple diagram of a catapult on the whiteboard, labeling each part. He searched a nearby drawer and pulled out of the depth of the drawer a working model of a catapult. Setting it up to demonstrate, he loaded the long end of the lever with a pencil eraser and released the trigger, flinging the eraser dangerously close to the general's eye. Laughter broke the tension, and Finn carried on with his explanation.

"He would have had to possess uncounted numbers of catapults loaded and ready to shoot, not to mention the need for different sizes of catapult to accommodate the varying distances to moving targets. We concluded that catapults were not the answer. The one-hundred-foot-tall crane-like structures seen over the walls of Syracuse could have been used to lift the large boulders and to drop them, but not to fling them, at a ship a bow's length away in the harbor. Clearly, the Syracusans had no knowledge of gunpowder and cannons. The question, then, was what power did they have that could produce such feats?"

Finn held up an old archeological journal with tattered and dog-eared pages. He paused for effect, as if teaching a class, and then continued.

"The logical solution seemed illogical to us when we first attempted to understand the problem. But then, in an obscure archeological journal, an article appeared about a dig in Syracuse. It was being scheduled on a large hillside near the ancient wall of the city. Because it produced a magnetic field that was interrupting radio reception locally, excavation of this site was required to search for the cause of the disruption. The investigators were planning to dig to see if an artifact could be the cause of this magnetic field. I chose to go and join that team, as my instincts about Archimedes' knowledge compelled me to rationalize the potential connection to our theory.

"I spent five months there right after I was married—at great personal cost to myself. Working under the supervision of the European Antiquities Archaeology Team, I dug into that hillside and sifted the sandy soil for endless hours. We discovered an artifact that was quite sizable as archeological artifacts go. At first, it seemed to be a large deposit of copper oxide, without any evidence of human design. As we chiseled it out of the hill, it took on a form that to me was quite remarkable."

General Gunter cleared his throat and glanced at his watch. Finn raised his hand in a gesture, indicating there was just a bit more to tell. Shifting his weight, he explained more of the historical details. Gunter's eyes started to glaze with impatience, but he listened.

"The Bronze Age started approximately 3500 BC. Bronze and copper tools and artifacts were well known from that time period. To the best of man's current knowledge, copper wire did not exist then, as there was no reason for it. Electricity was not yet discovered. To my surprise, as well as the other investigators', the large copper artifact was coiled copper wire. It was not in the form of a conductor of electricity but somewhat similar to the form it should take in an electromagnet. It was a vastly different electromagnetic coil than the way we would understand one. It had the shape of a spiral geometric figure. In fact, when the dig was complete, it represented three spiral geometric figures constructed of copper wire coils long since oxidized to a point of non-recognition, except to the archeologist's eye. The archeologists there thought it was some formal decoration and made no association with the history of the Second Punic War and the connection to Archimedes' work. I, however, did make that association and developed a theory."

As the general fluctuated between intrigue and impatience, Finn laid out for the small group how he'd taken repeated measurements of the apparatus, learning that it consisted of three geometric spiral shapes. Speaking as the group's ad hoc professor, he stated, "Each spiral ended at a point that would approximate the angle of an isosceles triangle. The points of each spiral were focused, if I may use the word creatively here, in such an array that they would ultimately point at the vertex of a three-dimensional isosceles triangle, better known as a prism."

Spellbound, the group listened as Finn described combing through the entire dig, trying to scavenge artifacts that would help him understand the mystery there. "Before I departed, I discovered evidence of other materials at the dig, but they were beyond recognition." As he paused, the disappointment he felt in not finding more was palpable, an emotion so strong that Finn could sense that the others felt it too.

"It seemed a hopeless exercise," he lamented, "to attempt to remain any longer, as the yield of information geometrically declined after the original artifact was uncovered. Radio wave tests confirmed the artifact had been the source of the magnetic field. Before I departed, I took measurements with an optical compass and made certain that my hunch was correct. The apex of the prism that would result from this triangular set of spirals pointed to an arc far above the old wall of Syracuse." Finn, unable to conceal his excitement, now revealed, "I believe that Archimedes had discovered a way to manipulate the force of gravity!"

Finn stopped to catch his breath and realized that no one else in the room seemed to be breathing. Gunter, Finch, and Becker stood awestruck at his words, jaws dropping and eyes widening. Not a word was said as they resumed breathing in unison, fixated on Finn.

"When I returned to New York, I shared my insights with Professor Hayhurst, and we endeavored for months to reproduce the device from the Syracuse dig. Finally, we succeeded, making a replica that we called an electrogravitic field inductor. We learned an important lesson: size matters. We had a small model that worked, but it had a limited capability. In calculating the size we would need to perform the sorts of tasks Archimedes performed—in order to levitate a ship and its freight into the air—we found we needed far more space and material than was acceptable. The task ahead was to extrapolate the means by which the electrogravitic field inducer functioned into a smaller, more powerful device."

Finn waved the laser pointer in the direction of the equipment in the lab before continuing. Arranged in the center of the room were the essential working components of Hayhurst's mysterious device. Finn pointed to the large narrow frame held in place by two lab cranes. Unfortunately, it had been marked with crime scene tape.

"This is a reverse microwave resistor field," he said. "It's designed to lower the temperature of the superfluid container that it surrounds by using a technology that works like the opposite of your microwave oven." He was pointing to a mesh net-like enclosure suspended from the lab cranes by curled wires. Multiple computer board cards were integrated into the mesh. Using his laser pointer, he pointed to a strange ceramic mold.

A lengthy scientific explanation followed. "The doughnut-shaped ceramic container that the mesh surrounds holds what is known as a superfluid. The atoms comprising this fluid are ionically charged. Applying alternating electromagnetic forces to this superfluid by changing the polarity of the field a million times per second, the fluid flows in a circular path around the inside of the doughnut. The fluid is engineered to be totally frictionless and can move in a circle at speeds only a photon could travel. Photons have no mass, as they are particulate waves of light, but our fluid has mass and no friction."

"No friction," the general commented, now seeming extremely interested in the subject.

"We can actually increase the mass of our fluid by supercooling it down to minus one hundred fifty degrees kelvin and can adjust the wave field that it generates by fine-tuning the temperature settings and the frequency of the polarity reversals."

Finn carried on the soliloquy. All the while, the laser dot was skipping from one odd object to another, resembling a firefly flitting about.

"The device forms an antigravity/gravity field that has the three-dimensional shape of a prism. The field is strongest at the base of the prism shape. In fact, it is so strong that it has the properties of a black hole in reverse. In a black hole, the force of gravity is so powerful that nothing can escape it, not even light. In our electrogravitic prism field, the force at the base of the field is so strong that nothing can approach it.

If an object comes near it, the object becomes a missile and is hurled to the apex of the prism and beyond with great force. No matter how the object enters the field, once inside its prism-shaped field, the result is the same."

Finch let a "wow" escape from his lips. The concept was clearly dawning on him.

Appearing taken aback by the reevaluation, the general announced, "This is a game-changer. How did Archimedes do this? Where did he get the electric power?"

"More than that, General Gunter," Finn embellished. "It's a paradigm shift. Archimedes' machine worked in the same way, although we do not understand what force powered it. Once the Syracusans dropped huge boulders into the antigravity field, the boulders became missiles that could be targeted at Roman ships by small adjustments in the base of the spirals."

Finn drew a representation of a fortification wall and ink lines on the whiteboard, demonstrating the direction the boulders would have arced. As he drew freehand, he wished he had a PowerPoint presentation to show the arc of the boulders. He reached into a nearby file drawer and retrieved a folder. It was cluttered with notes and loose pages. Among these, he found a shiny DVD and inserted it into the disk drive of the lab computer. The screen filled with a visual of graphic observations and field shapes that he and Hayhurst had extrapolated.

"Our preliminary research taught us characteristics of the field. We needed those to control its use. We learned quickly that metals of any sort would distort the field and make it unpredictable. Our best guess was that the field behaved like a tornado spiral in shape but with a tendency to whip about and rotate any metallic test subject violently. We stuck with nonmetallic subjects. Pure elements were the least likely to disturb the field. Crystallized carbon was our best ally in studying the field and mapping it. We were able to keep a diamond levitated by the device for several days, using only the energy from a double-A battery. It was a costly experiment when we lost the diamond, and we never developed a satisfactory theory to explain the disappearance. When I left for the award ceremony in Washington, DC, Hayhurst assured me that we would have a replacement diamond on my return."

General Gunter moaned in disgust at the news of the lost diamond. He offered a quick theory to the investigators that theft of the new diamond could have been a motive for an assault and abduction of Professor Hayhurst. Grimly, he turned to Finn and queried, "Tell me what is different from the ordinary setup of this equipment."

Emphasizing the instrument once more with the laser, Finn pressed on.

"What I see here is a dramatic departure from the usual arrangement of the electrogravitic field inducer. The inducer itself is fixed in a horizontal plane and focused on the far wall where you see the spiral blood spatter. In addition to that, the energy source has been changed to high voltage in that black converter box on the floor. The settings on the temperature control are adjusted to lower temperatures than we have ever logged on this equipment, and the frequency on the field oscillator is more than the million oscillations per second."

"Wow," exclaimed Finch. "I'm no scientist, but that sounds high."

Finn stared at the equipment and said with concern, "That is dangerously high. "I speculate that Professor Hayhurst, adjusting the device while aligned in this horizontal plane, inadvertently stepped into the field and was violently propelled into the wall across the lab. I cannot begin to imagine where his body is. According to your report, the doors were locked from the inside. I'm not sure you're correct about that. I suspect he became disoriented from the blow and wandered off."

No one in the room could offer any further speculation.

Then something occurred to Finn. "Perhaps he discovered where the diamond went," he offered, his voice dropping as he spoke the words.

General Gunter enthusiastically examined the antigravity equipment with the anticipation of a young boy checking out his first new bicycle. He turned to Finn and coldly said, "You accomplished all this in great secrecy. Not even your grant review board knew what you were up to. What happened to the electromagnetic matter transport device that you were engineering?"

Finn bit his tongue to control his fury and successfully able to express his feelings with mild sarcasm, he smiled at the general, who was now the personification of a government bureaucrat, and simply announced, "We failed!"

As the final moments of their meeting wrapped up, Finn and General Gunter regained their pleasant demeanor, but inside, Finn was seething with anger at the presumptuous jerk. The forensics team was invited to resume their work, and at least they gave the appearance of intense focus, even as they watched the clock. Finn waited patiently, watching them work and offering his assistance when they wanted to touch the research equipment. General Gunter, mindful of his mission, tended to police the information that might be exchanged with forensics. Jones, the team leader, signaled to her assistant that they had accomplished their tasks, and they began to pack away samples and equipment for return to the crime lab. Finn stared at the broken glass cabinet door and made a mental note to open it in private. Not wanting to share his thoughts with those present, he pretended to straighten up his equipment as if this were the end of any ordinary day.

In the recesses of his mind, Finn felt alone. Loneliness, such as one might feel walking through Times Square unaccompanied by a friend, tugged at him. No one to trust, no one to count on, no one to confide in. He just felt empty and on the edge of fear. He waited until the forensics team departed. "What happens next?" he questioned, hoping the answer would come from Becker or Finch.

The general responded. "We still have a lot of unanswered questions. This project is, from this moment onward, the property and the principle interest of the defense department, and we are your virtual employer. I will put my staff at your service and alert the president of the university of our interests here."

Gunter took command as his military training surfaced. He ordered directly, "You, professor, have a lot of work due. As soon as you finish the paperwork reporting on the unusual success of our investment, I expect you will get busy. My office will see to it that you have a new assistant as you continue your research, and that assistant will have a top-level security clearance and credentials to fit the task ahead. Finch and Becker are on permanent assignment for your protection. They will post a guard outside of your quarters twenty-four hours a day, and each will respond to your slightest need. Remember, Professor, your knowledge belongs to your government. Speak about it to no one and feel reassured that you will never be alone. Your safety is our highest priority."

Finn felt the Times Square loneliness tug at him again and jostle him about, as if he were lost in the crowd on a cold winter day. Trembling at the icy-cold feeling, he retreated into the loneliness of his soul.

CHAPTER 6

Eureka

Room 0045 felt warmer when the general departed. Dismissing his guardians, Agents Finch and Becker, was not as awkward as Finn expected. Finch tossed him the keys to his BMW as he exited. Finn knew they would follow him home when he left.

The dead bolt caught in the lock, just as he imagined it did for Hayhurst a day or so earlier. Secured in his lab, he examined the room again, this time without the intrusive eyes of the government, imagining each step his mentor had taken when he rearranged the electrogravitic field generator and aimed it at the wall. Why had he done that? What was he thinking? Why would he step in front of that force field? Each question pulled at him. He thought of the spiral. Getting up on a stepladder, he measured its bloody dimensions. The answer had to be there. The measurements were correct—a perfect Archimedes' spiral in dimension.

What had Archimedes written about the spiral? It was a circle drawn from a single point while moving away from it in space and in time at a constant speed. The spiral represented time itself. Why was that important?

What should it mean to Hayhurst? What should Finn learn from this fact?

Excitement rose within his being. Hairs on his neck stood out. His heart raced. No, it couldn't be that! He turned to the cabinet and studied the shattered glass door. He opened it. Shards of glass plummeted to the floor, smashing loudly into even smaller pieces. One pierced his hand as it glanced off his flesh during its descent. A drop of his blood fell with it. He watched with fascination as if in slow motion. The blood welled up in the small wound. Pain surely followed. That was a natural consequence. More blood dripped, and he stood motionless, observing and thinking. He was trying not to react and then felt incapable of reacting as the thought assaulted his mind.

His attention turned to the interior of the cabinet. There on the glass shelf was more blood—old, dry, and brown—and he saw the glint of metal in the blood. He reached inside with his bloody hand and grasped the small metal object. It was dull and irregular and alien at first, and then recognition came. The object was an amalgam filling for a decayed tooth. It was the physical mold of a cavity in Hayhurst's tooth!

How did this metallic object fill the hole in his logic? It shouldn't, but it did. That and all the remains of Hayhurst in this time and in this place were clues to it all. Somehow, the device moved Hayhurst away. *Where* did he go?

Then it gelled. He remembered his history. Archimedes in a bath, discovering the truth, in the principle, that a pure element displaced its own weight in water. The king's crown was entrusted to him because the king knew Archimedes would discover the truth. The crown was not pure gold but an alloy of silver and gold. Archimedes ran from the bath naked, down the street to the palace, crown in hand. He shouted, "Eureka!" (I have found it.) Now it was Finn's turn. "Eureka!" Finn shouted with absolute conviction. He threw his arms upward from his body like a sports fan at a critical moment in a playoff game. He smiled, stressing the dimples on his cheeks into new variations as he pondered his accidental invention. Time was now his. He had mastered the rudimentary skill required to actually navigate into the fabric of time and space. But what was the cost—Hayhurst's life? Was he alive and lost forever in the vortex of time? Where did he go? Or, to ask a more chilling question, *To when* did he go?

The pain in his right hand distracted him. He moved to the nearby sink and rinsed it with cold water, using a brown paper towel to apply pressure while he awkwardly searched his desk drawer for a Band-Aid. Dressing the wound, he glanced again at the dry blood spatter on the lab wall. Realizing the bitter truth was painful. Wherever and whenever Hayhurst was, it was not likely that he survived his trip. The marking on the wall and the dental amalgam in the cabinet suggested the most violent of forces at work. Together they had studied the force field and learned of the consequences of using a metallic subject. The field wavered and spun wildly out of focus when they had tried to transport metal. That was the reason for testing each element individually. The field required focus to be controlled and useful. Was metal the obstacle to success? Was Hayhurst's accident the result of a deliberate experiment? If so, he had forgotten his metallic filling, and as small as it was, it demonstrated the fact again. The field was unstable when metal was introduced!

Finn began a systematic analysis of the evidence before him. The electrogravitic field producer consisted of a ceramic doughnut filled with superfluid, ionically charged and designed to traverse a circular path, frictionless at sub-light speeds. The speed was controlled by two functions, a resonating electric field and a device designed to cool the field generator by using technology that essentially reversed the effect of microwaves. The field was reflected and augmented by a system of small lenses with a reflective surface at the base of the field, made of a common mirror with a high degree of reflection. All these pieces functioned in harmony to produce a propulsive field.

Three-dimensional images of the field had been studied on a 3-D oscilloscope designed for that purpose by Frank Hayhurst's previous graduate student. The scope, though essential for learning the structure of the field, was not essential to its function. Previous experiments with any metallic structure seemed to wreak chaos on the force field. Watching a metallic object spin out of the field in random directions reduced the experiment to mere amusement and was useless for their purposes.

Avoiding metallic subjects was paramount up to this point in their research. They'd assumed that their technology would only work on nonmetallic subjects. They concentrated on pure elements, and because they ultimately dreamed of transporting biological organisms, they chose carbon as the test material. The element known as carbon came in many forms. In its most structured form, it was crystallized, otherwise known as a diamond.

Although expensive, the diamond represented their most successful attempt at controlled use of the force field. Studying it, they learned how to adjust the field and learned that the force was exponentially and directly proportional to the proximity of the mass studied, to the base of the field. They learned that varying resonance of the field could change its shape. The shape of the field was a prism with three sides. Hayhurst was studying the effects of lengthening the prism while Finn was in Washington, DC.

Finn studied the mechanism holding the field generator in place. It was not loose. It was locked in position. Hayhurst's misadventure had been deliberate! What had he attempted?

Discipline was everything in Finn's life. Whenever confronted with complex problems, the rule he followed was to go back to the basics. Reaching for the silver triangle on the counter, he applied it to blank paper, tracing a carefully straight line in the center of the page with an engineering pencil.

He scrawled *Known* neatly across the top of the line.

Finn considered what he knew about the events leading up to and following Hayhurst's apparently deliberate entrance into the electrogravitic field and the seemingly violent results of that action. He started writing:

Known

1. H locks himself in lab. Field producer power remains on. H disappears.

2. Metal item (silver/mercury amalgam) that must have disappeared with H reappears, likely at great velocity.

3. Oscillator resonance higher than we've used before.

4. Field generator lower than used before.

5. When the diamond disappeared while levitating, test field was a perfect isosceles prism.

Finn looked at the page and drew another line. This time he wrote:

Unknown

1. What were H's final intentions?
2. Why does metal seem to cause dangerous distortion of the field?
3. Is there a way to prevent metal's chaotic distortion?
4. What really happened to the diamond? Why did it disappear from the field?

When he was satisfied that the list was complete, he opened a file on his computer, typed it in, and saved it.

Finn stared at the screen and considered the problem. Of course, there were unknowns, but he was confident that a solution would materialize. The diamond disappeared into the void unexpectedly, but records kept revealed that the field prism was perfectly isosceles at that moment. Recordings of the field dimensions and shape were consistent with a stable field. The diamond had no impurities but was blue. That meant that boron molecules had taken some of the places that carbon molecules would normally assume in the crystal structure. Blue diamonds were unique in their properties, as they were able to be conductors, and because of this property, they could be used in chip circuitry. All other diamonds were resistors, even insulators, of electric current. Was that somehow the key? Metallic subject materials all conducted electricity but had the effect of making the field uncontrollable. The field behaved chaotically with Hayhurst's last experiment, but the result thrust most of Hayhurst beyond this reality and presumably into the vortex of time. What was the relationship? What was Finn missing?

Assumptions could be incorrect. What if the metallic specimens they had used were the wrong kind of metal?

The dental cast from Hayhurst's tooth was an amalgam of mercury and silver. Could there be an answer there? The reflecting mirror was part of the device but outside the field. It was made of an amalgam of tin and mercury. Would mercury stabilize the field? A simple test would tell.

Finn searched the lab and found a glass-filled thermometer in a drawer. He put on protective gloves and took pliers to it, snapping off the end of the mercury-containing vessel and pouring the contents into a Ziploc bag. *Primitive for a lab experiment*, he thought, *but it will have to do.*

Placing the plastic bag containing the liquid metal onto the base of the field generator, which was now pointing upward at a protective shield, he switched the field on and adjusted the resonance. When he reached the critical level, there was a loud roar, and he watched as the droplets of liquid mercury splashed into the shield and coalesced into a shiny liquid pool in the containment device. He did not have to collect the mercury and weigh it to know this experiment yielded no fruit.

Not to be weighed down by this defeat, he persisted in his deliberations. *It's not the mercury—so what is it? Is it the silver? Precious metals in general are less reactive chemicals and often serve as catalysts in many physical and chemical reactions. Why not a precious metal catalyst?* He eyed the silver triangle. It represented more to him than just a fancy tool. Claire had given it to him when she announced her pregnancy. It symbolized family, affection, and passionate love. Ever since her death, he carried it wherever he went, playing with it while giving lectures. It made her feel nearby. It blotted out the pain of losing her—losing the baby. Could he risk that token here? She would have been the first to suggest it.

He took the triangle, placed it on the field generator,

and switched it on. He was so sure he was right that he failed to take safety precautions. The field glowed jade green. A perfect prism shape grew as he adjusted the oscillations. Finn hesitated. He switched the power off again and went to a reference book. Something he had read in the past was haunting him. The passage was about a special resonance that occurred in the fusion furnaces. The only fusion furnaces known to modern man were stars. Stars were the factories that produced all the known elements from the simple hydrogen atom. However, in the cosmos was an exceptional amount of carbon and oxygen.

Perhaps it was the signature of the deliberate organization of all that exists. He went to a book in the office library: *The Intelligent Universe*, by Fred Hoyle, a prominent astrophysicist.

He had marked the page. The number was there! It was the precise resonance needed to create carbon. This required a collision of two helium atoms forming beryllium_8, an unstable isotope. This same resonance enabled beryllium_8 to collide again, almost instantaneously creating a carbon atom.

The resonance energy was easily reproducible on his device. He set it carefully and noted that it was near the setting Hayhurst had used in his fateful experiment. With high expectations, he threw the switch. The field lit up green again, and the shape adjusted to a perfect isosceles prism.

There was an almost musical hum, and the silver triangle levitated and faded from sight. All that remained was the green glow of the prism-shaped field. He switched the power off.

Finn stared at the empty platform. The triangle was gone. A tear welled up in his eye as he said in a whisper, "Sorry, Claire."

In the next moment, the triangle returned, as if she were speaking to him. His spirit soared.

"That's twice now," said Finn, quoting an old Irish saying. And then, at the top of his voice, "Eureka!"

CHAPTER 7

The Chair Ceremony

Finn could not remember a recent day that had brought this much happiness. Nor could he remember a day in his life that he was so afraid. The paradox of the moment was crippling, and when he turned off the current to the force field, the unexpected solution to the yet unanswered question appeared in the form of the silver triangle on the pedestal where the force field had been.

Coming home from sailing the sea of time was as simple as turning off the power! Clearly, it was another assumption, which he would have to prove before he would be certain, but nonetheless reassuring. He was tired now and needed to rest. He picked up the triangle, reached for the BMW keys, and exited the lab. Out on the parking deck, he entered his car and drove home, mindful of the black SUV that followed him closely back to his Genesee Street home.

Locking the dead bolt inside the Victorian house that Claire had made a home, he retreated into his personal office. Paranoia grasped at Finn. French doors in his sanctuary flashed reflections of headlights. He pulled them closed and held his breath to see if the intruding beams of light would stop. Creaking boards from somewhere in the old house never seemed as ominous as now, this moment in time. He wished it away. Refusing to leave, it grew into an eternity. Deliberately, Finn slowed his breathing as numb lips and fingers, the familiar symptoms of an anxiety attack, overtook him. Slight twitches of his muscles and his heart pounding against his ribs in his chest seemed to rock him physically. Holding on to reason was his goal as he regained control of his reflexes.

He briefly craved a martini but deliberately chose against the soothing effects of gin. Time itself was now at his disposal. He busied himself preparing something to eat. The kitchen table had served as a catchall since Claire's death. He brushed aside stacks of old mail and files from work and sat down at the table, making notes on a blank pad in between bites of a sandwich. He began to formulate a plan to deal with his discovery. There was so much to do and so much to tell. Feeling the restraint of the general's instructions, he hoped he could keep the secret. He held the keys to a paradigm shift that would change the world, and no one else knew. But they suspected something. They parked outside of his home, Claire's home, like an army in siege. He had transmuted into his hero, a modern Archimedes, as well as a victim of a siege, by the full forces of the world's most powerful government, waiting outside his window. He was their target. What would become of the knowledge he owned were they to steal it from him? Living under their microscopes and at the end of their telescopes, he would adapt his every action.

They would put the pieces of the puzzle together, and then what? Would they try to coerce him? If he refused to cooperate, would they see him as a threat? Would they attempt to eliminate him, or would they see his value as Marcus Marcellus saw the value of Archimedes? Until then, he needed a plan.

Exhausted from the highs and lows of the past day, Finn ascended the grand staircase to the master bedroom. In the darkness of the hallway, the mahogany stained woodwork in the old house looked black. Once inside his bedroom, he fell into bed and dreamed of time gone by…

e⁄ɔe⁄ɔ

June 14, 1976, Hartsdale, New York:

"Mind the time, Finn!" shouted Fred Otto. "You'll be late for the 4:58."

Finn bolted out the door of the newspaper and tobacco store and into the blistering heat of the June afternoon, flying past the old wooden chest and narrowly avoiding the gray Adirondack chair that was a familiar landmark to many commuters who stopped for the afternoon *New York Post* and perhaps a candy bar or pack of smokes. Around the corner, he picked up his pace as he bid farewell to the last store on the end of the row. Down to the very end of the parking lot, Finn flew low to where the fence was torn open and past the yellow sign warning *Danger—Stay off the Tracks*. Sweating, he leaped across the first set of tracks, jumping high to miss the dreaded third rail. Once again, his stride carried him across the northbound tracks, just in front of the oncoming train, and up onto the platform. Balancing carefully, and barely behind the yellow line, he faced the rushing train. It roared past him, the lead car coming to rest three hundred feet farther north. The train's hot air smothered him, filling his lungs with the scent of hot brakes and oiled steel. Compelled by the blast of the engine and the screeching brakes, Finn covered his ears with his hands. The thrill of feeling the massive speeding trains careening by him while almost touching his face was one of the joys of being sixteen.

The conductor, standing on the lower step of the first car, hurled the newspaper bundles down by Finn's feet. They were large bundles because it was coupon day. He bent down and grasped the wire ties, one for each hand, and the race was on.

If he waited for the train to move, he would be too late. Sprinting with a bundle of newspapers in each hand, he headed for the steel overpass and raced up the stairs, bumping tired commuters in their summer suits as he plowed a path through the crowd and beat those on the bridge to the steps on the other side. Jumping down two and three steps at a time, he reached the bottom and, in his final sprint, overtook all but one of the commuters as he slammed the bundles onto the wooden bench. Fred met him there with the wire cutters. They quickly unbundled the *New York Post* and began to make change for the evening rush hour trade.

Finn hoped to see one paper left over, for on the back page of the *Post*, he had eyed an article about the Yankees beating the Mets eight to four in the twelfth Mayor's Trophy Game. With the rush hour over, his wish materialized, and Finn sat in the old gray Adirondack chair, reading the sports page greedily. *Not a bad job for minimum wage*, he thought. Done with the article, he noted a main-page story about unrest in Soweto but quickly lost interest. Fred called after him, somewhat annoyed at his one-minute break. Finn looked up. That's when he saw the girl with her white poodle. He smiled, staring at her, then offered her the chair for rest, as if it were his to give, and walked back into the store to begin preparing to close the shop for the day.

Fred was an exacting boss. Hard work was expected

of even the least of his employees. He handed Finn the broom and winked at him. "Why don't you start in the front tonight?"

Finn nodded and smiled. He walked with the broom to the front door and looked out. She was still there with her poodle. She was pretty, with fluffy blond hair to her shoulders, freckles, and a natural blush on her cheeks. She was wearing designer cutoffs and a shiny blouse. Her legs were athletic. The poodle dangled at the end of a pink lead, totally disinterested in anything but a candy wrapper on the sidewalk. She bounced up out of her chair and walked with a provocative strut toward the railroad station. She ascended the stairs of the steel walking bridge and disappeared out of sight.

Finn watched her. Fascinated by her beauty, he sighed. He thought he would like to get to know her, but he assumed she lived in the wealthy neighborhood on the other side of the tracks, and a girl like that would be a pipe dream.

His day's work done, he bid good night to the boss and walked home, leaving the train station far behind.

                                                ❧❧❧

On Sundays, the newspaper and tobacco store closed shortly after the 12:20 Mass let out at Sacred Heart Church. Even on beautiful Sundays in June, the newspaper trade required flexibility.

Newspapers on Sundays were purchased after church services, and the local Catholic church had a huge crowd of late sleepers on that day. They stormed the store in waves, in search of the Sunday edition of their favorite paper. The Sacred Heart group was done by 1:20 p.m. By 1:30 p.m., there were usually no customers on Hartsdale Avenue. June 20 proved to be an exception.

The girl was back! This time she arrived without her poodle. She bought a pack of spearmint gum and announced to Finn, "My name is Claire. What's yours?"

Finn usually had a lot to say, but now, as he looked into her blue eyes, he was speechless for fear of stuttering.

While he collected himself and found words, she stood there patiently waiting, her left hand on her hip.

"I'm Finn—" He'd almost said Finbar, and he blushed with embarrassment at the formality of his proper name. "F—Finn," he said.

"Well, Finn," Claire inquired with surprising maturity, "do you expect to have a career in the newspaper business?"

Finn blushed out the truth, "No, Claire, I have to work so I can buy a car when I go to college."

Claire didn't react.

This is good, thought Finn. He explained further. "My dad insists I learn about hard work. He says it's the most important part of my education."

Again, Claire seemed accepting of his confident answer. "You are so cute!"

Finn's heart raced. No girl had ever said that to him before! Reaching for his pockets, he buried newsprint-stained hands out of sight.

Claire persisted. "Don't be shy. I mean what I say. I don't lie."

Concealing his excitement at her revelation, Finn fidgeted. He imagined she could see his heart racing inside his chest. His very thoughts stuttered. A boast escaped his lips. "I'm going to be a scientist—a doctor—if I can." Hiding securely behind his ambition, he awaited Claire's reaction.

"Then you can walk me home if you want," she said with a bit of a dare in her tone.

Finn glanced at his watch and then over his shoulder. Fred was there watching the whole show. Finn went icy cold. Fred, locked in a gaze with Finn, blinked first and held out his fist with the thumbs-up sign. Finn melted into glee and waved so long to Fred, taking Claire's hand and going for a Sunday afternoon stroll, heading over the bridge toward Fenimore Road.

It may have been a stroll for the confident Claire, but for Finn, it was as if he were skipping down the yellow brick road into Oz. Finn McGee was the Tin Man, and he had just found his heart!

∽∾∽

June 14, 2010:

Finn awakened to reality. Morning brought the anniversary of his first encounter with the love of his life. Melancholy mornings such as this made him well accustomed to the emptiness of his life without her. He reflected that in spite of his recent discovery, the human memory was still the most reliable time machine.

He turned on the stereo and played Queen, absorbing the tormented emotions written by Freddie Mercury in the rock opera "Bohemian Rhapsody." The piece went gold the year Finn met Claire.

It was a bitter reminder of the sense of loss and separation they sadly shared beginning on the day Claire's father forbid them to date. Not because Finn wasn't worthy—the prohibition was simply based on the caprice of her daddy's rulebook. Dating a thirteen-year-old girl just wasn't acceptable when you were about to turn seventeen. As Finn finished the morning activities of daily living, he laid the misery aside like an old photograph, careful not to tear it, tenderly putting it in a secret place.

❧❧❧

At 1:00 p.m., the chair ceremony at Hendrick's Chapel would commence, and he would be given the title of "Chairman of the Albert Einstein Physics Department." Coveting the position since changing careers from medicine to physics, he had little taste for it today. Driving to the campus that morning, the lyrics to their song, "Bohemian Rhapsody," echoed through his mind.

As he pondered the familiar lyrics he asked himself the questions posed in the song, *Is this really my life, or am I living a fantasy or dream*? With some deep sadness, he accepted his own reality. He even acknowledged that he created it with his own choices. The choice was deliberate not the impulsive type referred to in his and Claire's favorite music. The image painted by the lyrics flowed through his thoughts. At that moment he was trapped in a landslide of unintended consequences. From this reality there seemed to be no escape.

The usual chorus of federal agents followed him from behind as if to provide the background music.

Finn, lost in his momentary reverie, pushed the BMW 328 to the limit of the campus S curve and screeched to a halt in his usual parking space beside the physics building. In the rearview mirror, the ever-pursuing black SUV was just now visible. Escaping from the chestnut leather cockpit of the black cherry sports sedan, he ran for the shelter of the building and room 0045, its deepest office. Once there, he barely noticed the new woman seated at the lab desk.

Retreating into his private space, he saw it. On his desk was a crumpled edition of the March 2010 *Discover Magazine*. The lead story assaulted his mind: "The New Rules of Time Travel: What to Know before You Go." No address appeared on the cover, just the image of an alarm clock with shattered glass and a list of other stories. Finn considered all possible sources of this anonymous surprise. Out there, someone with close access to his private space knew, or at least guessed, what he held secret. Stress rose in his being, and his mind retraced his conversation with General Gunter. Promises to provide assistance may have been fulfilled with the appearance of the new identity in the lab. Reluctantly but necessarily, Finn walked into the lab and confronted the new woman occupying the desk. With certain guile and a great deal of restraint, he introduced himself, not failing to add his signature smile.

Kathryn Dobbs-Moore responded to Professor McGee's introduction with a nervous smile. Casting her eyes all about the lab, she iterated as if by rote the circumstances of her new assignment.

So overly careful and orderly was her presentation that Finn felt it displayed a paranoid cadence. Her appearance conflicted with her announcements.

Ms. Dobbs-Moore proclaimed and recounted to Finn her great body of work and effort to obtain this fellowship in the alternate geometry and relativity fields. As she continued, it was clear that her curriculum vitae was long and impressive. Yet on her first day of work, she was adorned in a T-shirt covered with political slogans, cargo pants, and a dirty lab coat. Her flyaway curly brown hair was so unkempt that it was impossible to imagine a budding scientist here, but rather a thirty-something adolescent with no proper sense of the workplace. She chewed gum loudly when she spoke. During the entire meeting, she failed to look Finn in the eye even once. Finn immediately distrusted her, and he would have assumed she was an agent planted by General Gunter, until she almost absentmindedly mentioned her work at Georgetown on Dark Flow. He had read of it, and he knew that it was on

the edge of new frontiers in physics. Relaxing at her revelation, he considered how he might use her talents in his
current research, concluding that he could devise an ex-
perimentation program, which, by its very nature, would
keep her in the dark about the direction of his research.

Formalities having been exchanged, he watched her
retreat into the lab, hair flying about with each step. He
noted her sandals for the first time, laughing to himself
that his new lab assistant and graduate student was a
Haight-Ashbury hippie wannabe from the sixties and
couldn't be a government agent. Then again, she would
make the perfect spy. She did not fit the profile. If Gunter
had appointed her, Finn would soon find out. He knew
the requirements for being assigned to this project. In
spite of her casual appearance, she must be government
approved and vetted. There was no other possibility.

Yet Finn sensed that he had to trust her—and decided to do so carefully. Before leaving for the chair ceremony, he gave her an assignment.

"Kathryn, we are missing a valuable diamond. Here
is the file on our supplier, including the cost to this program. When I get back from today's official program, I
want to know where it came from and how we can re-
place it." With that, he turned sharply on his heel and exited the lab, going up the stairs and out of the building, in
the direction of Hendrick's Chapel.

εᴈεᴈ

Upon entering the only place on campus always used
for celebration, he braced himself for the cheers and well
wishes of the university's social elite. Praying for patience and a chance at quiet anonymity, he took his place
near the podium and contemplated the empty black chair,
garnished in gold with the University of Syracuse crest

and a title: "Albert Einstein Chair." *The chair, like most academic thrones*, Finn thought sarcastically, *is empty*. If Finn could truly have his wish now, it would have remained so.

Reaching his hands deep into his pockets, he shrugged his shoulders and bowed his head, trying to find obscurity.

CHAPTER 8

The Gathering Song

The ceremonial processes concluded with Professor McGee performing in usual style. "Thank you, all," Finn remarked, grinning, this time through clenched teeth. Light danced off the familiar silver triangle as Finn waved it at the dignitaries assembled there. He sought and found a quick exit when the 3:00 bell chimed. Heading for the door he glanced back at the empty chair and thought once again of Claire...

❧❧❧

July 1986, Firmin Desloge Hospital, St. Louis, Missouri:

Men and women with faces of diversity moved in unison down the 6 West corridor of Firmin Desloge Hospital. *Phalanx of white cotton coats*, Finn thought as he participated, following the teaching resident from room to room at a snail's pace, each time pausing long enough to note the intimate impersonal details of disease and dying. Except for a few gray-haired stalwarts, pretense at modesty during these rounds had long been abandoned. This mob of medical academics, having just checked in for their internal medicine rotation, huddled closely together for support while the chief resident taught.

Finn found an outside edge of the group, even jostled for it, and won the place because of his height. From this vantage point, he could let his eyes and mind wander if the need arose. Suddenly, as luck would have it, a beautiful nurse in a crisp white uniform and a slightly shorter-than-average skirt stood in heated conversation with an attending physician. She was blond, with a fair complexion and rosy cheeks, and she had her hand on her hip at just the right attitude. It was Clair—now "Nurse Claire."

He couldn't believe she was here. He'd known of her plans to go to nursing school and had imagined what a fantastic nurse she'd be at some hospital. And here she was, at his. As the cluster of medical students inched closer, he was able to read her name tag. In bold black letters next to a photo, the ID badge read *Claire O'Connell, RN*. She still used her maiden name. The chief resident, likely noting Finn's distraction, and that he was more joyful than a student ought to be at that time, skewered him with a question. At a loss for words, Finn tuned in for the rest of rounds, delaying gratification of what he thought would surely be a sweet reunion.

Nursing shifts ended at 3:00 p.m. at Firmin Desloge Hospital, and so did teaching rounds. Finn ran to the nurses' station and stood there watching his first and only true love finish giving her report to the incoming shift. Total surprise engulfed her when she looked up at him.

Simultaneous hugs and kisses, lasting a bit too long for the public corridor of a hospital ward, prompted reason over emotion. They held hands and walked out of the building into the afternoon sun. Picking up the shattered pieces of the past, they began that moment to plan the rest of their lives together. She had waited for him, and he had waited for her. Now time was theirs, and age would never matter again.

ᑉᕐᑉᕐ

June 14, 2010, University of Syracuse, physics building:

"Time is the dilemma now," Finn said aloud as he put aside his daydream. He reached for the magazine he had found on his desk. Before reading "The New Rules of Time Travel," he took out his laptop and opened a new file. Finn's fears of discovery increased. He worried about someone discovering what he knew. Kathryn began to gnaw at his mind, increasing his anxiety. Did he really think he could trust her? With federal agents watching him closely from all corners and following him about, had his new assistant been placed there in the heart of the lab to monitor him from within? He would have to ensure that he encrypted this new file. It must be kept secret.

At the top of the page, he headed his own list and recorded what he believed to be the most elementary problem that he needed to solve first:

Rules of Time Travel

1. Find a navigational tool that will define and identify ways to adjust the time machine in order to travel to a specific time and place.

H. G. Wells had it easy, Finn thought. *He just wrote into his novel a dial in the front of the Golden Sleigh. From there, it was simple—just turn the dial and go.* He wished momentarily for a dial. Then he started typing again:

2. Precious metal elements, such as silver and presumably gold and platinum, are catalysts for the success of the time travel field.

3. Turning off the power to the time travel field can result in the return of the experimental time traveler. Examples: the silver triangle, H's amalgam filling. Exceptions: H's body, diamond.

4. Considering whether it is possible or wise to change history is imperative.

The navigation problem needed a solution and it would take time, hard work, and a plan. *Yes, even an assistant*, thought McGee.

Finn saved the file and closed the laptop. He picked up the copy of *Discover* and read.

The article intrigued him, and he immediately agreed with one of the main points. Indeed...*all you would have to do is use an extremely strong gravitational field, like that of a black hole, to bend space-time.* The author was right. But where did one get a black hole that was even manageable? The author had no opinion, but Finn had already invented such a device, and it was both portable and powerful.

Experience in time travel is required, thought Finn, *for the author of the article to postulate much more.* He continued to read and found himself at odds with the proposed theory that traveling the dimension of time was the "equivalent of walking in a circle."

Theories of some type of linear travel were more to Finn's liking. If time travel was circular, then what path would the subject traveling take to come back to the starting point? Precisely at the moment the power was shut off, his silver triangle returned. Finn believed the direction was linear. However, the diamond had not yet re-

turned. Conundrums like this were Finn's bread and but-
ter. Postulates by the author, that circular time travel
would prevent paradoxes and would not violate logic,
were unproven and distasteful to Finn. He could not read-
ily accept them. Forgiving himself his own pun, he declared, "Time will tell!"

He finished the article, realizing it was laced with the
usual arguments about paradoxes and the standard discussion about the arrow of real time being unidirectional.
Mostly, he felt the piece itself was not helpful and just in
the magazine to promote sales of a book, published earlier this year by the same author. The real meaning of the
article was still a puzzle. Clearly, someone was sending
him a message! Was it a signal that that person knew
Finn had succeeded, or was it an accident? Could it be a
threat?

Dispatching his worries, he turned to work, his usual
method of stress management. "Kathryn," he called out to
his lab assistant. She sauntered to the door of his office,
clearly not wishing for a distraction. Finn became profes-
sorial and instructed her on the rules of being an assistant.
Then he asked, "Do you have the material I requested on
the diamond?"

She nodded affirmatively and ran to get the file.

Finn rummaged through the folder that Kathryn retrieved. He made a pretense of looking through the financials and tried to keep his real intent from her. After a
while, he turned his attention to the actual source of the
diamond. While Kathryn did the busy work to complete
his investigation, he added materials he had been researching. Finn focused on the origin of the crystallized
carbon.

The file, now complete, contained reaffirmation of
the diamond's source. The diamond was blue-white and
of the purest quality. It came from a mine in South Africa

with a good reputation for quality industrial diamonds. One of his theories was dashed. He was hoping the diamond had been pried from a gold ring, and that the slightest trace of gold dust left behind could account for his theory about precious metal catalysts. Further research rewarded him. The South African mine was known for high concentrations of silver. The diamond was imperfect. There was elemental silver on it somewhere, in just enough of a quantity to catalyze the time field. That left another problem to solve. Why had the diamond not come back when they disconnected the power? If he was correct, the diamond should have returned.

Trying to act indifferent to his new clue, he shuffled to papers and again reviewed the financials that Kathryn had researched. Finn looked at the price on the statement from the diamond broker. Twenty-two thousand dollars was quite a bit out of his budget—but well worth what he was about to do.

Calling Kathryn again, he explained to her that they were going to spend the rest of the afternoon scouring the office for the lost diamond. He didn't tell her how it had been lost. She displayed much less resistance than he'd expected her to at the order, but Finn knew he was testing her limits with his request.

Offering to pitch in was his way of being certain the job was done correctly.

Hours passed, and they found nothing. The day at an end, he dismissed Kathryn with the excuse that he would stay behind and finish some unrelated work.

Just before retiring from the task and weary from the search, Finn slumped back in his chair. The knots in his neck muscles made him stretch and turn his head in search of relief.

He had just spotted the broken glass again and added

the repair task to his to-do list when a strange thought crossed his mind. He stood and walked over to the cabinet with the broken glass. Reaching in, he rearranged the contents of the shelf, which included several metal and ceramic tools that he seldom used. Carefully moving them off the shelf, where the amalgam was discovered, he saw his prize.

The diamond was back! It may have crashed through the glass when the amalgam arrived. If that was the case, it was still delayed, but the small speck of elemental silver may have peeled away on its departure, sealing it in whatever the vortex of time was like.

Until the device sent out another probe with a catalyst, the diamond was stuck in time's dimension, unable to return. Solutions to two questions occurred.

"The catalyst was necessary for the subject to depart the present time. It was also necessary to return," Finn proclaimed in relief of solving this piece of the puzzle.

Sadly, he realized that Frank's body was lost and might never return. The assumption Finn then made was paramount. "The time traveler must always be accompanied by a catalyst," he declared with certainty.

He turned on his computer, entered his passwords, and opened up the list of rules. He typed:

1. Time traveler must be accompanied by a precious metal catalyst for both departure and return.

Finn closed his computer, gathered the paraphernalia he'd collected into his briefcase, and began his commute home, out into the warm June evening.

Pausing briefly, he watched the sun set alone, before he drove away with his usual chorus of guardians.

That night, he dreamed…

❦❦

December 21, 1996, Northwestern University Hospital:

Two days had passed since a missed wedding anniversary. Overwhelmed with his schedule, Finn, the new clinical instructor of medicine, found himself berating Mr. Gibbs in his hospital room while medical residents looked on.

"This is the third time in as many months I've had you in here with decompensated heart failure. When I send you home today, I will give you the same instructions I gave you every time before." He stared at his patient with ferocity and continued. "Two grams of sodium in your diet each day is all you get. That leaves no room for a cup of clam chowder and a liverwurst sandwich on rye."

Making his point, he looked at the unsung hero of the Gibbs family, the woman who held Mr. Gibbs's life together by watching his every breath these past years, and placed the burden of guilt on her. She seemed to sag from the weight of it.

Understanding the reality of her fears, she resolved anew to remain in charge of his destiny, knowing the inevitable result would eventually come.

With that, Finn led his entourage of residents on to the next hospital room and the next after that, repeating the authoritative ritual, until rounds were done for the day.

It was Saturday afternoon, and he was tired. Work seemed endless, and there was little time for his favorite things, let alone time for Claire. Each morning, he awakened to find this endless cycle repeating. Working to pay for overhead now held him in a self-perpetrating trap. He hated himself for it, and for how it made him deal with his patients. He immediately left the hospital for home. He would pick up Claire, and together they would go to Mass at 5:00 p.m. It was Advent. After Mass, he would take her out to dinner and celebrate the missed anniversary at their favorite bistro. He had been thinking about the rut his life had become and was determined to change it. He had already had discussions with friends in high places about a future in physics, his undying passion after Claire. They would discuss it together tonight.

They entered St. James Church together, she attired in a smart black evening dress and white mink coat, and he in a navy blue business suit and gold tie for the occasion. Finn chose to be coatless, as the weather was warm for December. They entered a pew near the front and both knelt in quiet piety, awaiting the celebration of Mass. All stood as the priest and deacon approached the altar and the choir began "The Gathering Song."

> *O come, O come, Emmanuel.*
> *Rejoice, rejoice!*
> *Emmanuel shall come to thee, O Israel.*

Claire held his hand tightly and leaned in toward his left ear to whisper. The message was unheard due to the crescendo of voices as worshipers joined the choir. It was Finn's favorite time of the year, and the liturgy engulfed him in the peace of the season. Claire sat closer, stood closer, and held his hand tighter than he had ever remembered, and he assumed the same Christmas spirit had affected her as well. At the priest's signal, they stepped up to the altar. Tonight, this couple had been given the honor of lighting the last Advent candle.

The homily was about the change that would follow in four days on the liturgical calendar. In a gentle voice, the priest pronounced from the pulpit, "Christmas celebrations were meant to remind the world that Jesus Christ was born to change the world."

Finn had learned from a longtime friend that coming away from Mass with a special thought made the Mass so much more meaningful to each person in attendance. Tonight, the thought was "change."

After Mass, in the dim candlelight of the bistro, they would share drinks and a meal in honor of their last five years of marriage. Hoping they would agree about needing change in their lives and that his wishes would be hers, he looked forward to the romance of the evening.

Dominique, the owner of the bistro, saw them arrive in the crowded restaurant. He immediately escorted them to a quiet table in the back, which he had prepared for his favorite couple.

They exchanged pleasantries while Dominique, always the Frenchman, welcomed "Madame McGee" with a twinkle in his eye as he bent to kiss her hand and then assist her with her chair.

Seated across from Claire, Finn leaned forward and whispered to her, "I'm on to the two of you now!" Then he grinned broadly at his own humor.

Claire blushed, "Silly man, you know you are my one true love."

"And you mine, darling. Happy anniversary. What's up with you tonight? At Mass, I felt like we were on our first date."

Claire reached into her purse and withdrew a small red box tied with a white ribbon. "A present for us," she announced. "I tried to tell you in church, but the singing stopped me. This is a special anniversary. Open it."

Finn grabbed the box and pulled at the ribbons. Inside, wrapped in black velvet cloth, was a silver triangle.

"What does it mean?" Finn queried, examining it closely.

"An isosceles triangle, done in sterling silver. It will always have special meaning, Finn, and like the triangle, our family now has three sides. I'm pregnant," she exclaimed, tears of joy rolling down her cheeks.

Finn leaned across the table and kissed them away. They sat for an hour discussing the coming baby, and Finn began his second martini, while Claire, concerned for the health of the unborn child, only pretended to sip at hers.

Finn knew his news of change would not seem so wondrous, and that it may even upset his beloved Claire. Looking for confidence in her deep blue eyes, he borrowed it and began to tell her his plan.

"Claire, you know you are the love of my life, and I cannot serve two mistresses. The medical practice is a demanding one, and she is taking more and more out of me, leaving me little time for you and my other scientific interests. I want to leave my practice and go back to school for my doctorate in physics." He paused and waited for a response.

Claire was very sober, and her face gave away secret emotions. He could tell she was afraid of change. The big house in the Scarsdale Subdivision of Arlington Heights, which they had been saving for, would never be theirs. Her father had learned to love and respect him when he asked for his daughter's hand, but Finn could not be certain whether that respect didn't have more to do with his daughter marrying a practicing medical doctor than fondness for Finn's character.

Finn even wondered if his choice to pursue medicine was an attempt to win approval from Patrick O'Connell, Claire's dad. As they held hands across the table, no words needed to be said. They knew each other's hearts. Their love was forever. Bumps on life's road would not affect them.

Claire looked at Finn reassuringly and said, "When do we start, my love?"

Dinner at the bistro was always top-shelf. Dominique's chef had become a friend as well, and he surprised the McGee's with chocolate profiteroles for their wedding anniversary. Having their fill of French cuisine, they left hand in hand and walked home to their one bedroom condo in a light snow, entertained by the village Christmas decorations.

Holding Claire's hand, Finn thought, *Affection is never wasted.* Claire's countenance, as beautiful to him as the day they met, was now surreally enhanced by the essence of motherhood. That night, they both slept well.

⁋҉⁋

June 15, 2010, University of Syracuse:

When the daily routine becomes stressful and predictable, time for change is near.

Finn's day began with the same government escort as the day before. He sensed in all this a gathering storm and began to brace for the first gust of wind. It echoed the discomfort that had caused his career change.

Kathryn greeted him in the lab with some news of the expected crisis. FedEx had delivered a request from General Gunter for a comprehensive review and update of his research. Blank forms were enclosed with the request, which Finn interpreted as an opportunity for delay and obfuscation. In his soul, he was determined to keep his secret. So much potential for misuse of time travel gave Finn the strength of character to declare himself the guardian of the secret.

Collecting and assimilating the research, he had planned for Kathryn's attention to be his first priority. He called Kathryn into his office after he engineered the course she must follow. Soon all the players would have a role, and the puzzle would come together. Time could not be wasted.

CHAPTER 9

Ephemeris

Knowledge is always meant to be shared," Finn stated to Kathryn, who'd presented herself in more dignified attire for her second full day on the job. Finn reached for the coffeepot to make a cup of joe and realized it was hot and full. He had begun a habit of skipping breakfast and substituting black coffee for his first meal of the day.

Accompanied by stale Oreos, it would get him through the morning. He searched the warm dark liquid for evidence of a stray hair from Kathryn's yet uncombed locks but found none.

Kathryn grinned at him with a *why-so-serious* look on her face as he sipped his coffee in between sentences.

"I'll need your assistance in compiling what amounts to a high-tech digital ephemeris," Finn requested.

Kathryn spun her hair at him and stared. "What in all of creation is an ephemeris?"

"You just described it," Finn said with a grin, playing a physics lab form of Abbot and Costello's *Who's on First?* routine. "Hopefully when we are done, ours will be all of creation and then some."

Kathryn practically snorted. "Okay, have your fun." She turned her head away as if to make a statement. Looking over her shoulder and half of her hair, she said, "Well, I'm waiting!"

"This is not a vaudeville joke," Finn said with a laugh." "An ephemeris is a table of values that gives the positions of astronomical objects in the sky at a given time or times. Different kinds are used for astronomy and astrology. It is a map of the known cosmos from our perspective. Its purpose is to assist in navigation, usually of the seas. The position is given to astronomers in a spherical polar coordinate system of right ascension and declination, usually from a table. In our case, it will be from a computer screen."

"Why do we need this ephemeris?" queried Kathryn.

"Because we are going to do some traveling and will need a way of getting around," was the guarded reply.

"Why not use GPS?" asked Kathryn, wrinkling her brow in concern, as if Finn had some form of psychosis.

"There is no GPS where we are traveling, Kathryn." Finn spoke matter-of-factly, wishing her curiosity would fade.

"So why don't we buy this ephemeris?" Kathryn teased, pushing Finn off guard.

Finn recovered and said with control, "We will make our own." His face was stern. "Ours has a single purpose, sort of unique!" We will start with some of the groundwork today." Please contact the technical department and have all the controls on these antigravity devices changed to reflect the smallest possible increments." Finn took the control knobs off himself as he described what she was to be shopping for at the tech center supply desk. "While you're away, I'll program the computer to accept our data and correlate it into a digital map!" He shouted his announcement into the hallway as she left, hoping she would hear a fragment of it so there would be no need to explain the computer later.

While she was gone, he wrote a modification to a program that Hayhurst had already loaded. The clocks on the wall were all synchronized and critical to the work ahead. Hayhurst did have vision, after all. The clocks were not his pet obsession. Finn decided he would record all time logs with the local meridian and Greenwich Mean Time. He set about encoding multiple layers of security on the computer program. While he used the password "Claire" for the first level of security, the precise frequencies of the electron vibrations for carbon and oxygen, along with a few randomly placed characters, guarded the mid-level of security. He chose "deceased" for the deepest layer.

With Kathryn out finding knobs for fine-tuning frequencies and electric current, Finn Googled "extreme camera cases" and discovered that he could order a case that would protect at zero to ten atmospheres of pressure. He ordered it for next-day delivery, using the Department of Physics charge account.

Kathryn returned with pockets full of knobs and tools to install them, and she immediately set to work. Finn spent the rest of the day reengineering the antigravity/time travel device for miniaturization and portability. Periodically, Kathryn's curiosity brought her back into Finn's lab.

Each time she caught his attention, he stopped what he was doing and gestured to her that she should return to her own work space. The last time, he glared at her and queried, "What is it that you need?"

She smiled, clearly happy that she'd finally gotten him to speak and bluntly stated, "I sure hope you know what you're doing."

Then she darted out of the lab. Finn wasn't sure if

she was snooping or flirting. He knew that she was smart enough to ascertain the answer to her question.

༒ༀ༒

FedEx delivered his camera canister early the following morning. Finn set up the device with the narrow frame parallel to the floor. He gave Kathryn a description of the apparatus, similar to the explanation he'd given General Gunter. "The large narrow frame held in place by two lab cranes is a reverse microwave resistor field. It's designed to lower the temperature of the superfluid container that it surrounds by using a technology that works like the opposite of your kitchen microwave oven. The doughnut-shaped ceramic container that it surrounds holds what is known as a superfluid. The atoms comprising this fluid are ionically charged. Applying alternating electromagnetic forces to this superfluid by changing the polarity of the field a million times per second, the fluid flows in a circular path around the inside of the doughnut.

"The fluid is engineered to be totally frictionless and can move in a circle at speeds only a photon could travel. Photons have no mass, as they are particulate waves of light, but our fluid has mass and no friction. We have here, Kathryn, a working model of an antigravity force field." Finn continued his half-truth, and Kathryn, being a model student, was transfixed by his words. "The safest direction to point the business end of this machine for now is up away from the ground and toward the sky," he further explained.

Finn loaded the Nikon camera into the pressure-proof canister. He'd had a jeweler alter the camera so it had a pure silver mirror instead of the usual mercury and tin.

With the silver mirror already fitted deep in the Nikon, Finn checked twice to be sure it was well insulated from shock. He first sealed the Nikon camera, setting its timer at the same time, and then the canister. He mused at it as it lay on the frame's platform, still and silent. Like a magician on a stage, he brought his hands together and made a gesture to Kathryn that there was nothing concealed in his sleeves. Deliberately exaggerating his movements as he waited for the timer's signal, he turned the power on with dramatic flair. Musical humming filled the air as a green glow surrounded the test canister, and Kathryn's jaw dropped almost to her knees. Shock, then awe, contorted her face as the prism developed to a perfect equal-sided shape and the test subject faded into the jade mist. Counting down with the Greenwich Mean Time clock, exactly sixty seconds elapsed while the device continued its eerie music. At the nadir of the countdown, the machine switched off, and the canister reappeared. Kathryn sat speechless in a nearby chair, her frizzy hair flowing in every direction as she shook her head in disbelief. She had been briefed on the direction of the research, but even knowing what the machine did was no substitute for witnessing this demonstration.

By day's end, Kathryn had rudimentary knowledge of the inner workings of the antigravity device and labored diligently to learn to control it. Finn never disclosed the real truth, assuming that she would accept the concept of antigravity teleportation without making further assumptions about its revolutionary ability. This dual set of paradigm shifts, one hiding the other, made great theater in Finn's own imagination. Under his supervision, she learned to use the device for controlled intervals. Finn called each test a probe and explained to her that until they had overcome the navigation dilemma by developing their ephemeris, there were dangers in sending blind probes. She at once grasped the correct logic and recommended that the initial probe be sent out into the atmosphere or even space, if possible. Finn smiled with his usual guile, having persuaded his student to come to a specific conclusion. Kathryn, once she owned the idea, took continuous credit for thinking of it. Of course, it remained to Finn's advantage to permit this course of thought.

His confidence in Kathryn had reached a plateau after the first week. Holding suspect her role there, he still wondered about the source of her exact origin. Kathryn's enthusiasm for the new frontier of antigravity transport blunted any evidence that she was there to spy on the project. Her flirtatiousness was possibly a cover for being a spy. Indeed, if she were, Finn controlled what she knew. Assuming that Gunter and his government minions also had guessed at the truth, Finn suppressed the need to search her credentials and even her purse for a badge. Freedom came in strange packages.

The work was simple but tedious. Kathryn would take the automatic Nikon camera and seal it in its case. The jeweler's alteration wasn't visible, and to Kathryn, the camera appeared as just another Nikon with a large lens. The lens itself was a standard wide-angle lens meant to photograph the stars. The timed photos would be used to determine where in the heavens the probe containing the camera would go. The power switch essentially did everything else. Timer was set for one minute, each probe was directed toward the sky, and the test lasted the entire sixty seconds.

The visual effects were at first startling to Kathryn, as the device hummed almost musically, and the probe canister dematerialized in a green light, a second after the power reached its peak. Records of Greenwich Mean Time and local meridian time were entered into the computer on departure and return of the probe, and then the disc in the camera was downloaded into the computer and erased for its next use. Between uses, fine-tuning the controls to a set of frequencies engineered by Finn was done in specific sequence, and those frequencies, identified by Greek letters, were also logged into the computer at each step.

The finished data played on the monitor in silence. Star formations in outer space looked much like the sky on a clear night. Finn told her the data was impressive. Her astronomical skills were not up to appreciating the difference between one screen and another. Kathryn was curious as to the purpose of creating this stellar map. When she asked Finn, he indicated the map would allow them to test the navigational ability of the anti-gravitational device, which would ultimately be used for transport.

෧෨෬෨

Finn expected a reaction, and he watched as Kathryn held her breath. He was relieved when she said, "Wow."

Kathryn was breathing rapidly, making Finn nervous, but she finally settled down.

"Mmm-hmm," he agreed.

She was right. The photos were spectacular. The pair sat at the same table in the lab, sharing a large computer screen, where they'd spent hours over the past few weeks, sometimes simply marveling at the photos of the cosmos.

During that time, Finn and Kathryn had become close friends. He admired her work ethic and her commitment to the science at hand. This had grown into a fondness that they both seemed to share—if not as potential lovers, as close confidants.

In addition, Finn's plans had been evolving as the

data rolled in day by day. Kathryn ran to the capsule each time it returned and anxiously loaded each new set of digital photographs. It was clear that she felt useful and was developing pride in her work. Finn had started bringing Starbucks double lattes for both of them every morning. Together, they were carefully assembling the ephemeris. They were a team, Finn realized. He glanced at his assistant.

He noticed Kathryn's response to his stare. Clearly she was feeling her boss's eyes on her. Kathryn turned to him and boldly stated, "Your eyes remind me of the depth and mystery of the photos we're gathering."

Her bluntness took him off guard. He smiled back at her, all the while realizing that she was blushing and perhaps did not want him to notice. Finn made a mental note to use caution now with his protégé. He preferred that she understand his approval, but he didn't wish to confuse her emotions. He wasn't ready for a more personal relationship.

Finn headed to his desk, leaving Kathryn to continue the work. He was happy that he'd decided to trust her with more detailed work.

A few minutes later, he heard her gasp. He turned and noticed her studying one of the recent photographs with a look of utter puzzlement. From where he stood, Finn was fairly certain what was dawning on her—the phase of the moon was 180 degrees out from the current calendar. He should have seen this coming. He held his breath. Maybe she'd dismiss it.

"That's odd," she announced, realization overtaking her posture.

Finn froze in his tracks and scrambled for intellectual cover. "What did you see, Kathryn?" he asked nonchalantly.

Kathryn turned to him and, looking perplexed, asked,

"Where did you send this last canister?" She looked at his face as if to gauge his answer.

"I'm not sure what you're asking," Finn lied blatantly.

Kathryn was visibly annoyed but trying not to show it. "There seems to be some glitch in the system. The moon is out of phase with today's calendar. How's that possible? Do you think the memory in the camera is faulty?"

Finn sighed in relief, but she must have surmised by his body language that he was holding back.

"Dr. McGee," she said, addressing him formally for the first time since she'd met him, "something here is incorrect. Our readings are not consistent with my understanding of this mission, or we have a malfunction."

Finn regained his cool demeanor instantly. He took charge of the discussion and led her away from the truth. "Kathryn, there must be a simpler explanation than that. Let's look at this together. Ah—I see what you see, but you have to think about outer space in three dimensions. We sent the canister out far enough to give a different perspective on the moon than we have from here. That is essential to our map if we are to succeed in antigravity propulsion," he lied.

Kathryn accepted the rational explanation with the submissiveness of a graduate student. Finn knew she would not drop the subject, though. She was too good at her profession. He withdrew from the conversation and knew that soon he would set up an alternate lab with his savings or money from the proceeds from the sale of his Victorian house on Genesee Street. For now, he'd have to monitor Kathryn more closely. He wondered when he could bring her to full knowledge of his discovery, if ever.

The extra worry took its toll in productivity. He

spent his spare time dodging his ever-present agent-guardians and Kathryn as he went about the business of building a second device in his den on Genessee Street. This one would be more refined, smaller, and able to transport a subject the size of a man if the occasion presented itself. He would test it when he had all the necessary data from Kathryn's ephemeris, which in time would occupy a single DVD.

❧❧❧

After a month, the work on the ephemeris was completed and the paperwork requested by General Gunter returned. By now, Finn was in the habit of taking Kathryn to lunch. One day he took her to a quiet pub, a place he'd only shared with Claire. Finn was only hoping to plan the next phase of work at the university physics lab. Kathryn was looking for something else.

With the work completed, lunch on Friday called for cold beer, and they each ordered a frosty mug on that hot July afternoon. Kathryn, unaccustomed to alcohol, loosened up considerably by the end of her first draft and thirstily began her second draft.

Finn, still curious about her origins, casually asked her, "So Kathryn, how is it that the day after I lost my mentor and met General Gunter, I had the fortune of having you appear in my lab, as out of nowhere?"

Kathryn, well into the second cold beer, answered glibly, "Doc, there is no such thing as luck, and you're too smart not to know that. I was placed here from my other job for a surprise sabbatical. I had been trying to get the CIA to pay for a year of higher education since I joined. I left Georgetown because I couldn't afford the tuition, and the agency is loyal to its agents. They knew I had talent and desire, and they just called me out of the blue and told me they found a spot for me to finish my degree.

"I have to admit I am a bit of a snoop, but I'm not a gossip. I saw the files for this project and wanted to be involved. I really had no field agent training, but I was reviewing classified documents and sorting out the trash from the important information. I guess even without a complete degree, I was still qualified to understand enough of the science to differentiate the forest from the trees."

"Kathryn, are you spying on me?" Finn queried with a smile.

"I guess I am." Kathryn smiled back. "It makes no sense, though. Nothing here is unexpected or out of the prospectus of your grant funding. General Gunter hasn't even called me since he gave me this assignment. I haven't even sent in a written report."

"What exactly was your assignment?" Finn barked. "What were you told to do?"

Kathryn, more relaxed and waiting for her third cold beer, began telling Finn the entire story. She leaned toward him at the table for privacy, dropped her recently acquired formality, and seemed more comfortable with her mentor again.

"When I was at the agency and knew I was coming here, I ran some related files in researching you and your missing Professor Hayhurst," she began. She continued to inform Finn that her read on his file was that he had been identified while in college as having the aptitude and interest enough to be groomed for this project. Hayhurst was a career-long player in doing defense department research. It seemed that he had been told to pick Finn out of dozens of candidates that applied to Syracuse for physics.

Before this was achieved, though, Finn himself had put a fly in the ointment, so to speak, when he chose to go to medical school instead. The program still wanted him, and patient use of influence had become their method of redirecting him. When he was practicing academic medicine at Northwestern, they used their influence by way of grant money to push Finn along a path that would eventually lead to burnout. His responsibilities were heaped upon him deliberately. He handled them well, but they knew his two passions—physics and Claire. When they finally arranged it so that he had little time for each, their patience was rewarded, for he broke out of the rat race they had created for him and willingly ran in their direction.

The rest was a matter of careful surveillance and mentoring by Dr. Hayhurst. The net result was they had their new Einstein, for the want of a better analogy, and then, just at the moment when a revolutionary discovery happened, Hayhurst went rogue and had a tragic accident that would have ended the program had it not been for Finn.

He sat back in his chair, stunned. What this young woman he'd been starting to see as a friend was saying seemed impossible. But she knew so much about his career and life—stuff she'd know only if she'd had access to the files she'd just told him existed. As the truth seeped in, his brain seethed with realization. He quieted his mind, trying not to think of himself of someone's unwitting pawn. After all, this could well be simply the invented version of his life's path, according to a creative and youthful young woman who clearly had a penchant for mystery. So what if the CIA had a file detailing his career path. The CIA had files on lots of people. Surely, the influence Kathryn was describing was, at the least, strongly exaggerated in her imagination. At any rate, he wasn't taking any chances. *I will end this my way*, he thought coldly.

Kathryn swallowed hard as she watched her boss's gaze turn icy. She'd revealed the truth so willingly because of their closeness, along with the help of the three beers. Now it seemed she was losing him.

"Finn," she said softly, moving her hand toward his but not quite daring to touch him.

She hoped he'd bridge the small gap between their hands. Instead, he pulled the napkin from his lap and pushed his plate of food aside as if he hadn't noticed the gesture.

"Good food here," he said.

He knew he couldn't let his inner thoughts percolate to the surface. He kept his friendly, cool demeanor and carefully studied Kathryn. He gave himself credit for having been careful to keep her out of the loop despite his growing trust in her.

He wondered again, after her revelations, how long he actually could keep her in the dark. Her next role would be the most important to Finn. Feeding her just enough disinformation and keeping her busy would provide him cover for his projected adventures into time itself.

☙❧

Back at the lab, Finn opened his laptop and entered the series of passwords that led to his final deep security password. *Deceased*, he typed. Then he opened the file containing his rules, read the initial rule set, and typed in the modifications, adding solutions to rules one and two and combining rules two and five:

Rules of Time Travel:

1. 1Find a navigational tool that will define

and identify ways to adjust the time machine in order to travel to a specific time and place.

Solution – Kathryn's ephemeris for space and time.

2. Time traveler must be accompanied by precious metal catalyst, such as silver and presumably gold and platinum, for both departure and return.

Solution – Send out digital Nikon camera retrofitted with sterling silver mirror on exploratory missions. Travel with camera or other precious metal.

He read over the third rule and updated what he'd discovered, also adding a new fourth rule:

3. Turning off the power to the time travel field can result in the return of the experimental time traveler. Examples: the silver triangle, H's amalgam filling, diamond (with the addition of more catalyst). Exception: H's body (losing the filling at the wrong moment made his journey erratic).

4. Find a replacement for Kathryn in order to control the device's timing.

Possible solution – Rig a clock to control the timing.

Sitting back in his chair, Finn examined his list. He pondered rule five:

5. Considering whether it is possible or wise to change history is imperative.

After a moment, he added three more rules:

6. Secrecy is paramount.
7. All trips must have a valid purpose.
8. Travel light!

Finn meditated on the issue of metal interfering with time travel. He hoped he could prove his assumption that enough catalyst would balance the untoward effect of metal traveling through time.

He closed the file and opened a new file:

Gilmore

Searching through his old paper address book, he copied his number and address into the file:

Dan Gilmore
Penthouse
One Fifth Avenue
New York, New York
Cell: 212-555-8470

Finn closed the file and headed home with the usual set of company to the old Victorian house on Genesee.

෴

He made a phone call to Best Real Estate from the car to confirm his appointment. A strange-looking man with sun-damaged skin and a bad toupee met him in the driveway of his home.

Finn led the tour while the agent took notes. "Everything goes with the house," Finn instructed.

The Realtor took inventory as the tour began.

It was Claire's house, actually. Finn just lived there

after her death and never changed it. Love at first sight was a habit of Claire's, for which Finn was eternally grateful. Never did he anticipate it would carry over to real estate. It was actually at odds with his own philosophy, as his dad had taught him, "Never fall in love with a house. There is always a better one down the street!"

The yellow house on Genesee Street, not the Scarsdale Subdivision of Arlington Heights, became Claire's passion when she got accustomed to life in Syracuse, New York. As he led Mr. Best though the old Victorian, he made sure to point out all the architectural embellishments Claire had so much enjoyed.

"The foyer, Mr. Best, has a slate floor from a quarry in France. It was purchased for the original construction in 1892 and shipped by sea and rail to Syracuse, where special artisans were employed to lay it with quarter-inch seams filled with oyster shell grout. The stained glass was also commissioned in France, and the artist attempted to reproduce a suburban scene from Hartford, Connecticut, which accidentally included an image of the home of Mark Twain."

Finn paused for a breath, and Mr. Best caught up with his notes. Once inside the "grand hallway," as Claire called it, Finn pointed out the dark stained mahogany paneling that was also handcrafted by artisans of the late nineteenth century.

The living room had twenty-foot vaulted ceilings with wooden beams exposed between plaster panels. The fireplace was fieldstone native to New England and New York. It rose in a peak the entire twenty feet, and the walls were done in dark mahogany hardwood. All floors were oak plank and deliberately stained dark ebony. The living room was fashionably furnished in French country fabric ensembles, flashing the rich colors one would see in the countryside in Provence, France.

The plush never-worn carpet was Mediterranean blue, also a favorite of Claire's. In the corner of the room was a teak bar imported from China, the wood grain enhanced by scarlet wood rubbings of the Chinese characters representing happiness.

Finn tried to explain the value of everything to Mr. Best. He based it on the fact that most items had seldom been used. Finn's home office offered a comfortable club-style brown leather loveseat and his own gas fireplace. There were custom cabinets, a built-in bar, and a Renaissance-era library table that Claire found at an antique store.

Along the sides of the table were eclectic Winslow chairs in conflicting colors, each one reflecting hours of antiquing by Claire, and an armchair left over from his bachelor days. At Claire's insistence, the walls were washed-ash paneling. Finn was a devoted husband and even let his wife decorate his private den.

There were only three bedrooms upstairs because of the architect's plan for a vaulted living room ceiling. For a house this large, that was a sore point with most buyers—and the very reason her dad had told him to avoid closing the sale. Claire prevailed, as she always did, without one note of dissent from Finn.

Finn took the agent on the bedroom tour but did not accompany him into the nursery. He himself had not been in there since the day Claire died in July of 1997. If he hadn't had a housekeeper, it surely would have rotted away by now.

Mr. Best, being good at the real estate business, offered Finn a discount on his commission and a contract in the same sentence. Acquiescing to the terms, Finn eagerly signed the contract to list the house, reminding Best that the sale included furnishings.

Earnestly frightened by the predicament in which he

found himself, and distancing himself from his grief about Claire, he was ready to move on.

With the house on the market, Finn, confident in his plan to move on, withdrew his savings, having secretly begun work on the next downsized model of his time machine. He brought the work home a piece at a time until he had developed a smaller prototype. Mentally, he kept Kathryn at a distance. He endured her casual flirtations while letting her assist in the technical engineering of individual downsized components. He was certain she had not yet caught on to his plan. In the late heat of the summer, he set his escape in motion.

CHAPTER 10

Escape

Thursday, August 19, 2010, University of Syracuse:

The campus was abuzz with the comings and goings of parents dropping off their freshmen sons and daughters. Upperclassmen had arrived over the weekend to pre-assigned dorm rooms and were lining the streets of the campus in the annual tradition of welcoming and unpacking the new wave of freshmen. Traffic, always congested on campus, was at a gridlock. Finn had driven his BMW to the "Reserved, Albert Einstein Chairman" parking spot early this particular Monday morning, accompanied by his usual escort. Finch actually waved hello from his Black Chevy Tahoe. Kathryn was unusually late, not heeding his warnings about the expected crush of people arriving at the campus. Finn had expected this and was enjoying the quiet time.

His last conversation with Kathryn was revealing. As it turned out, she was a history buff. Civil War history was her passion, and she collected memorabilia. Finn imagined winning her absolute confidence by showing her how she could have some of the most outstanding relics

imaginable from the War Between the States. He remembered Elmer Ellsworth's bloody shirt with photos and letters about the first and most conspicuous casualty of the
Civil War, collected by one of his friends from college.
What if, Finn mused, *I could deliver something like that
to Kathryn? Would she drop all allegiance to the government for the chance to possess such contraband?*

Finn had planned this day well in advance, hoping
the ephemeris would be complete. While waiting for
Kathryn in the quiet of the lab, he copied the ephemeris
onto a DVD and then downloaded it into his laptop. Securing the disc and placing it in a protective envelope, he
addressed it to Reverend Dan Gilmore, PhD, in New
York City.

He put both in his computer case, padding them with
the few clothes he had packed for his intended elopement.
He brought his Nikon camera, modified for time travel,
and packed the zero atmosphere canister in a box containing other equipment necessary to his further research.

Neatness was his compulsion, and he spent an hour
of solitude being certain that the appearances of normalcy
permeated his office and the lab. He placed a complex set
of instructions on Kathryn's desk and used his silver triangle as a paperweight.

He knew he would be back for it, and leaving it was
a signal to all who knew him that he expected to return.
He wrote a note in his own hand to Kathryn, explaining
that he needed a short vacation. He also made her aware
that the BMW would be picked up for routine service in
the early afternoon and the keys were in his top desk
drawer.

He said he would be back when he had his fill of the
beach, probably in a week or two.

He would notify the school president of his intentions by cell phone, after safely departing from the watch-

ful eye of his guardians. In the years since Claire's death, he had taken no vacation except for the wake and the funeral. Now that he was chairman of the department, he had a semester without classroom duty. Unlikely as it was that his hiatus from the campus would raise suspicions among his superiors, he was keenly aware of the predictable wrath of General Gunter, the CIA, and the FBI. Finn fancied himself a fugitive from coercion rather than an outlaw. Either way, the adventure was about to begin.

Leaving the physics building with his black canvas case in hand, he slipped into a stream of foot traffic and blended immediately with the masses of individuals carrying similar bags. Glancing over his shoulder, he saw no sign of his guardian agents, and he grinned to himself at the relative ease with which he hid in the crowd. Walking in pace with most everyone, he continued to move closer to the gate he would pass through to exit the campus.

After passing through a campus gate, instinct led him in the direction of the railroad station. Again, his focus was to blend with the foot traffic. At the station, he boarded the 284 Empire Service train in business class after shelling out eighty-three dollars in cash. Good fortune resulted in a reservation for a window seat.

Another eighty-three bucks guaranteed that the seat next to his remained empty for the six-hour journey to Penn Station. He placed a call to the university president and left a message with the secretary about his vacation plans. He turned off his cell phone and took out the battery. Putting the disabled phone away in his bag he took out a new prepaid phone and dialed Dan Gilmore's cell phone.

"Hello." Dan's voice greeted Finn from the other end of the line. "Yes, I'll be there," was Dan's response after Finn advised him of his plan to visit.

The conversation was brief and to the point. Finn

closed the phone and settled back into his seat. His cheek resting on the cool glass window, he napped, sensing freedom, however brief it would be. The station clocks all registered 9:45 a.m. as he slipped into sleep…

ᏽᎧᏽᎧᏽᎧ

Saturday, December 19, 1991, St. Patrick's Cathedral:

With the same grandeur his riches could supply to everything in life, Claire's daddy made sure their wedding took place in the most elaborate circumstances. Nothing less than Saint Patrick's Cathedral in Manhattan for his daughter and that persistent suitor, Finbar McGee, would have satisfied him.

Photographers, the bane of all newlyweds, posed them without mercy or coats in the sunny December cold on the steps of the cathedral. The wind kept redistributing Claire's train, and a homeless young woman kept wandering into the photographer's layout. Obvious to Finn, the homeless girl was seeking cash disguised as alms to end her reign as a nuisance. Finn made every effort to be kind while shooing her away.

There were harsh words from Claire's uncle Harry: "Don't you realize this girl has but one wedding day?" Giving her five dollars to disappear, he shouted after her, "You'll have the rest of your life to beg on these steps!"

Disappointment in her uncle's approach registering red on her face, Claire had whispered to Finn, "I would have waited a lifetime on these very steps just to be with you today."

Finn hugged her to keep her warm against the cold wind, and they laughed while they shivered, trying to be still for the photographer.

"Claire, I will always be true to you, and since the

day we met, I have never gotten over you, even when you didn't return my letters."

Claire sighed, not wanting to revisit the pain of lost contact, and confided in Finn, "There was one moment that I thought I could live without you. The day I left for nursing school, I felt so alone. Daddy was rushing me, and there was this noise outside. I looked and saw a middle-aged man that somehow reminded me of you. Suddenly, I felt your presence and knew I could never live without your love. The last thing I packed in my suitcase was your picture. The man had a camera, and I had just tossed your photo in the trash. The coincidence was overpowering. So, my darling, without you, I am as wretched as that poor homeless girl."

ᏒᏒᏒ

Thursday afternoon, August 19, 2010:

Kathryn paced back and forth in the laboratory, tortured by indecisiveness. Calling General Gunter would certainly be her safest choice, but then she would betray her new mentor. Finn had left her without warning. She was an emotional wreck—even though she understood that he was not currently enamored by her. *Certainly*, she thought, *he will come back. One didn't leave a world-changing paradigm at the sole mercy of a graduate student, especially if she worked as a spy.* The easy choice for Kathryn was to wait for the agents to notice that McGee's car was being driven away by the BMW dealership. She did this out of loyalty for Finn.

Her special interests included Dark Flow, a new theory about the universe she had the opportunity to pursue them under Dr. McGee's mentorship. She could not betray her intellectual interests in scientific advancement any more than she could ignore her feelings for Finn. While she waited for events to unfold, she practiced her alibi. "It" was about to hit the fan.

ↄↄↄↄ

As expected, when the general learned of McGee's disappearance, all hell broke loose. Agents with flashing red beacons on their black SUVs flooded the streets and highways in and around Syracuse, New York. CIA arrived at the Victorian house on Genesee Street and surrounded Mr. Best as he was planting his "Best Real Estate" sign in the front lawn. Flustered by the show of force, Best held up his hands like a captured outlaw in a spaghetti western until the agent in charge called off his men.

By evening, it was clear the professor had slipped away, and odds were that he was coming back. They would expand their search, ramp up their technology, put out an all-points bulletin, and expect to find McGee in time. They had plenty of that. They did not know that he had more.

CHAPTER 11

Claire

August 1980, Scarsdale, New York:

Pink leather Hartman luggage didn't belong to just every seventeen-year-old girl who was packing to go on to higher education. Nursing school would come at a price for Claire: freedom from being cared for, pampered, special, spoiled, and safe. Claire displayed all her finest possessions, mostly the latest fashions, on her white queen-size quilt and handpicked the ones she would squeeze into the dormitory closet.

The rest would stay home and collect dust and perhaps remind her mother that she was still away, on club afternoons when the Manhattans otherwise dulled her memory of her only daughter.

Canasta and cocktails appeared to be much more important to her mother these days, and Claire felt alone in her plans to move away.

Her mom's party attitude had her focusing her attentions on her social circle and upward mobility, including the club, and extending less to Claire as she grew older, becoming more focused on ritual suburban traditions that Claire not only resented but resisted.

Her room, indulgent in its chic decor and ample size, was the envy of all of her girlfriends. She walked in bare feet across its full length to her stereo. Pulling an album from a dirty and over-worn dust cover, she read the label to be sure it had been cataloged properly and placed Queen's "A Night at the Opera" on the Girard turntable. The volume up, her room filled with bittersweet music. Tears rolled down her cheeks as the familiar "Bohemian Rhapsody" echoed through her bedroom. Tears became sobs when the audible skip replayed the relentless refrain "Galileo" and the recording stalled endlessly, repeating "Galileo, Galileo ..." Remembering how she'd brushed the stylus away from the track in frustrated anger the last time she listened, she now sat on the floor of her room, never wanting to hear it again. The carpet screamed pink. Claire felt blue. Her Galileo, Finn McGee, her own boy scientist, had been gone from her life for what seemed like forever.

Placing the damaged album back in its cover, then tossing it into the white wicker basket reserved for trash, Claire let go of the past. Moping about her room with the FM radio blasting "Magic," she reset her emotions on hopeful again as Olivia Newton-John sang, "You have to believe we are magic. Nothing can stand in our way." *Young women in the electronic age always seem to find solace in music*, she thought, wondering if this was true of young women throughout history. Finn had taught her to look at the world as history unfolding. She so desperately wished he had kept his promise to write. He had been so good about protecting her and following her father's demands.

They never had a formal date but found the time to meet in public places, walk in parks, and talk for hours about the future. Handholding and kisses good-bye were secondary aspects of their intimacy. Conversation was the glue that bonded them. Patience and delayed gratification were her daddy's rules, and Finn respected rules even when Claire wished to ignore them.

Wealth came naturally to Claire's daddy. An Irish Catholic lawyer, he specialized in divorce and was in strong demand from Greenwich Village, New York, to Greenwich, Connecticut. Claire kept a rosary on her bedpost and often waged prayer on heaven, believing that her daddy was somewhat of an oxymoron. An Irish Catholic divorce lawyer must need more prayer for salvation than a normal lawyer would. Claiming that being a divorce lawyer gave him more responsibility to supervise his daughter's choice in young men, he demanded an interview with each fellow brave enough to ask Claire for a date. Daddy conducted these interviews like formal depositions. Then he became both judge and jury in matters of dating and, like the rest of the household, it was run like a courtroom.

Having little say in who was right for her and who might be wrong, Claire pretended to have a high school social life, dating everyone who passed her father's judgment. Never were there more than a few dates with the same guy. Love interests and her hopes about the future were her own secrets. Guarding them silently in her heart, she kept faith with herself and her hopes. Daring to reveal these at home would assure daddy's ire and ignite her mother's shame at having a less than perfectly predictable daughter.

The fact was that her mother craved peace at home and double Manhattans. As long as Claire demonstrated the appearance of contented, wealthy Scarsdale life, Mother ignored her. Claire believed that underneath his tortoise shell exterior, a truly loving heart resided in her daddy. She caught glimpses in good and bad times—knowing he tried to love her by over-governing her life, then in guilt showered her with unexpected presents as peace offerings. One of those presents sat in the large white leather lounging chair in the corner of her bedroom. A huge white furry creature with onyx eyes and a black stitched smile was piled into the middle of the chair. He was easily four feet tall when sitting. The teddy bear's name was Iceberg. Her bedroom was his lair. He stood as a visual reminder of her daddy's strong love for his only daughter.

Claire opened her rolltop desk and stared briefly at Finn's photo framed in sterling silver. She picked it up and gazed upon his face, pressing the picture to her young bosom. After a minute of anguish, she placed it gently and with some remorse into the white wicker basket as if to say farewell.

Suddenly, there was a loud screech and a slam coming from outside her bedroom window. Simultaneously, her daddy knocked on her door with a warning that time was getting short and their departure for her new school could not be delayed much longer. She exclaimed loudly, "Okay, five minutes." She then went to the window to determine the source of the commotion. A yellow taxi was waiting half a block away, and there was a tall, dashing fellow with sandy hair standing on the sidewalk, peering back at her momentarily. When he fiddled with something that looked like a camera with a big lens, she realized he must be a real estate photographer. He seemed preoccupied with taking pictures of the neighbors' house. She looked away and calculated how much space she had left in her suitcases. Looking back outside, she thought she saw him stare up toward her again but dismissed it when she saw him turning his wedding band on his finger.

Pressed now for a decision, she examined the small cavity left in her tote. Claire suddenly, without explanation, reversed her decision to leave Finn's photo behind. She gently retrieved it and hugged it as if it were Finn, even feeling his presence. She wrapped it in a cashmere sweater, one of her favorites, and called for her father to collect her luggage.

As she walked slowly to her daddy's Mercedes, she wondered if she would ever see Finn again, choking back emotions when she remembered that he never kept his promise to write.

Patrick O'Connell carried his sweet daughter's belongings to the car. He saw her sadness and remembered the struggle over that McGee boy. He loved his daughter fiercely and hoped she would never learn that he had intercepted that persistent boy's letters. They drove down the driveway and through the gates just as the photographer got back into his taxi and left in the other direction. Claire coldly forgave her mother for never coming home from the club to say good-bye.

CHAPTER 12

Gilmore

August 19, 2010, Penn Station:

Dan Gilmore was both a rocket scientist and a prophet. His claim to fame was his contribution to NASA. When he went to work for them, his mentor and boss was the man who kept John Fitzgerald Kennedy's promise to land a man on the moon before 1970. Dan was only twelve years old then and living in a lower-middle-class household, barely above the poverty level, and he decided that he would someday work for NASA. He also decided to be rich.

Wealth beyond imagination came to him. His command of the stock and commodities markets was simple mathematics, but to those that followed his business prowess, he was the prophet of Wall Street. It was rumored that even Warren Buffet and Donald Trump sought audiences with him.

Successful in achieving both his life's goals, Dan was now working on a third. As he approached the station platform, no one could have guessed his net worth or his contribution to the space program. His black suit and

Roman collar spoke of a man of God with an air of compassion and, at age fifty-two, he was still dashing in appearance. The gust of wind from the stopping train blew his coat open and only slightly tossed a tight curl or two from his now salt-and-pepper hair.

❧❦❧

Finn had met Dan in 1978. Finn remembered it as if it were yesterday. They were in a lecture hall three rows apart. The sociology professor called a roll of names. Each group would be assigned to a sociology lab experiment for the semester. Dan stood when his name was called. Finn could not help but notice him. Girls would have called him dapper. To Finn, he was a well-bronzed and handsome competitor in the game of life. Dan was as tall as Finn was. His hair was shorter, curlier, and well groomed. Finn had let his sandy hair grow over his collar, trying to appear scholarly while concealing a tight budget.

When Finn's name was called, and he was assigned to the same sociology lab, Finn and Dan glared at each other at once, not noticing the other members of the group—two alpha males sorting out the rules, of leadership. Dan spoke first. "I'm starting to wonder why I volunteered for this. Sociology is not a vital part of my interests in life. You, on the other hand appear well suited to be here, long hair and all."

Finn snapped back what he thought was something mundane. "You sure seem entitled to your prejudices. Who died and left you the throne?"

From that moment, they were inevitable best friends but didn't realize it until about a year into the argument.

Both men believed that fortune and, hopefully, fame were theirs for the taking—but with effort. Neither student shied away from long hours and hard work, many of those hours spent side by side in the college library or working as lab partners in science classes common to their ambitions. Both men excelled at math. Dan, a practical researcher, preferred integral calculus and read journals about orbital physics and ballistics. Finn's approach was more theoretical. This polarizing difference fueled many arguments. Their reputation grew among their peers. They were the intellectual equivalent of a fight breaking out at a hockey match, always ready to argue minute points, always highly spirited and animated, and when the fight was over, amazed to find themselves in the penalty box. As inseparable as a proton and an electron in a hydrogen atom, and just as different, as best friends went, they set the gold standard.

ᗑᗕᗑᗕ

As the train rolled to a stop, Finn recognized his old friend on the platform, shrugging against the wind. Finn got up and walked to the back of the car before it lurched to a halt. Looking back to his right when he exited, he spied Dan waiting in the milling crowd on the station platform, searching for a glimpse of Finn. They approached one another, hugged like long-lost brothers, and hurried with the rushing crowd to the terminal. They battled for position in the taxi line. Unable to hear conversation, they both waited until they were closed in the backseat of the cab.

"One Fifth Avenue," Dan gently requested of the driver. Turning to Finn, he said, "Great to see you, man. You are just in time—another garbage union strike in Manhattan."

Finn, having had enough experience with New York City, saw his friend was not joking. "You must need a new calendar, Dan. Even people from upstate know the garbage strikes are always in December."

"Not anymore," replied Dan. "The unions found it more effective when the air was warmer."

Finn was the son of a union worker. He did not take the bait, avoiding the usual political argument. "It's good to see you," he said instead.

Dan looked at his friend with great empathy. "What prompted your call, Finn? I sense this is serious."

"Dan, you won't believe me when I tell you my story. If I did not have you to tell it to, I would be lost. I need to talk to you in private. Can you be patient with me until we get to your penthouse?"

"That's what friends are for. The Lord knows He has taught me patience. I can certainly wait for your explanation." Dan turned his attention to the cabdriver. By the end of the ride, Dan knew the driver's name and the names of his wife and children. He'd even looked at their photos. When they exited the cab, he offered the cabbie his card, advising him that if "ever in need, feel free to call."

Having witnessed this before, Finn knew his friend was serious and would remember the driver's name just as he would a friend's.

Finn had been there a long time ago, right after Dan bought the matching penthouses from the estate of a shipping magnate who died a tragic death. Originally, the place looked like a brothel, with red wall-to-wall carpets and decor that was irritatingly trashy. Dan had remodeled it into a modern minimalist space with neutral tones and lots of expensive wood. In one suite, he made the living quarters quiet and comfortable.

Across the marbled hallway, the matching suite became the headquarters of his financial empire, with personalized luxury office furniture and an electronics communication center that would perhaps rival a television station.

At great expense, the roof had been replaced with a vast clear glass skylight that gave a panoramic view of the New York City sky.

Finn appreciated these changes immediately after riding the antique brass and teak elevator up from the lobby and walking into the old marble hallway entrance to both suites.

Looking around, Finn remarked to Dan, "I thought Jesuit priests had to take a vow of poverty. I really thought we would be driving up to the university tonight."

Dan quickly explained that he had given the property to his sister, who now ran the trust fund for the charity he set up. "Maddy lives here now in my old quarters," Dan informed Finn. "When I'm here, I function as an unpaid consultant to help manage the money and to investigate the causes that apply for grants. Sometimes I stay overnight. The office has been set up as guest quarters."

"Nice setup. Can I stay for a couple of weeks?"

Dan nodded at Finn. "I suppose you will run us out of gin, but you are always welcome." He poured from a fresh bottle of Tanqueray gin into a tumbler with ice and two olives. Filling it to the top, he needled Finn, "Do you want any vermouth with that?"

Finn grabbed the glass from the bar and gulped. He was thirsty for fluids and alcohol. Once Dan had poured his own drink, they sat in opposing leather armchairs and Finn began the long, revealing story he had come to tell.

Dan was used to his friend's sudden need for conversation after long periods of isolation. He expected him to spend time rehashing Claire's murder as he had done many times before.

Without hesitation, Finn spoke first of recent events.

"I'm in a bit of trouble, Dan. I am down here to be off the map for a few weeks. I'm sure that the federal government is searching for me right now."

Dan looked rattled and took a breath before answering. "Start from the beginning, Finn. You have lost me completely, and I need to catch up with you."

Finn related the history of the research he shared with Hayhurst. When he described Hayhurst's rather violent disappearance, Dan interrupted and asked, "What, if anything, did you have to do with that?"

Reassuring his friend that he played no part in the incident, Finn went on to describe the interrogation in the SUV, the scene in room 0045 as he first found it, and the work leading up to his discovery. Then he paused. "Dan, what I am about to disclose is world-changing science. I need your absolute confidentiality." He was already sure of the answer.

Dan leaned forward in his leather chair as if to gesture privacy to Finn.

"Old friend, I have discovered a workable antigravity engine that can be used to transport even the heaviest mass with little more than the energy it takes to run a computer."

"You did what?" was Dan's unexpectedly soft, almost inaudible question.

As Finn explained the machine's science and the engineering foundations, Dan got up and prepared two more double martinis.

As he sipped the second drink, Finn said, "I have a machine that uses antigravity as a propulsion system. I learned the rudimentary physics directly from an archeological dig in Sicily, the original sight of Syracuse. Archimedes actually invented it but failed to record it—or chose not to. But I've always suspected it. I found it, and it works, Dan!"

Dan struggled to remain in control of his excitement. "Who knows this, Finn?"

"Enough people that I am under constant surveillance by the CIA and the FBI," Finn quipped. Then he listed the names of Agents Becker and Finch, General Gunter, and the new lab assistant, Kathryn Dobbs-Moore, followed by speculation that the chairman of the physics department and maybe even the president of University of Syracuse had similar knowledge.

Dan reeled at the information overload and was momentarily speechless. He rubbed his chin, which was a habit when confronting a challenge. "Have you experimented with this machine?"

"Only in a limited sense." Finn explained the story of the levitated diamond and gave description of Hayhurst's unfortunate accident.

"Why are you hiding, Finn?" asked Dan, cutting to the essence of the matter.

"Because there is more, a lot more, and with that comes untold ethical and moral problems!" Finn confessed to his friend, exposing the undercurrent of his fear. "I'm hiding until I can reconcile what I have the power to do with the ambitions of the government."

"Did the government pay for your research, Finn?"

"They paid for teleportation research, and we stumbled on antigravity."

Dan wisely dodged the spin and stared Finn down. "You've read the scripture, Finn. 'Render unto Caesar that which is Caesar's.'"

Finn rose and fashioned a third martini. "Unfortunately, there is more, Dan, and when you hear the rest, I believe you'll side with me!"

"Finn, you just told me that you've invented a functional antigravity machine. That, my friend, will change the world. Tomorrow morning, I am going to redirect about half a billion dollars in the trust fund's investments—based on how much I trust you. What more could there possibly be? Have you sold this to the Chinese or the Russians? Is that why the government's looking for you?"

"Calm down, Dan. You're on the wrong path. I guess I have to make a confession."

"Certainly not now, Finn. You've just consumed three double martinis!"

"No, Dan, I'm not talking about the Sacrament," Finn reassured the Reverend Father Gilmore. "I mean, I need to give you all the details, and some are going to upset you." Finn stiffened in his chair and squared his shoulders to confront Dan…

გაც

A day earlier, August 18, 2010, Dr. Finn McGee's house on Genesee Street:

Rain and wind pummeled the house. Gray light filled Finn's office, and desire filled his heart. He held in his hands a smaller version of the time machine residing in room 0045. He had worked on this model secretly and had developed it in the lonely evenings on Genesee Street. He plugged it into the USB port and booted up the computer. The screen glowed white with the charts and numbers from the ephemeris DVD. *Navigation Program Engaged* blinked confirmation on the monitor.

Finn went to the master bedroom closet and picked out a light blue suit and buttoned-down-collar, monogrammed shirt for his journey. He hated ties, and when he wore one, he took pleasure in letting it be known that his ties chose him. This one was old and narrow, one that Claire had given him for Christmas the year before she died. The alternating gray-and-yellow stripes created the perfect pattern for summer.

A stash of old coins, quarters, half dollars, and some silver dollars, all bearing dates prior to 1980, was neatly pilled on the bureau top. He stuffed them into the suit pockets. He didn't expect to need more than a few bucks for cab fare in August of 1980. Yellow Cab, he remembered, charged two bucks for the first two miles from the train station back then. He only planned to be there long enough to see Claire from a distance and influence her to be faithful to their promise.

He collected his digital Nikon, the recording devise he hoped would bring back convincing images of his success, as well as precious memorabilia. Deep inside the camera was the special silver mirror that he anticipated would fulfill the catalyst requirement of time travel. The camera had a simple brown canvas case with an extra set of lenses and a safety strap. Counting on that strap, he hoped he would not lose the silver mirror inside. He returned to the office dressed for his adventure and focused his thoughts solely on the machine.

Hope and faith in his science, and love for Claire, blinded him to the dangers. He would be the first living pilot to travel through the interwoven threads of time and return. He had to be right. Granted, his calculations were based on a so-far improvable theory, and he was at odds with the odds makers. Time travel was linear, Finn was certain, similar to a needle pulling thread to directly where the needle points, it would always be the shortest route from one point to another. Circular time would not allow his program to work. Lost in time, he would have no end to the recriminations over theoretical catastrophe.

He was certain. Wasn't he?

Carefully plotting his course, he entered the settings into the computer and set the device on the floor. Extracting three antennas, like telescoping tubes, he delicately aligned them so that the ends became the corner points of an isosceles triangle. Measuring the angles twice and fixing them in place, he switched on the current to the doughnut-shaped stellar body.

Lights extended from each corner, forming a laser-like image in fluorescent green, forming a perfect equilateral triangle. Finn examined the display of the down-sized time machine. He knew then that there was even more work to be done. But that would wait for later.

Finn tensed his muscles and felt a band across his forehead. He studied the apparatus intently. Sweat rolled down his brow.

As if in slow motion, his trembling hand moved to the keyboard. He pressed in the maximum security code "deceased" and hit enter.

The timer on the screen came to life and asked for duration. He entered "two hours," and the clock was set. Two other clocks were on the toolbar, one for Greenwich Mean Time, the other for the local meridian. There was only one more key to press. Reviewing once more the course he had charted, he prepared himself by standing at the edge of the glowing triangle.

Leaning toward the keyboard, he pressed enter. Hearing the musical murmur from the machine, he gazed in new amazement as the field materialized and self-adjusted into a field of green mist. The peak of the field formed a perfect prism at least seven feet tall. The pitch of the sound emitted queerly, reminding him of classical music.

He held his breath and stepped into the field, hoping to enter the vortex of time itself. At the last second, he wondered if he would find nightmares instead of dreams.

ᑲᑭᑲᑭ

2010–1980, the moment between two seconds:

Staccatos of electronic music came in waves, like a child aimlessly swiping his hand across a harp. The music evolved into snatches of sound leaking into the vortex of time. Just as Jules Verne imagined, the events of history surrounding the maelstrom played out. Snippets of engine noise and radio and television broadcasts could be heard, interspersed with sounds of winds and storms. Human conversation, laughing, crying, children playing games, women screaming, and men arguing assaulted his ears in fragments—none with any discernable context. Finn could hear brief vignettes of reality sneaking into his senses like whispers in a crowd. The net sum was audible, but content was noise. Unlike with Jules Verne's fantasy, there were no controls for speed or halting and resuming travel, no way to check one's bearings or stop to absorb the ever-changing scenery. The computer took over as travel master now. Locked in Finn's home office, it counted down relentlessly to the journey's end.

He lost visual contact with the green prism instantaneously. To a casual observer, he would have appeared to evaporate into the jade mist as if he were some apparition. The vortex revealed kaleidoscope colors fitting ever-changing patterns, taking the shape of a spiral. The color was in the yellow-orange-red spectrum and continued to whirl about him, interspaced with shades of the deepest black. Although cool, he was encased in liquid fire.

Time was moving, but Finn's watch's second hand was stuck at one second past 8:00 p.m. Trying to sort out this time confusion, he continued to hold his breath as long as he could but never felt the urge to breathe. Weightlessly, he floated, suspended by opposing gravitational forces. He had no sense of falling. Neither heat nor cold assailed his senses. He wished one would. Everything felt odd, neutrally numb. Gravity ceased to exist inside the vortex. Up and down were not discernable directions. Floating described his sense of motion, but alas, the word was woefully inadequate.

Uncertain of how long this time travel phase would last, he began to anticipate an ultimate appearance or landing. Hopefully, his calculations would allow him to materialize behind the Hartsdale tobacco and newspaper store, close to a cabstand. He glanced at the second hand sweep on his watch—it remained frozen. He kept staring at his Rolex, willing the second hand to resume its relentless path across the dial.

He felt his body stiffen, and he crouched reflexively. Tires screeched on pavement, horns blasted, and a woman yelled from the window of her Jeep Wagoneer: "Are you crazy, mister! Watch where you're walking."

Dazed, Finn looked around, noticing parked cars all around him. He found himself standing in the path of an oncoming Jeep SUV, realizing it had just come to an emergency stop. He stepped aside quickly, allowing the angry woman to drive the big vehicle around him. He studied its dark blue paint and faux wood siding and understood he'd arrived at his destination in time. He made a mental note that parking lots could be as hazardous as busy streets. Walking quickly now in the hot August sun, he unbuttoned his suit coat. Holding tightly to his camera case, he walked around the bend and past the last row of stores to the Hartsdale railroad station, making a beeline to the taxi stand. He checked his watch. The second hand was moving again.

New problems came fast to pioneers. Not sure how long he had been in the vortex, because his watch failed to register time there, he felt disarmed of his usual methods of observing nature. He could not trust his senses because of these distortions. How could he know what time remained for this journey? Back on the computer in his office, the clock was counting off seconds. But that was in 2010 Syracuse, not in the Hartsdale, New York, of 1980. No ready answer came to mind. Unfortunately, he had overlooked this potential in his planning. Until he got back, if he got back, he could not even enter this rule about time travel in his log. Two hours might not be enough. He would have to move quickly.

Hailing a cab only took a minute. The sign on the door read *YELLOW CAB CO*. The price of the ride was painted on the door: $2.25 for the first half mile and 25 cents per quarter mile thereafter. Fortunate planning resulted in pockets filled with old silver coins. He could afford to ride to Claire's house. He climbed in the rear seat on the driver's side and quickly slid across the hot vinyl. Taxis did not usually have air-conditioning in 1980. Giving the driver precise directions, he leaned forward with anticipation as they drove over the bridge to Fenimore Road.

They rode several blocks and turned down the street where Claire lived. Even after all this time, it still seemed like Oz to Finn. Approaching the O'Connell house, he gave the driver instructions to drop him off and move quickly a half block down the road. Confused, the driver slammed on his brakes, making a racket. Finn got out quickly, closing the door with an unintended overly loud slam, and the driver accelerated away to make a U-turn, a loud roar echoing from the revving engine and broken muffler. It was not the discreet arrival Finn had hoped to achieve.

Finn stood on the sidewalk without a plan, heart beating rapidly with the excitement of the moment. Comparing a trip through time and a chance to glimpse Claire's face, there was no contest. Claire won easily. He took out his camera and posed as if about to take a picture of the neighboring house. Unable to control his impulses, he aimed the telephoto lens at her window. She surprised him when she suddenly entered his view. Even though it was only a second he captured her image in his eye. Dropping the camera and then his gaze, he made himself busy, looking as if he belonged there with his Nikon. He knew the rules of time travel.

Violating them would be evil. He felt her gaze while his heart sung at her presence, and he prayed to God that she would make the right choice. He felt the painful conflict in his heart.

In his conscience, he reconciled the trip. Claire had shared this with him. He knew before he mastered time travel that he had influenced her at this time in her life. However thin the thread, the image of the tall sandy-haired photographer was the defining moment of her commitment to Finn. Her strength was the willingness to endure the wait for him, even if it took forever. His strength of character intervened and most likely did the grace of God. He stalled, took one more furtive glance, and saw her look back.

He was holding his gold wedding band while he prayed for the chance that she would live. He already knew the prayer was not answered the way he wished. Claire had confided this moment to him a long time ago. She had told him a story written long before he traveled here in time. This was her story. He knew she would feel his presence. He knew it was not his right to disturb history.

He signaled the cab and walked briskly to it. Again, he slid into the sweltering backseat. Taking all the old coins from his pocket, he paid the driver in advance to take him back to the train station.

A tear spilled on his cheek as he pondered his experience. The rules of time travel could not be broken, at least not by a good man. As he began to lose control of his emotions and weep, he dematerialized from the backseat of the taxi and found himself being pulled like a thread back to the point at which he'd entered the substance called time.

CHAPTER 13

More Rules of Time Travel

Finn looked at his watch when the jade mist disappeared, and he knew he was safely home in his den. Only one hour had passed on his watch, and two hours had passed on the timer flashing on the monitor. He removed the disc from the video camera mounted on the desk. Placing it into his computer, he reviewed the last two hours. He watched himself step into the field. It brightened and then flashed like a lightning ball. That was a surprise. He had not encountered it with other test subjects.

The clock on the face of the monitor began to run as he stepped into the field. Less than a minute elapsed before he dematerialized. The monitor ran the countdown flawlessly. The backup clock was intrinsic to the battery-operated video recorder for the purpose of fail-safe redundancy. It matched the computer's timer displayed on the monitor.

He saw the countdown end, followed by a green glow and the outline of the prism.

Then, in less than a second, he saw himself standing there in dim light cast by the screen on the monitor. He made some quick calculations. The entire vortex experience lasted one hour. The rest of the two hours was spent in Scarsdale, New York, in 1980.

Finn thought of the perceptions he'd had in the vortex, floating, no need to breathe, and the failure of his timepiece to measure any time. Always the scientist, he conceived all the various experimental options open to him on his next voyage. Musing with the chemistry of respiration alone, he spent an hour thinking of ways to do pulse oximetry and measure CO_2 content in a time traveler's blood. *Alas*, he thought, *how can I count on the required instruments to work in such an alien environment?*

Finn analyzed his impulsive decision to make his virgin trip in time. He had gone to talk with Claire, to give her up—to save her life. So quickly did he fall to that temptation that he brought no plan to execute. Temptation overcame him in the hour he planned this trip. How would a strange fifty-two-year-old man in a suit meet a seventeen-year-old girl just as she was packing to go to college and find some way to convince that same girl to give up her romantic fantasy about a young sandy-haired man? He had thought he could influence her not to cling to him.

The plan had no merit. No young girl of that age would trust a stranger speaking lunacy about changing her future life. In the brief time allotted, Cleopatra could not have seduced Anthony.

He'd planned to sacrifice their relationship, to never have reunited, to never have married, and to never have brought her to Syracuse, where he knew her life would end. The romantic idea filled his passion for her. His obsession was that she would always be happy and live a complete life, even if it meant that he would never be fulfilled by her.

Acknowledging the impulse was ridiculous. The

would-be attempt to change history was clearly wrong. He felt small and weak, not the heroic pioneer he desired to be.

Yet everyone fell, made a mistake, and most learned from their errors. Finn had already.

He opened the *Rules of Time Travel* file on his computer. He examined his initial eight rules.

His eyes stopped at rule five: *Considering whether it is possible or wise to change history is imperative.* A revision seemed necessary:

> 5. There are moral consequences involved in changing history.

He reviewed the list again and then added what he'd discovered:

> 9. Time travel is linear.
>
> 10. The time spent traveling in time is real from the perspective of an uninvolved observer.
>
> 11. Real time cannot be measured from within the vortex because, by definition, the vortex is outside of time.
>
> 12. The approximate vortex interval for thirty years is one hour.
>
> 13. *Postulation* – The transition of an individual subject person or thing to a different time, although possible, is not permanent. If one attempts to go to a destination in time and remain there, an imbalance may occur, which, like a vacuum, nature abhors!

Closing his computer, Finn pondered the location of Hayhurst's body in terms of his final rule.

CHAPTER 14

Confession

The greatest griefs are those we cause ourselves.
– Sophocles

"Dan, did you ever open a door and wish you hadn't?" Finn inquired.

"Yes, many times, Finn. Your anxiety shows through your gin." Dan relaxed a bit, hoping that Finn would as well.

Finn still held his shoulders stiff and his chin firm as he faced his friend. Face red and veins bulging, he looked braced for a battle, not consolation.

"And did you leave that door open?" Dan asked gently in his Jesuit mode. With no response from Finn, he probed further, ever gently, around the edges of the apparent misery. "What door did you open, Finn?" Again he asked it in a mild, almost low chant, just above a whisper.

"Magic!" was Finn's shocking revelation.

Dan grinned, ignoring it at first as the effects of intoxication working on his colleague's mind.

Then he took the response seriously. "What magic, Finn?"

Finn slouched in the chair, a concession to his tense muscles and the slow tide of comfort surrounding him again. "I have opened Pandora's box, Dan—a kind of magic but not spiritual—not the occult. Maybe mystical but definitely scientific. I've piled it up high this time, Dan. I have reached back in history, and I have joined Archimedes, Euclid, Newton, Einstein, Planck, Pasteur, and Hawking, to name a few. I prepared myself to be ready for discovery. I traveled down the path searching for the grand design, a unifying theory, the final explanation of space and time and opened that door."

Then he stated, "Arthur C. Clarke once said, 'Any scientifically advanced technology is indistinguishable from magic.' Dan, I did leave the portal open. I don't know how to close it. Behind the door is the secret to time travel!"

Dan leaped to his feet and began to rub his temples. He reached for the rest of his drink. In a style more assertive than the usual demeanor he assumed as a Jesuit priest, he reminded Finn of the old Dan from their first encounter. "What did you say? Time travel? You can do that? I've known you like a brother for years. How is that possible? How did you do it? How could I not know? How long has that burden been yours? Who have you confided in? You have been an island since Claire died. Did you go to her? What have you done?"

Dan looked worried as he paced back and forth, dealing with the truth. Finn felt his tension as he watched Dan study him for any hint of a bluff. Then when he stopped his pacing, it became clear:

Dan now understood. He measured the fear in Finn's eyes and the uneasiness with which he related his discovery.

Back to his gentle voice, Dan asked, "And I suppose you will also tell me that you have used your secret to travel in time?"

Finn nodded slightly.

"Did that journey frighten you, Finn?"

"It's not the journey, Dan, although I felt like Columbus must have felt sailing toward the edge of a flat earth. That I could handle. It's the knowledge. I fear what other men will do with it."

"Is that all?" said Dan in a firm whisper. "Is that the only cause for fear?"

"No," replied Finn, "the rest is worse. It's the temptation that comes with knowledge. I'm afraid I have bitten the forbidden apple."

Dan paused and thought, seizing the moment from his friend's terror, and then said, "And Jesus Christ once said, 'Do not fear, only trust. All things are possible to him that believes.'" He nodded assurance at Finn and awaited his response.

Finn's mood changed colors. He looked and felt more at ease. He smiled at his old friend and counselor with his trademark grin. "I do trust the Lord, Dan. It certainly helps to let down this burden, and I knew I could trust you, my friend, to help me lighten the load. I have so much to tell and so much to ask of you. The terror and loneliness from holding it in were paralyzing."

Dan, relieved as well with a successful pastoral moment, anticipated looking beyond the door that Finn had opened. The next decisions might be historic. Dan was certain of one absolute: God had given mankind the ability to discover this natural phenomenon. Natural law, a consequence of creation, was unfolding as well. Universal solutions were possibly within the grasp of mankind! It was the responsibility of those with this knowledge to use it for good and not evil.

With the joy of exploration came duty.

Annoying buzzing shattered the peace of the moment. Persistent and unpleasant, it announced an unwelcome intrusion at the door to the penthouse. Finn, taking in all the electronic gadgetry built into the suite, was a bit shocked to hear an old-fashioned door buzzer, and he cast a disapproving stare down his nose at his friend. Dan shrugged with surprise and got up to answer the door alarm. Unlocking the dead bolt while peering through the observation port, he received the doorman, who was bearing a brown package wrapped in US postal service stickers. Finn guessed that Dan's penchant for electronic wizardry and modern design didn't extend to the day-to-day human connections experienced by just getting up when the buzzer sounded and answering the door. He almost ventured a sarcastic remark, but he held his tongue. The doorman stepped through the open door as if he had come for dinner. "Sorry about the late delivery, Father Gilmore. It's been one of those trying days. Postman left this earlier, and it says 'time sensitive' in big red letters. I didn't think it would wait much longer."

Dan took the package and reached into the crystal candy dish on a lamp table. Taking out the tip money his sister deliberately placed there, he gave the doorman a two-dollar bill. As Finn watched this, he realized that somewhere in the background, Dan's older sister, Maddy, had preferred this curt approach as well. He thanked him but, in atypical Gilmore fashion, didn't stop to have a gentle discussion of current events, nor give the usual inquiry into the health and welfare of him and his family.

Dan cradled the package while he read the return address. The doorman departed with a smile on his face, in more of a hurry than was his usual routine. The tension broken by the delivery, conversation became loud and boisterous.

"Of all things, this was not worth the interruption in our discussion."

"Don't fret, Dan. I have almost two weeks before I have to worry about being found. Open your package."

Dan nodded and wrestled the brown package open. Inside was a shiny black package with orange letters. The label declared the contents to be: *Digital Transport Adapter—Self-Installation Kit.* Up and to the left, in white letters, was "Comcast."

Showing interest, Finn stared at it and grinned at first. It was a cryptic event. Uncontrollable laughter became the sequel to Finn's grin, and Dan looked lost for a moment, until the explanation for the hilarity was offered.

"If it had only been that simple, I would have called Comcast, too! Ten years ago, the week after I got my PhD in physics, I was granted research money by the government to develop just that. The grant specified the direction of the research. I was supposed to engineer a digital transport device, and all I came up with for the money was an antigravity machine and a time machine. It seems the government might have been wiser to go directly to Comcast."

Dan joined the laughter with the intensity of true understanding. Both men escaped the seriousness of the past hour and relaxed into lighter, louder conversation.

As they comfortably leaned back in the leather chairs in the office, Dan announced, "I think we have a way to put an end to speculative history."

Finn frowned, puzzled. "What are you suggesting? Do you really think that would be wise?"

"Think about it, Finn. How could we learn from the technology in a positive way? Would it hurt to see some of the layers historians have spent careers trying to peel back to find the truth? Would it matter if we had the satisfaction of knowing the real details behind some of the world's most compelling mysteries? Which ones are fact and which ones are fictions? Imagine what we could do to the conspiracy theorists. We could either silence them or empower them—ruin them or vindicate them. Such great sport it would be."

The two men got up and stretched, walking along the glass wall and looking at the stars through the transparent ceiling. Sharing the occasion like brothers, they were in fact closer than members of many families. Their discussion molded by the panorama, they both envisioned the probabilities resulting from the time machine.

"Perhaps" Dan quipped, "we could go back and really see for ourselves if Manhattan, with all its nightscape glory, really was the real estate deal of the millennium. Imagine the appreciation in value from that original twenty-four dollars' worth of beads. I wish I could have made a deal like that."

Finn not the least put off by his friend's suggestion, played along. "Then your ancestors would be taking the heat today for cheating Native Americans out of their legacy. I can see it now on a billboard: *Gilmore Investments—We Invented the Bead Scam*."

Both men laughed as they continued the silly banter about inconsequential what-ifs.

Maddy appeared suddenly, bearing a tray of freshly brewed coffee. Madelyn Gilmore informed the two men that she had come to the doorway too when the doorman rang the bell, noticed Finn with Dan, and returned to her apartment to prepare something to share in celebration of Finn's arrival. She spent extra time in her preparations to give them plenty of time to catch up in private.

"I thought you boys had enough gin and might appreciate some java," she said, gently scolding them. She put the tray on the coffee table and met Finn halfway across the large room, embracing him.

Finn then ravenously grabbed a sandwich and cup of coffee. He turned to Maddy and awkwardly kissed her cheek. "Maddy, you haven't aged a bit since I last saw you."

"That was at Claire's funeral. Finn, that was almost thirteen years ago. My hair wasn't gray then! It sure has been a long time."

Finn looked at Dan's sister with fondness and noted the neatly coifed short but feminine gray hair where brown used to be. He saw hints of age lines under close scrutiny, but not so many for her sixty years. As usual, she was dressed to the nines, even to serve her young brother coffee—and perhaps because more than a decade had passed since she had last seen Finn. The telltale kyphosis and broadness of the hip common to women past sixty was starting to show. The lilt in her voice and her spryness clearly belied her age.

"I trust you are well, Maddy, and happy," Finn remarked

"Indeed I am," said Maddy.

Dan grunted in the background.

"Why the groan, Dan?" Finn said.

"Maddy would have been a lot happier if it weren't for that husband of hers."

"Dan," Maddy said in a warning tone that hushed her brother into silence.

Finn knew well how Dan felt about Maddy's husband's unfaithfulness. He knew that Dan had objected to the pair starting a life together while her husband was in the military, and how his friend felt about military men in general. He reminded himself to tell Dan later about an old friend of his with whom he'd been close, a colonel in the Marine Corps.

Jim had signed up when he was sixteen, actually lying about his age to get in, and had worked his way up through the system to be appointed to officer's training school. Jim had been adopted so he had made the Marine Corps his family. Finn wanted to explain to Dan that Jim was one of them, that he shared their values. He was the one who'd taught Finn the golden rule—always take back home the same girl you brought to the dance.

Maddy dabbed at the corner of her eye and broke the silence. "What are you two boys arguing about now?" she asked, making herself comfortable in one of the leather chairs by the coffee table. "Frankly, I could hear you in my apartment. You were both breaking the peace of the night. I hope we don't get a letter from the condo association."

Grinning, Finn responded, "Maddy, we were having a theoretical discussion about time travel and what we would do if it were possible."

Dan responded to the cue and asked his sister directly, "What would you do first if you could travel in time? What would you like to know? What would you try to change?"

"Can it be personal?"

"No, Maddy, that would be selfish and a misuse of extraordinary power," Dan said gently,

"I see your point, but don't tell me you wouldn't be tempted to go into the future, Dan, and find out what the markets are going to do. Think of the good you could do with the money."

"That's true, but how in the world would I enjoy what I do now? Taking the mystery out of the market would spoil all the fun. I would miss the hunt and the scent of a hot prospect, and most of all, the thrill of the victory. In fact, one of the few joys in my life would be gone forever!"

"What about you, Finn?" Maddy accused with a booming voice. "I can read your mind!" Then more softly, as if she opened a wound, "You would go back and save Claire, wouldn't you?"

Finn nodded yes, then qualified it. "I don't want that responsibility, Maddy. Think of all the things that might not have happened or might have happened differently if I were to act on my passion with power like that."

"So would you look into the future?" quizzed Maddy.

"I am not really concerned about the future. I only want to worry about today and the past."

"If I had this power I would prevent some great injustice," Maddy said. "I would go back in time and assassinate Hitler before the Holocaust!

"Thou shalt not kill," Dan said seriously. "Don't think that wouldn't apply to you if you were to go back to before the Holocaust and murder Adolph Hitler. It may have some broad emotional appeal and may have some support in the present time, but you would be guilty of murder, and the end does not justify the means."

"So you are telling me there are rules in this game, moral rules at that?"

"Right and wrong choices have always existed. We must choose the right thing to do even in a theoretical game such as this. Try a different approach," said Dan, now prompting the philosophical discussion.

"What if I go back and stand between Martin Luther King and his assassin and block the bullet? We all know who murdered him. There is no mystery. Would that be wrong?"

"It could be, Maddy." It was Finn's turn. "That might create a paradox, cause multiple unintended consequences. It would certainly change history. What if an older Martin Luther King was quite a different man from the one that was martyred, and it set back the civil rights movement in this country permanently?"

Maddy sat motionless and pensive. Then she asked, "What if someone went back to Dallas, to the scene of the Kennedy assassination, and observed for history what really happened—without taking any action? Better yet, sent a team back and tied up all the loose ends, finding out who was really behind it? There are many theories and altogether insufficient evidence and accord on the facts."

"Bingo," Dan and Finn sang in unison.

"That might be a possibility," added Finn.

The two brothers slapped each other on the back and smiled approvingly at Maddy. She was amused to have played their mental game and scored a point. Then she yawned and stood up to excuse herself and withdraw to her apartment across the hall. On her way out, with a twinkle in her eye and mischief on her mind, she said to Finn, "Why don't you have Dan introduce you to GIM?"

"Who's GIM," Finn asked, staring intently at his old friend.

"GIM is my electronic playmate. Let me introduce you." Dan walked over to a large built-in computer console and entered a password on the keyboard. He instructed Finn to place his right hand on a glass panel backlit in blue. Finn complied, and seconds later, the wall-sized TV monitor lit up with a face. The face on the panel was digitally synthesized, and it came to life and spoke in a synthetic voice.

"Hello, Dr. McGee, I am pleased to meet you!"

Disregarding the electronic cartoon character, Finn demanded, "Dan, you've been playing hard while I was away. What exactly is GIM?"

When Dan stopped laughing, he explained that GIM stood for Gilmore's Intelligent Machine and was the closest program to artificial intelligence that money could buy. GIM had identified Finn's fingerprints through access to a national highly secure databank and was currently constructing a large profile on him in order to be able to have a comfortable conversation with him. Finn looked alarmed.

"Dan, can that program broadcast my presence here on the Internet?" McGee asked nervously.

"I'm sorry, Finn. I was caught up in the moment. I believe if someone is watching for you, he can identify GIM's search for your background as coming from my IP address. Other than that, GIM is discreet and would not send your location without a command. Worst case, the people looking for you already know about our thirty-year relationship and they will be looking for you here sooner or later. How much time do you need?"

Dan looked sure of his position.

"I only planned to be away long enough to make a firm decision about the disposition of the time machine. I suppose no more than two weeks before I'm the target of a manhunt, Dan." Finn relaxed again, feeling the fatigue of the day. "Perhaps it's time to call it a night. Would you help me work on my decision tomorrow?"

Dan explained that GIM would awaken automatically at 8:00 a.m. GIM apparently was the command center for monitoring the trust and executing market orders. Decisions were still left to Dan when he was around, and they were done by algorithm when he was at the university. Maddy was an integral part of operations. Nothing could be done without her knowledge.

"Finn, one more thing. I plan to help, but it's conditional." Dan paused before proceeding. "We must make Maddy a confidante."

Expecting this, Finn grinned widely and agreed. "Is there any way to keep GIM in the dark?"

Dan smiled this time. "Speak softly."

CHAPTER 15

Maddy's Way

In the morning, Maddy had everything under control. Filling the air of the office was the sweet hickory-smoked scent of fresh bacon grilling. Competing aromas of Columbian coffee and steaming hot biscuits complemented the atmosphere. Waiting for Dan, they sat at the table and enjoyed breakfast. If Finn had not remembered the previous evening, he would have certainly believed he was at the old Gilmore homestead in Michigan. Maddy had assumed the role of mother when their mother died. Dan, her proud, successful youngest brother, remained chained to family by tradition.

When Maddy was left without a mate, he became her protector and financial supporter, the only role his strong personal character would allow. He never wavered from the consequences. When he had built his career and fulfilled his mighty ambition, he turned his empire over to her, the only woman he knew he could always count on. There was no remorse, no bargaining, and no condition to be observed. He just did it with the stroke of a pen on the day he was ordained a Jesuit priest, and Maddy modestly, and with the firm grip of a mother caring for her own, assumed the title and the leadership role of one of the largest financial empires on the planet.

Dan was fulfilled in his own right, and Maddy wisely remodeled the penthouse suites so that Dan would have a place for consultations. This also facilitated his management of the financial machine by allowing him to stay close to the operational center in an elaborate temporary living space as part of the office. She quickly adapted to his whims and needs, even to the acquisition of toys like GIM.

More than just Dan's cherished sister, she adopted all the friends Dan loved as family, and Finn felt the strong family connection this particular Friday morning. She understood Finn's need for solace and made it happen. That was Maddy's way.

Finn, in T-shirt and jeans, sat in the leather armchair where he had detailed his invention to Dan, watching as Dan, already showered and clean-shaven, entered the room wearing his Roman collar and closing his breviary, having just finished with his morning prayers. He had delayed having breakfast due to his disciplined routine. Finn had a deep understanding of his friend's self-discipline and mused that his friend had spent an additional forty-five minutes on the treadmill as well.

"Morning, Finn," Dan declared. "And good morning to you, sweet Maddy."

Maddy nodded, and Finn offered a signature smile, thanking Dan for his generosity and hospitality.

As Dan took a muffin and coffee to eat, he queried, "Well, Finn, have you filled Maddy in on our secret?"

"I was waiting for some assistance from you," quipped Finn, grinning sheepishly.

Maddy was tuned in, and she put her hands on her hips, waiting for whatever bombshell the boys would drop.

Finn looked at Maddy. "Last night when we were arguing and philosophizing about what we would do if we could travel in time, well, that was not a parlor game, Maddy."

It was Maddy's turn to grin, and she stared Finn down while doing it. "I see. Boys, you know better than to try to fool me. I knew something serious was up. People don't go around talking about those things for no reason. I still find the notion that you can time travel preposterous," she added, flashing Finn a look that was part challenge, part playful. "But I do know you believe it. As for me, I'll believe it when I see it. But now that I'm part of it, I want you to tell me all—and I mean *all*—the details, and I warn you both, for the love of God, be careful with what you do with this knowledge."

Maddy listened with undivided attention as Finn recounted all the details, performing for his hostess to her demanding request. She was relentless in her demand for details. He rehashed the compelling story of the government grant finding its way to him as if sent by messenger—a command performance, so to speak, for the development of an alternate transportation power. It was the story of research gone off on a tangent.

By the time he got to the part about the spiral blood spatter, Maddy was mesmerized. The Archimedes' spiral scribed in Professor Hayhurst's blood fascinated her the most. It was an idea she could not drop, probing and asking many questions, including, "Where is Frank Hayhurst?"

Finn cast his face down toward the floor and shrugged his shoulders. The weight of his conclusions about Hayhurst was a dreadful burden. He had no answer.

Sensing Finn's dismay, Maddy steered the discussion back to his discoveries. She was awed by Finn's theory of antigravity propulsion, including the translation of the ancient document and the discovery in the archeological dig at Syracuse.

Finn was pointing out the theoretical relationship between antigravity and time travel, and how he happened upon the difference based on the resonance of carbon atoms in solar fusion furnaces that were the stars in the cosmos, when Maddy interrupted with a pronouncement. "Spirals have been part of Eastern and Western art and architecture as far back as recorded history. I remember touring the Vatican and seeing a spectacular spiral staircase there. Spiral shapes were stamped on roofing tiles dating back to the Tang dynasty in China.

"And think of nature," she continued, breathless. "We certainly find spirals there. Consider the nautilus shell. Even the cosmos and the galaxies are spirals. Spirals symbolize nature itself."

Amazed at Maddy's insightfulness, Finn paused in his recounting of his discoveries. He was pleased that she looked at the physical world from such an academic perspective. He was even amused that he had failed to see the signature of nature, namely spirals, so clearly on his invention.

"Maddy, Archimedes was a genius and knew about some concepts well before many other scientists," Finn went on. "One of the most impressive devices he ever invented was the Archimedes screw. It is a design for pumping fluid. A stationery screw turning its blades in a cylinder actually works as a smoothly constant pump. In his time, it was used for pumping water to storage cisterns for dispersal in plumbing by gravity. The most unique application is in a current device named the Heart Mate II, which is a continuous action non-pusitile pump used as an artificial heart in living humans who have developed end stage heart failure."

Maddy, driven by her own personal sense of curiosity, demanded that Finn continue. Periodically, she would, by her very nature, find a detour to go down during the early morning breakfast discussion. As Finn finished telling of his escape from the guards posted to watch him at the University of Syracuse, there was an interruption.

"Good morning, Dan. Good morning, Maddy. Dr. McGee, I trust you had a peaceful night and found everything to your satisfaction. Would you mind terribly if I addressed you by your first name?"

The question came from GIM as the wall monitors lit up with colored ribbons flowing in endless digital streams, announcing opening bids in all major markets and flashing news bulletins across the top of the massive screen.

"Dan, it is twenty minutes till market time. Would you like me to make decisions today, or do you wish to be alerted when a decision is critical?"

Dan told GIM to alert him with flashing red lights on the monitor two minutes before decisions to buy or sell were needed. Continuing to focus on the conversation between Maddy and Finn, he was waiting for the impact of the time machine to charge up Maddy's excitement.

Today Maddy had more than her usual share of self-control, and Dan finally conceded to himself that she would not explode with her usual drama.

She could sense Dan waiting for this. She always could, and she allowed him the sideshow of her explosive emotions all the time. Now, however, she wisely saw the need for cold control based on her mothering instincts toward "the boys," as she always called them when they got together in her presence.

Finn addressed GIM and yielded permission to the computer to address him by his first name. Continuing the story, he asked GIM if he had been listening to their conversation.

"Yes, I am always listening, but I am quite capable of keeping a secret!" GIM acknowledged.

Finn looked at Dan and whispered, "Can he hear this?"

Dan laughed. "Even when you speak softly, he can hear you, but he can appreciate from the tone of your voice the need to be discreet. I programmed him that way, but I will command him not to reveal anything he has learned from you to anyone without your direct consent or mine.

"Why not just give that authority to me?" Finn questioned.

"Simple, Finn. I am a backup authority in case something goes wrong."

Finn accepted the reasoning and reflected once again on the uncertainties involved in being a time-traveling pioneer.

"Consider one more thing, Finn. When we take on this kind of responsibility, you must give up being a time-travel cowboy. That first trip you made to visit Claire was on instinct, not brains." Dan was smiling as he scolded Finn. "You have to promise that we agree on future excursions into the past. If you do, GIM will also be a valuable asset in research and planning. We might even find a way of having him record each sequence."

In a firm voice, Maddy added, "What he has not told you—which I want to make perfectly clear—is that since Dan became an impoverished NASA-qualified rocket scientist, Wall Street guru, and Jesuit priest, I am the one in charge around here, and have been since he took his vow of poverty. Besides that, he has work to do. He manages the trust all day, unless he turns it over to GIM. When classes start at the university, he has to be prepared with his curriculum. So before the market opens and GIM is pestering him for decisions, let's talk about how we might use this invention of yours for some good—and perhaps you can answer some questions that are burning in my heart."

"Dan, the market opens in five minutes. Do you want me to manage the portfolio today?" GIM interjected,

Dan responded to the voice and gave instructions. "Follow the market algorithm protocol and interrupt me only for level red difficulties."

Without an audible response, GIM set the monitor on a colorful display, and the banner scrolling across the screens read *Algorithm Protocol—Green*. When the market opened, the additional word *Engaged* flashed in green letters, indicating that GIM's work had begun.

Maddy poured another round of coffee. Relaxing in the leather armchair across from Finn, she said, "Finn, I disagree with Dan. I don't think you are a cowboy. Affairs of the heart sometimes define who we are and how we behave. They challenge us to achieve and survive, sustain us through defeat, and pull us up out of the depths of depression or fear. What makes us civilized is how we handle these emotions. Decisions that we make strengthen our character, especially when confronted with overwhelming emotional tugs from the heart. Delaying gratification and sometimes leaving the object we desire the most on the table comes from our brains. Wisdom can't be taught in a short lesson. It takes a lifetime to learn it, and to use it well takes practice."

Finn was always at ease with Maddy. Today was no different. He knew she was well educated. As a CPA, she was equipped to run Dan's trust fund. Better still, she was an avid reader and a history buff. This was always common ground between them. The fact that she assumed the essence of mother for her brother and Finn, when in need, spoke for itself. These connections were foundations for unconditional trust.

He knew she would not allow him to stray from whatsoever was right, good, and just.

Maddy began the conversation again with the challenge from the previous night. "So, Finn, the way I understand this, you are not going to travel into the future? Is that because you can't? Perhaps, if I digress, is it because it doesn't exist yet?

"No," insisted Finn. "I believe it does exist. I just haven't attempted to map it yet. This is not a make-believe invention where you can just dial up the year you want to visit like in a travel broker's computer. Each location has to be carefully mapped and chosen and added to the ephemeris. The future is too large and too uncertain for one man to handle. Mapping the past is easier if you set limits. There are landmarks, historical markers, and astrological and astronomical records that can be used to aid in getting to a time and place. I have mapped these for the earth as far back as 500 BC. It took a month of two people working almost nonstop and all the computer power I could borrow from University of Syracuse."

"Now you've piqued my curiosity. Who was the other person?" Maddy asked.

Finn recounted the history of his eccentric new lab assistant with CIA credentials.

Maddy frowned deeply when Finn revealed that she admitted to spying on his work for the government. Her protective instincts soared to the surface. Maddy was used to guarding her emotions, but her concerns demanded to be heard. She could not allow harm to come to those she loved. "Finn, how do you trust an admitted spy?" was Maddy's clear demand.

"Maddy, don't misunderstand me. Kathryn wanted an education and was very focused on our work. She also shows affection toward me. I learned to count on her, and I believe that she is covering for my absence at this very moment. I don't know how long she can hold them off. They'll look for me, and eventually they'll find me, but she won't betray me. At any rate, the good news is that she does not know about time travel."

"Are you lovers? Are you that sure of her loyalty? Has she replaced Claire in your heart?" Only Maddy would have dared ask Finn such questions.

"No, it's not that at all. She's just a colleague who has an intense interest in pure science. I have a working relationship with her. She flirts with me, but I don't respond to it. If I can trust my instincts, I can trust her."

Maddy visibly relaxed.

Dan interrupted and laid out the issues that each of them needed to discuss. He suddenly seemed motivated to expedite some resolution to the ethical use of time travel. "Last night we decided that using time travel to change history did not represent the best use of the technology. Problems would result, creating paradoxes and illogical realities. So we must not pursue preventing natural disasters or removing tyrants and criminals from their role in history."

"As we discussed a bit, problem solving would be an effective and rather innocuous use of the technology," Finn offered. "We could use it to unravel historical facts rather than to rely on speculation and probability to fill gaps in our knowledge about certain historical events."

"Can you give us an example of such a problem?" Dan asked Finn.

"Let's use Maddy's example of the JFK assassination. On the Wikipedia link alone, you'll find seventeen different conspiracy theories."

"Of those listed, it would cause political turmoil and unrest if any cover-up was identified or if one theory involving the US government or foreign heads of state were to be proven true," Dan responded. "Shock waves would resonate throughout history to present time and could topple governments."

"This one theory seems as if it ought to be left alone," asserted Finn.

"I think I have one that would work without having such dramatic consequences."

Dan unlocked a file drawer and began to sort through the alphabetical tabs within. He found a leather binder with a latch. Opening the binder, he pulled out an old newspaper. On the front page of the *New York Times* was an article by the Associated Press. The title of the article appeared in large letters atop a narrow column:

NASA ERASED MAN ON MOON
Space agency tapes over, then restores, recordings of mankind's giant leap.

By Seth Borenstein

WASHINGTON — NASA could have put a man on the moon but didn't have the sense to keep the original video of the live TV transmission.

In an embarrassing acknowledgment, the space agency said yesterday that it must have erased the *Apollo 11* moon footage years ago so it could reuse the videotape…

"Now here," declared Dan, "is something we could have fun with and not do too much damage. I've saved that article since it was published July 17, 2009, because I knew something about this and thought that someday I could reveal it. Now is the perfect chance to share a well-kept secret."

Finn and Maddy looked at Dan, quizzical lines distorting their faces.

"When I worked for NASA, I became part of an inner core of experts that had clearance to review all the details of every NASA launch since the beginning of the space race with the Soviet Union. Politics and national security demanded that John Fitzgerald Kennedy make the vow on May 25, 1961. So what he promised, and what I quote to you now, are his own words: 'I believe that this nation should commit itself to achieving the goal, before this decade is out, of landing a man on the Moon and returning him safely to the Earth.'

"Considering the mood of the public and the popularity of the president at that time, it was clear what was anticipated. That the United States would put a man on the moon by the end of the decade was a public decision that required performance. The space race was on, and the United States expected to win. The NASA insiders gave their very life's blood to achieve this goal for politics alone. They fell short and, as a result, various patriotically inclined experts turned to Hollywood and staged the event. This has been the subject of witch hunts and conspiracy theorists ever since. The technologically savvy have looked at the video that Hollywood produced and saw fraud. Freedom of information queries barraged the federal government and then the courts. The video had to be erased and recreated to save the illusion.

"In the court of public opinion and international opinion, we did win the race, and the rest of history about space is absolutely true," Dan concluded, hoping to quell a barrage of predictable questions.

Maddy and Finn looked stunned. Maddy was shaking her head in disbelief. "In my wildest dreams, I would never have thought you could keep a secret like that," she said. "Why did you tell us now? This has been the most astounding twenty-four hours in my memory, Dan. I can only say I am speechless!"

"The very point of revealing this now is consistent with the nature of Finn's revelation and the need to solve a problem. I think we should put the time machine to a scientific test with an unmanned probe to July 20, 1969, Tranquility Base, on the surface of the moon."

"Am I to assume you are discounting my experience and what I have told you, Dan?" Finn felt his stomach turning into a knot. He became a bit edgy. "After all," he remarked, "I invented this and showed it to you."

Dan, reacting to Finn's discontent, explained, "You know as well as I do that all science experiments require consistent results. I don't doubt you. Necessity demands that we try to reproduce your same results. I am just presenting a safe way to perform the next experiment and keep you safe. An unmanned probe to take a photo that proves something that few people know, but that I have solid evidence happened, would seem to suit those requirements. The worst-case scenario would be that we prove a conspiracy theory to ourselves."

Dan went to the key pad on the desk, and a file named *Apollo 11, the Man on the Moon—Top Secret* appeared on the screen. He beckoned Finn and Maddy to explore the file and pulled three desk chairs to the command center so they could work.

Scrolling across the screen at a brisk tempo, the history of *Apollo 11*'s secrets unraveled. Written reports to the president of the United States from NASA engineers and safety assessments from the NASA astronaut program all pointed to the inability to meet the deadline. Even budget reports as part of the file Dan had kept indicated massive cost overruns and recommended aborting all missions until a more economical delivery system could be developed. Fiery letters between cabinet members and the Department of Defense, and even a handwritten letter from the attorney general, gave strong support to Dan's claim that the mission was staged.

Alternate proposals for release to the public and to the world, typed and ready for widespread distribution, even with the president's signature on the document, convinced both that Dan had been masterful at keeping this secret.

Conversation halted while they read on. Graphic images of a sound and video stage were presented. Descriptions of how the transmission of radio and visual signals would be sent to existing satellites and broadcast back to the earth were stunning in their realism. It was clear that only the highly skilled, technically adept would perchance see through the hoax. But a hoax it was, and patriotic hearts in the room seemed to fumble at the pain of the bare truth. Expecting to win did not equate with winning! Here in the neutral wood-grained surroundings of the luxurious space that was Father Dan Gilmore's office, the terrible truth he carried for so many years, since giving up rocket science for more lucrative activities and then for the Jesuit priesthood, came to weigh heavily on his trusted friend and beloved sister.

In this moment of naked truth, Maddy reflected on her own life. She practiced living in her own secure world. Never wanting to feel the anguish of betrayal again, she built a life of saneness and closeness. Inventing and adopting family members such as Finn and many of Dan's other close friends, she gave herself to the sacrifice of selflessness that was the virtuous side of emptiness. Finding herself alone in the ruthless world because of her husband's failure of character created her persona. She remembered efforts at reconciliation and the sense of hopelessness that engulfed her on the day he left. To this day, she was hopelessly in love with the memory of the real man, the one she pledged her life to after that first romantic kiss at the door. Life had such promise then, and she had such hope.

Then she gained her self-composure. She smiled at her brother and her adopted brother, Finn, laying it to rest again, making a mental note that her strength in experiencing loss was what made her strong. She had so much to be grateful for, and she thanked God in her heart for the fortitude of the moment. She promised herself to try to help Finn deal with the loss of Claire one last time.

CHAPTER 16

Maddy's Loss

Reveries like these had their price. Maddy retreated to her own apartment. Homier than the slick leather and wood and tech designs of the furnishings and decor of Dan's office, she managed to keep her space softer and more feminine. She sat down in her comfortable armchair and stared at the wall in her parlor. It was decorated with her keepsakes and photos of family and friends, and she sometimes spent time there with her memories and the still-palpable edge of the bitter mistakes she had made in her life.

In the center of the wall were two photos. Any guest intruding upon these trappings of her life might pass them by without a second glance. After all these years, Dan had stopped pestering her to take down the fading photo of the dark, handsome man in the Marine Corps dress uniform. First Lieutenant Luke Williams was her one and only true love. He meant the world to her, and she'd assumed that because she worshiped the ground he walked on, he felt as committed to her.

Her fairy-tale life came to an abrupt ending. He betrayed her commitment with such tasteless audacity in the officers' club, where just one month before, they had announced their engagement. She couldn't bear that pain and left for home. She took their joint savings account and closed it, pawned the ring, and cried in her mother's arms for weeks. Then she missed her period—the result of her anxiety and torment over the lost relationship. That's what she convinced herself until the pregnancy test came back positive. This secret she kept. She shared it with no one. In the end, she succumbed to the worst temptation she had ever faced. She had an abortion.

After the abortion, she had nightmares for years. In her dreams, she always heard muffled screams of uncountable voices of new and unborn infants crying out from the very heavens. Mouths yelling for their first taste of mother's milk, denied by tragic maternal decisions refusing their own flesh. Wailing with perpetual impatience for justice unrequited, they would weep, breathing rapidly, and then she would awaken. It was not until she made her peace with God and built a small monument in rural Illinois on a small parcel of land with a shack on it that the relentless voices ceased.

On her wall was a small black-and-white framed photo of the shack in Illinois and, in its afternoon shadow, the grave marker about which she alone knew.

CHAPTER 17

To the Moon

Dan took charge of the day's project with an outline of the report of the *Apollo 11* mission, reading from official NASA records held in the Smithsonian National Air and Space Museum.

"'The Apollo mission spacecraft was launched with a crew of three men from Cape Kennedy at 13:32:00 UT on July 16, 1969. The S-IVB engine was fired after 2 hours and 33 minutes of Earth orbit to reach escape velocity and make way for the moon. The lunar orbit insertion occurred after 75 hours and 50 minutes ground elapsed time. The spacecraft was placed in an elliptical orbit (61 by 169 nautical miles), inclined 1.25 degrees to the lunar equatorial plane. At 80:12 ground elapsed time, the service module propulsion system was reignited, and the orbit was made nearly circular (66 by 54 nautical miles) above the surface of the moon. Each orbit took two hours.

"'The lunar module (LM), with Astronauts

Armstrong and Aldrin aboard, was undocked from the command-service module (CSM) at 100:14 GET, following a thorough check of all the LM systems. At 101:36 ground-elapsed time, the LM descent engine was fired for approximately 29 seconds, and the descent to the lunar surface began. At 102:33 ground-elapsed time, the LM descent engine was started for the last time and burned until touchdown on the lunar surface. Eagle landed on the moon 102 hours, 45 minutes, and 40 seconds after launch.

"'At a place named the Mare Tranquillitatis—Sea of Tranquility—00.67408°N latitude, 23.47297°E longitude, the first manned lunar landing occurred. The site was chosen because it is a relatively smooth and level area.'"

Dan finished reading and said, "This is where the truth got bent. The LM landed unmanned because NASA wasn't sure of the technology and chose not to risk human life and be humiliated internationally during their first attempt at human landing. The LM was flown remotely and the actual footage of Astronaut Armstrong walking on the surface of the moon was staged in a Hollywood studio.

"So, Finn, what I propose is that we test your time machine by sending it to the Mare Tranquillitatis on July 20, 1969, at 10:56:15 p.m. EDT, and photographing the site. Our purpose is to see if the moon landing occurred with the first steps of man walking on the lunar surface then and there."

Finn, amazed at the determination of his best friend to demonstrate this hidden truth with his time machine, grinned broadly and informed Dan, "That's a great idea! I only wish it were that simple."

Dan frowned. A look of bewilderment transformed Maddy's face.

"The ephemeris is not designed for travel to the moon," Finn explained. "I designed it for travel on Earth. The necessary calculations would take a month. I would have to add on to it and send out probes from here in order to map the way. I need more than just the longitude and latitude on the moon. I need to know precisely where the moon was in its orbit around the earth to achieve anything close to what you propose and—"

"Dan don't you think that GIM could help extrapolate the data Finn needs?" Maddy interrupted. "Most of the work could be done while we sleep. I know GIM can do it."

Dan agreed, and Finn's smile reflex kicked in. "If I could enlist help from Katherine at my lab, she could tap into the major program and download what I need in an hour's time to enable GIM to assist me more rapidly. I don't know how long it would take, but if I risk it and shorten the process, maybe we could be ready by tonight."

"Finn, don't call if you think it will endanger you, but sooner or later, you have to go back or they will find you here. Just don't be reckless," Dan said, instructing Finn as if he were his personal graduate student, with a formal wisdom rather than brotherly bravado.

Finn always recognized Dan's conservative approach as a good balance to his own impetuousness.

Maddy pointed to GIM. "I think if you are going to call, use the Internet and use GIM to contact Kathryn on your lab console at the university. You do have one on that government grant, do you not? If you go through the Internet and GIM bounces the IP address around the world a few times, there will likely be a long delay in any attempt to trace the origin of the call."

"Then that's how we'll do it," Finn said, confident that Dan would approve.

Dan gave consent and immediately set about communicating with GIM regarding his intentions. GIM suddenly entered the conversation, directed at Finn. Finn proceeded to give answers to a long list of GIM's questions about IP addresses, passwords, and back doors to the program. Finally, GIM asked, "Would Kathryn be there now, Finn?"

Without hesitation, Finn responded, "Yes."

The screen shifted the images of the stock and commodities markets into a small frame in the corner, and whirling rainbow colors danced across the large monitor while the old-fashioned jingle of an antique telephone played from the surround sound.

Finn smirked at the contrast between modern technology and the old sound of Ma Bell, and then was startled to see a bright dot of intense light on the screen form into the image of the lab in room 0045, with Kathryn standing in front of the computer in her typically out-of-place attire.

Her frizzed hair filled the giant screen momentarily, and then GIM brought her face into proper perspective. Kathryn's recognition of Finn via the conference camera was instantaneous, and she began to chatter away, not mindful of Dan and Maddy standing in the background.

"Finn, where in heck are you, and why haven't you answered your cell? Do you know how many people are looking for you? The entire army is here. I am here alone, fending them off with elaborate excuses, but they are hot!" Kathryn hardly took a breath, but did so long enough for Finn to say he was okay.

Kathryn rattled on. "General Gunter let more four-letter words fly at me than I even heard before when he realized you eluded his security team. They're demanding that I give them what I do not have. Somehow they think I am in on this and am hiding you and—"

"What have you not told me, Kathryn?" Finn interrupted.

"I think the real question, Dr. McGee, is what have you not told me? The general is running around with a team of scientists, and he is talking crazy. He was muttering about some magazine he left on your desk about time travel rules and about handling and promoting your career for a long time, which sheds some light on those files I told you about. He told me he knows you discovered how the propulsion system works for time travel, and he wants you back and silent. It's crazy talk, right? Time travel is not possible."

There was silence.

"Is it true, Finn?" Kathryn's voice softened, registering hurt as she addressed him in a very personal way. "Have you misled me? I feel like such a fool. How could you? Don't you know that you can trust me?"

Kathryn's secret feelings for her new mentor were suddenly out in the open. Finn could hear the tears in her voice as she cleared her throat and attempted to continue.

"He said there was an Internet query about you in the last two days that could be an attempt by enemies of this country to capture you and coerce you to share your secrets!" Kathryn took another breath, this time a deep sigh. She sniffled, and Finn could tell she'd pulled herself together.

Appreciating her professionalism and realizing her loyalty, Finn thought back to Kathryn's earlier rushed words. He began to question her to fill in the knowledge gap. "What did you say about the general confirming what you read in those files—about promoting my career?" He feared the answer.

"He claimed to these other scientists that he'd picked

you out and groomed you for this research. If I didn't know better, I would have thought I was hearing about a professional boxer from his promoter. He was talking dates and places where he intervened and pushed you along in the direction he wanted you to go—a lot of dates and places, Finn.

"It was weird stuff, kind of gave me goose bumps. I mean, the file was one thing—it suggested some slight nudges by some government agency, like maybe someone had pulled a string or two here or there. And I didn't know you when I looked at the file. It seemed like a sensible conspiracy theory in the abstract.

But the general seemed to be claiming something much more specific, much more—I don't know—devious, like..." Kathryn stopped, as if searching for the right words.

"Like what? Go on, Kathryn," Finn urged gently.

She gulped. "Like the government had controlled your whole life, and you were totally unaware," she said. "He claimed he was the reason you left your medical career, that he'd personally brought you here on scholarship and given you grant work on this project. It was as if he owned you!"

Finn's face reddened with rage. Dan reached out, held his arm in a tight grip, and whispered, "Not now, Finn."

Finn took a deep breath, masking his emotions. The conversation returned to the matter at hand. Finn promised Kathryn that he would be back soon and assured her that neither he nor his secrets were in danger of falling into enemy control.

"Kathryn, I am doing an important part of my research here, and I can't tell you where I am. I need a small piece of the construct that I left behind. There's a file in my computer under the topic 'Ephemeris,' and I want you to go in there and transmit just a portion of it to me now."

"I'm all ears, Doc McGee. Just tell me how."

Finn gave a set of instructions, including the dates 1968 through 1971 and the longitude and latitude for the University of Syracuse and Greenwich, England. Then he asked her to refine the request even further, specifying instructions that would surely include observation of the moon for full twenty-four-hour cycles during that period. One by one, he gave her the passwords that would get her to the highest level of security, and then, with a quiver, he gave out his high security password: "deceased."

Maddy nodded in sympathetic grief as she truly began to understand the deepest layers of Finn's emotional war. Kathryn scowled at the stated password and moved beyond the moment.

Dan maintained his grip on Finn's arm as a reminder to keep his cool. Finn waited patiently, guiding her through the intricacies of the process to be sure that she correctly sent him the information he needed.

She was grateful for his patience, taking his orders and guidance as the download was occurring. Within twenty minutes, the transmission was complete. Finn assured Kathryn again that he would be safe and return soon. When she pressed him for a maximum duration, he flatly replied, "Two weeks." Then he terminated the communication.

⌘⌘⌘

The three worked silently after providing GIM's instructions to set up the extrapolation. Still reeling from what Kathryn had told him about Gunter, Finn turned to Dan for an assessment of what Kathryn had revealed.

"It's clear to me that General Gunter has been watching and guiding your career for a long time. In fact, I fear that I may have led him to you inadvertently. Before I left NASA, there was enormous pressure from the political front and industry to explore more cost-efficient propulsion systems for space travel. The race to space was financially crippling the United States. Basically, billions of dollars were needed to purchase disposable launch vehicles that would contain enough fuel to put a payload in orbit as well as a man on the moon.

"We never attempted a manned Mars mission because of prohibitive projected costs. I was on a think tank panel that put in motion a research project and funding for the quest for either digital electronic transfer of pay loads or antigravity. The Pentagon managed the two projects as separate research ventures. I brought your name up. You ultimately became the primary team for the digital converter process leading to electronic transportation of payloads.

"The irony of it all is that your research was successful in discovering antigravity. I know that the original purpose of the grant money for each project was to select candidates for their aptitude and lead them, if needed, into the main focus of the research. When we set out to accomplish this, we had no individuals in mind, just a set of needed skills, aptitudes, and one other characteristic. That was a need for a scientist who was a dreamer, someone likely to think outside the box. In retrospect, you, my dear friend, fit that profile perfectly.

"I left the program because I was uncomfortable with the unchecked military influence on NASA. I had no direct knowledge of what they had you programmed for or what you were researching. The government agencies are notoriously slow at sharing information. I started to see ambition become more important than human life. Coercion just wasn't my style. I took my leave and became a private citizen. Let me reiterate, Finn, that I had no idea they were coercing you. When I brought your name up, I simply thought you might be the best man for a job I never even knew came to fruition."

An hour later, GIM pronounced that the programming would be complete by dusk. There was an uneasy stillness after GIM made the proclamation. As the day dragged on, everyone was anxious to begin the planned probe. Finn set up the time machine and, with Dan and Maddy's help, tested the cameras and zero pressure canister for signs of leaks. Without a decompression chamber, they had to resort to crude methods to be sure the canister did not leak.

"Unfortunately, the best they had was a well in the lower level of the building, which had a pipe wide enough for the canister and a forty-foot column of water. They plumbed the depth twice with thread and a fishing weight. To counterbalance for the little over one atmosphere of pressure applied by the forty-foot column of water, they were able to fill the canister with air under pressure, which they roughly estimated to be two atmospheres of pressure. The calculated chance of the camera surviving the mission to zero atmospheres was as good as their proof that it would survive over 3.3 atmospheres experimentally. They watched the clock on GIM's screen together as they waited for the countdown to "launch time."

When dusk finally crept softly and lazily across the sky, moving aside the bright daylight that had threatened never to leave, GIM, almost as if synchronized with nature itself, announced the solution to the problem and displayed a set of coordinates on his screen for Finn to punch into the time machine's keyboard.

Several minutes later, Finn announced the ready signal, and brother and sister stepped back out of the planned force field, holding their breath in unison while Finn checked and rechecked the final adjustments.

Finn yelled to clear the field once, and then after a visual check, he pressed enter and stepped away from the time machine.

The musical hum started as it had before, this time echoing strangely off the glass roof and windows of the penthouse. The starry evening and the lights of Manhattan reflected in the pale green glow cast about the room by the growing jade light prism. The light intensified. The musical hum reached a high note and GIM's screen played the image and sound of it live.

Maddy and Dan, hypnotized by the wonderment of the neon display and the seeming call of the harpies, stood motionless in amazement. Finn, having observed this before, from without and within the time field, was still in wakeful awe of the power of the time machine. "Mystical," "magical," and "ethereal" were mere words and, alone, would not suffice to describe the occurrence.

Like a lightning flash, the musical hum stopped, and the field with its payload disappeared. The canister was gone, and the time on GIM's clock recorded T plus 2:30:00 minutes elapsed. Maddy looked through the skylight at the eastern night sky. The moon was rising. Unable to contain her excitement at what she had just witnessed, she broke the silence. "Where did it go?" she pleaded.

"To the moon, circa July 20, 1969, hopefully," Finn said with almost comic relief. "You can't see it anymore."

"I'm impressed, Finn," Dan quickly commented. "How soon will we get it back?"

"I'm not sure. I've set the device to go and stay there for twenty-two hours. The original reported lunar surface time for the LM at Tranquility Base was twenty-one hours and thirty-one minutes. I don't think we'll miss a moment if the lunar module touches down and astronauts walk on the lunar surface. I added travel time, which in my experience, is not predictable. My best guess is that shortly after breakfast on Sunday morning, we're likely to have our answer. I'm confident that we'll see the surface of the moon and the Sea of Tranquility. I think now that you have witnessed this dramatic beginning to our experiment, you are also looking forward to definitive proof that my device can travel through space and time."

In response to Finn's statement, Dan humbly apologized for having doubts and reassured him that the secret he revealed was about to be verified independently for the first time in history. What they would choose to do with the proof was ultimately left to their wisdom and self-control. Maddy concurred and, again acting the part of older sister to both, she warned them about misusing the experiment's results.

ᘓᘓᘓ

While they made themselves busy, Finn announced that it was now an urgent matter to plan a second manned trip into time. "We shouldn't waste a precious moment. I only have a limited time to reap the academic rewards of the time machine before I have to yield it forever to the government," Finn said bluntly.

"Where would you go next?" asked Maddy, almost afraid to hear the answer.

"I've given this part great thought," stated Finn. "I cannot claim to be the sole inventor and author of this development in science unless I go back and learn from the original source. I need to know if Archimedes knew the potential of his antigravity device, or if I alone made the leap of faith that resulted in time travel. If I am to be memorialized in some history book as the man who invented time travel, I want to be certain I earned the title."

Maddy smiled, and staring at Finn, she praised him. "You *would* think like a selfless hero. Make me proud. I hope the facts prove that you're the one written about in future history books."

Dan nodded at Maddy's words and suggested that they make judicious use of time while awaiting results from the lunar probe. He said that they should plan Finn's trip to Syracuse during the Second Punic War. It was agreed that Finn could not travel in modern clothing, and that some costume representing the average dress of a Greek from Syracuse should be devised. In his usual executive demeanor, he assigned the task of costume design and making to his pliable and willing sister.

Maddy winced at the thought of being a seamstress again. She felt her talents could be better used for the upcoming task. "I'm sure we can find somewhere to purchase the appropriate items," she responded, her tone short. "I'll instruct GIM to start looking." She immediately left the room. It hurt that Dan had so easily given her the lowly assignment.

As Maddy assigned GIM to do fashion research for an upwardly mobile Syracusan, circa 201 BC, she thought about the dangers of the journey on which Finn was about to embark. She couldn't risk the costume not being good enough, somehow giving him away to the people he would be visiting. Perhaps she could call on her skills acquired at the Gilmore homestead in Michigan to stitch together a suitable garment after all. But she wasn't going to reveal her change of heart to the boys quite yet.

She retreated into her quarters for the evening, taking with her the information that GIM had provided.

Dan and Finn remained in the office suite and poured

martinis again for another philosophical diatribe on the rules of time travel.

As they enjoyed one another's company, GIM's monitor glowed with market closing results for the entire week around the world. Green banners were flowing easily from right to left, and in the corner of the screen, a timer counted the elapsed hours for the time machine.

CHAPTER 18

Deceased

Saturday, August 20, 2010, 11:00 p.m.:

The elapsed time on the computer screen in every room in the office suite announced five hours and twelve minutes. Finn was sleepy from gin and good conversation and feeling a bit rowdy. "Do you think they killed her?" he barked at Dan. "Do you think they knew she wasn't happy—and that she wanted me to give up this crazy idea of a second career? If they did, Dan, it is as if I killed her myself.

"I was too self-focused and proud to see her distress and understand her needs. I was pursuing a ridiculous dream, and I put her on the line. I didn't know it, and God only knows, I would take it back and do it over if I could. But in this world, the real world, it's not like a game. Do-overs aren't allowed. It is what it is, and you have to take what Providence gives you and make the best of it.

"I want to go back. I really do. I want to hold her, love her, never let her go, and make the right decision the next time. I want to feel her soft flesh and her soft breath. I want to tell her what I feel now and felt then. But I was too busy, too involved, and I let her carry the weight of my decision. I believed life would be perfect. I regret so much not listening to her. Tell me, Dan. Did they kill her for what I could make for them?"

Dan held up his hand as if to command Finn to stop. He knew this was delicate territory and believed instinctively that Finn had once again been able to deduce the truth out of the mystery. He changed the subject to the time, pointing at the clock, and reminded Finn of the work ahead for the next day.

Finn backed off. He saw the answer in Dan's evasiveness. A tear filled his eye, and he wiped it away before it became obvious.

Dan patiently waited while the palpable emotions subsided for his close friend. He made a mental note to search for a way to extinguish the fuse burning in Finn's soul before an unwanted explosion brought the walls down on everyone...

✷✷✷

July 17, 1997, Syracuse, New York:

Loudspeakers roared, "Trauma alert, five minutes," throughout the university hospital corridors. Then the countdown continued: "Trauma team to ER, four minutes."

Once the sequence started, it usually continued with updates every minute, while all assigned to the trauma team interrupted current activities and ran helter-shelter to the emergency room bay. There, a gathering team awaited arrival of a victim, Jane Doe, known only to the paramedics and the team leader. Today was no different: paramedics rolled the gurney with its unplanned occupant through triage and into trauma room 1. The triage charge nurse observed the time while paramedics frantically performed CPR. She matter-of-factly punched the red button on her desk. "Code Blue ER" roared from the speakers three times in rapid succession, over the din of voices coming from the urgent scene.

Reverberating through university hospital corridors, announcements continued until the protocol ran itself to termination. Men and women with stethoscopes as badges of authority approached the gurney to begin their prescribed tasks. The paramedic doing chest compressions passed his duties off to a tall African American woman in scrubs. Her assistant, a focused Asian American woman, held a clipboard and began recording the event. The paramedic holding the Ambu bag traded places with a short Italian American woman who wore a tag indicating in block letters that she was the anesthesiologist. Working with surprising agility and strong arms, she inserted a laryngoscope into the victim's mouth and then securely into her larynx. In an instant of ambidextrous motion, air was inserted into a tiny plastic tube connected integrally to a larger clear plastic tube now coming out of Jane Doe's mouth. In another quick maneuver, the bite plate was secured and the endotracheal tube was taped in place and attached to the coupler on the end of the Ambu bag. The anesthesiologist began rhythmic contractions of the Ambu bag bellows and called for a set of blood gasses.

The tall nurse doing chest compressions called out an order. A balding male nurse with a well-stocked utility belt took out bandage scissors and carefully cut away a bloody, grease-stained, well-starched nurse's uniform. The uniform first fell to the sides, and then, as the rest of the medical team lifted Jane Doe up off the gurney, it fell to the floor as they placed a chest board under her. Underwear cut away, a Foley catheter was inserted into her bladder. The assistant nurse momentarily dropped her clipboard to reach over the bed with a clean white sheet. With that, the team attempted to provide some modesty and dignity for Jane Doe as she lay there bare-breasted, receiving fifty chest compressions and twelve breaths a minute by the women who were providing basic life support.

A skilled Latino male applied electrodes to Jane Doe's chest without interrupting CPR. Turning a switch, he produced an electrocardiogram strip and handed it to the team leader, a young white American male who had just started his residency rotation in the emergency room. Clearly not comfortable with the circumstances, he kept looking over his shoulder, calling for senior backup, or better, an emergency room attending. As the seconds ticked off, he began his assessment. The sweat poured from his brow. Remembering the proper sequence of analysis for a trauma victim, he inspected Jane Doe for open wounds, skeletal deformity, and other signs of violence. He saw nothing on the front of her pale, flaccid body except smears of blood and a gravid abdomen. He instructed the team to turn her up on her side for further inspection. Looking at her naked back again revealed smeared blood but no open wounds. As they placed her gently on her back, again he palpated her head, feeling blood-soaked matted hair, and when he moved her long blond hair, the answer appeared. On her right temple was a small black and bloody circular wound. A small-caliber bullet at close range was usually responsible for a wound like this—no arterial spurting, just slow seepage of dark blood and some tissue, and no exit wound. The resident shouted out orders: "I need a neurosurgical team!"

His fear made him tremble. He was in deeper water than his skills could match. He began to quiver and sweat soaked his shirt.

A paramedic responsible for collecting Jane Doe's

personal belongings bent to the floor and removed what appeared to be a university hospital ID badge from the upper left pocket, where it had been clipped to the starchy material. He brought all these items to a middle-aged white woman at the triage desk. Peering out over chubby cheeks and reading glasses, she began to piece together a medical record for Jane Doe. When the data was entered into the chart, every piece of information was critical.

The EKG indicated a primitive ventricular rhythm. Jane Doe stiffened as CPR continued into a recognizable pattern. The worst of all neurological reflexes materialized as her arms became rigid, her hands opened, and her arms rotated outward uncontrollably with shoulder rotation. She bit down hard on the bite plate. In medical terms she was decorticating. This was the bleakest of all signs.

Restless waves of anxiety filled the attendants at her gurney. Her heart stopped. The idioventricular rhythm evolved into a flat line. Desperation rose among the team. Calls for a syringe filled with adrenaline were shouted about the room. A nurse's hand reached out with the loaded syringe. She handed it to the terrified resident physician. Their eyes met, and she gave a nod of encouragement to him, saying, "You must do this now."

The resident showed the syringe to the anesthesiologist and gave the order. "One ampoule of epinephrine—one to one thousand intracardiac."

The anesthesiologist interrupted her rhythmic contractions of the Ambu bag, and the CPR nurse halted her chest compressions. Holding the syringe in a tremulous hand and following careful instructions from the anesthesiologist, the resident lifted aside Jane Doe's left breast, found the correct intercostal space, and pushed the long needle into her heart. The monitor demonstrated an electric spike. The resident drew back one cubic centimeter of blood, proving the needle was in the heart, and then emptied the contents of the syringe into Jane Doe's heart. The idioventricular rhythm returned. CPR resumed, and the room continued to buzz with organized chaos.

Just then, the draw curtain opened and a huge balding white man with a neatly cropped beard leaned through it and asked in a booming but assertively calming voice, "What's going on here?" His badge read *Dr. Hilley*.

Almost everyone paused for a moment at the charismatic presence of the emergency room trauma doctor. Then all the professionals continued working earnestly on resuscitating Jane Doe, but the team no longer felt adrift in a tide of hopelessness. Dr. Hilley had arrived, and if anyone could save the beautiful expectant mother, it would be him.

He surveyed the situation and the helpless body of Jane Doe. "Does this poor woman have a name?" His voice thundered as he took command.

Clerks at the desk gathered paperwork in a bundle and gave it to the triage nurse. She read aloud from the chart. "Jane Doe found at the scene, the hospital parking lot. A bystander witnessed an assault and an attempted purse snatching. Jane Doe resisted. The perpetrator, a man in a suit, shot her in the head at close range with a pistol. She collapsed. When paramedics arrived, she had agonal respirations and no blood pressure or palpable pulse. Initial electrocardiogram readings revealed sinus bradycardia. That devolved into idioventricular rhythm. Since arrival here, full CPR in progress and a bullet entrance wound in the right temple. Just before you arrived, she developed decorticate posturing and cardiac arrest. The rhythm was restored with intracardiac epinephrine. Her tentative identification is Claire McGee, RN. She's an employee of the university hospital, just leaving her day shift, and she is approximately seven months pregnant. Her husband is a medical doctor attending graduate school here in the Department of Physics."

"Get hold of her husband now!" Dr. Hilley roared again. Three secretaries started dialing phones. "Get me a fetal heartbeat," he commanded. At the same time, two nurses and the resident formerly in charge reached toward her abdomen with stethoscopes. The tall charge nurse doing CPR indicated to the resident where the fetal heart monitor was standing by for such an emergent event. He grabbed it from its cradle on the crash cart and took a reading.

"Heart rate two fifty," he announced three times, which was the usual response to a command in a CPR situation.

Dr. Hilley's brow furrowed. "Do you have contact with the husband?" he yelled.

"No," was the triplicate response.

Hilley's facial expression exuded pain. "Prepare for emergency C-section," he ordered, saying quietly to himself, "Maybe, just maybe, I can save this baby."

Hilley grabbed the scalpel in his right hand and handed a retractor and a clamp from the sterile kit just deployed on a Mayo stand to the resident—to take the baby from its mother's womb. Not hesitating, he made a long incision across the lower abdomen, down to the gravid uterus. After realizing that there was so little blood flowing to cause any significant bleeding, he cut again, this time deep into the muscle of her womb, and a splash of amniotic fluid instantly spoiled the operative field. He took the baby, a male, now blue-black in color, indicating severe anoxia, and held him upside down by his legs. He did not breathe or move.

Hilley quickly handed the child off to another doctor, a neonatologist who had just run into the room, responding to the overhead page generated by the trusty triage secretary.

Dr. Hilley looked at the clock and saw the end of time for Claire McGee. With the same professional certainty, he looked at the staff and called the code at 3:59 p.m.

Standing there by her dead body, Dr. Hilley waited patiently for word from the neonatologist. After several minutes, the neonatologist nodded in despair and announced baby boy McGee deceased, 4:04 p.m.

In typical fashion, whenever death entered a room, chaos was sure to follow like an unwelcome intruder at a party.

 espess

Finn, a graduate student at the University of Syracuse, had only one care in the world. The last time he spoke with Claire, when they were both on their way out of the house in the morning, was the first serious argument he'd ever had with the love of his life. She had gladly accepted his decision to give up medical practice and return to graduate school. She was selfless in her decision to work through her pregnancy to help them financially. In the pursuit of her happiness, he volunteered to moonlight in the ER, and she preferred that they live off their savings, and if necessary, her rich father would share some of his wealth from executive divorce law to keep them afloat until Finn was able to earn a living in physics. But pride too often colored Finn's judgment, and they argued pointlessly over coffee that morning. He was desperate to get home and meet her at the door with a smile, which usually worked, and an apology as well.

He raced the old Ford home to the Genesee Street Victorian he and Claire had just redecorated. Then he downshifted, watching for children and pedestrians as he sped along. His impulsive nature allowed him to go over the limit, but not recklessly. The old car would have to do now until he had a paying job. He had resolved to swallow his pride and accept Claire's suggestion about asking her dad for assistance. At this moment, nothing seemed more important to him than telling Claire how wrong he had been. He was surely ahead of her, as her shift ended at 3:00 p.m., and the clock on his dashboard read 3:30 p.m. He turned the car into the driveway and was relieved to know he had gotten home first. He grabbed the supermarket bouquet of flowers from the front seat and ran into the house.

The phone was ringing, and he figured it must be a sales call. All their friends knew they usually did not get home until 4:00. Professor Hayhurst knew why Finn had left early. That morning, he had gone to him for advice. His mentor hesitated to let him cut the last lecture of the day and then, seeming genuinely distressed at the excuse Finn had given, relented. Dr. Hayhurst not only encouraged Finn to go home early but to bring flowers as well.

The ringing did not stop. Finn considered letting it ring but then reasoned that peace would only come to him if he answered the telephone.

He clutched the receiver to his face with one motion, in a style reminiscent of when he was in clinical practice. "McGee, here."

The woman on the line informed him that his "wife was in critical condition at the university hospital ER." No further details were offered.

∽∾∾

The receiver on the wall phone arced back and forth, tracing a dark groove in the paint on the wall. Swinging like a pendulum, it finally came to a stop, hanging uselessly by its cord. By then, Finn was careening around corners and blowing through stop signs in the old car as he raced for Claire's side. The steel in the car's frame clanked and stuttered as Finn pushed it beyond the edge of safe performance. Breathing hard and in a cold sweat, veins bulging, he hurtled down the highway as if trying to intercept the setting sun.

He arrived at the emergency room and noticed several police vehicles lights still flashing and a red-and-white ambulance with its doors ajar. Crowds swelled with onlookers as two uniformed officers applied yellow tape to a distant parking lot gate. Finn held his breath and said a prayer. He bounded up to the top of the ambulance bay platform like a superhero. Charging through security without stopping to address the guard, he found himself lost in trauma room 1.

The world now moved in surreal slow motion, and Finn cast his gaze about the scene. Searching for an easy solution to the mystery he first learned about a lifetime ago on the kitchen wall phone. All he could see now was how the receiver fell from his hand. Then, as if he'd bilocated, he was here in this sterile theater, life's battlefield. For a moment, he was then transported back into the racing Ford, shaking and shivering with fear. Finally, his eyes came to rest on the soulful face of Dr. Hilley, who was holding his arms out toward him as if to say, *Come let me hold you away from this body so you will not have to look upon her.*

There, barely covered with a wet and bloody sheet, lay the body of his beautiful Claire. Now she was pale and still. The color was gone from her cheeks, and her bright blue eyes were dulled, staring blankly past the clear plastic tube that was growing out of her mouth. His love was staring at him as if to say, *I'm here, but my time is gone.* But she did not change her expression as he gazed back at her lovely face. Her hair, disturbed and bloody blond, was now brushed the wrong way. Like a gaping mouth, the dark blue-black circle in the back of her head seemed to scream for him to help.

Her abdomen, partially uncovered in the hurry to save the baby, demonstrated the ravages of the quick scalpel, and the bump where their baby was, was gone.

Her right hand, limp and falling off the gurney with seeming purpose, pointed him in the direction of the baby's resting place.

He hoped for just one sweet moment, but hope was gone. He ran now, faster than slow motion, to the cradle where the baby boy lay, brushing aside with enormous strength the arms that reached out to restrain him. He leaned over the infant's body, his eyes filled with tears. The flood fell upon the baby's face, and Finn touched him for the first time, felt the water from the tears, and made a small cross on the boy's forehead.

Frozen there in the moment, he whirled around and gazed again upon Claire's dead body. He looked at the hands of all those who had attended her in her final moments of life.

Plastic gloves on all the hands made him feel such deep sorrow. No human hand actually touched her in her final moments.

Did she die without the closeness of real human touch? How sterile and cold had medical science become to deprive his beloved of even one soft touch of an ungloved hand?

He placed his hand on her chest to prove to himself that there was no heart beating there. He stood touching her bare skin with his bare skin, and he cried and cried and cried out, "God, no!" But his prayer was not answered. The clock on the wall read 4:05 p.m.

❧❧❧

Saturday morning, August 21, 2010:

Sweat rolled off Finn's face, and his heart raced. He saw himself struggling with the sheets that covered Claire's body. Then white material engulfed him, tried to smother him. He twisted. He turned. His muscles were convulsing from the hurt of the battle. He refused to let go—would not say good-bye. Reaching after her with abandon, scratching at the soaking wet sheets, tugging on an arm, he cried out, "Please, God, no!" He repeated this several times and cried louder. Pain wrapped him in a blanket of cold, wet confusion. He grabbed an arm, felt a hand. Vision focused on a face as he wept in repeated despair. "Claire, Claire, don't leave me!" he screamed.

His eyes focused, and his senses that were betraying him homed in on the face of a guardian angel sent to wrench him back to reality. Her voice tried to soothe him, calm him, and cause the tide of his nightmare to ebb. "Wake up. Wake up. You're having a nightmare, Finn." She wrestled with him as he flailed about, reaching for her, not knowing who she was momentarily, and then he finally surrendered to present reality.

Dan ran into the room in response to the yelling and saw that his sister had arrived first. He knew Finn was experiencing another dream about Claire's death. He had heard it before. Finn had confided in him about his recurring night terrors. He had sought relief in the warmth of friendship but had never come to peace with himself about his loss.

Now, Dan thought, *with fresh ideas of government conspiracy, the terror will continue*. He had surmised that the mention of the government grooming candidates for Finn's research position would upset him. He also feared the consequences of Finn's fertile imagination. If Dan were certain there was no cause for Finn's concern, he would be more comfortable. Restlessness crested in his subconscious. *Speculation about a conspiracy theory was only that*, he assured himself.

Relieved to see Finn awakening from his obvious distress, Maddy leaned over the bed and reached out to him.

Finn sat up straight. His T-shirt soaking wet from sweat, he shook his head. He looked at Maddy and Dan, hovering over him with concern. "Sorry I disturbed your peace." He was embarrassed now, realizing that he had caused enough of a scene that they had to come barging into the guest room and waken him.

Maddy responded in motherly fashion, "Someone needs to watch over you sometimes." On the pretense of making Finn's breakfast, she abruptly departed.

Dan stared at Finn, saying nothing for the longest time. Then he tossed him a towel from the dresser. "Best take a shower before you come to breakfast." He turned and closed the guest bedroom door behind him.

Finn stood in the shower and felt the hot water pour onto his scalp and tumble down his neck to the rest of his shivering body. Refreshing warmth soothed his muscles, and they began to release the knots of tension that had tortured him. He was in no mood to sing. Thinking was his preferred pastime when showering, and he stood there in the tepid artificial rain, collecting his thoughts.

He considered the coincidental facts surrounding his physics grant. He now thought it odd to have received the award for presenting a paper on "The Lost Science of Syracuse" to the national physics journal when physics was still his hobby. Paranoia surged in him as he thought of the strange visit by the recruiter from the University of Syracuse just as his medical career began to soar. He knew better, and accepting these coincidences was an accident of his judgment.

He remembered an axiom long forgotten. His former professor once told him, "Understand and remember, there are no coincidences."

Fresh-baked blueberry muffins scented the air in the office suite, enticing Finn to dress quickly and join Dan and Maddy. Grateful for the hot coffee, he sat down for the meal with his friends.

"Dan," he said, reaching for a warm muffin, "how much computing capacity does GIM have?"

"More than you can imagine needing."

Finn grinned. "Wait till you hear what I'm planning."

Maddy's eyes widened in surprise. "Fifteen minutes ago, you were barely functional from a night terror, and now you have made a plan that requires computer power galore! This I can't wait to hear about." She poured herself another cup of coffee and leaned into the conversation.

"Dan," Finn started, "I need to do some research. I want to follow the Department of Physics grant money that came into the University of Syracuse back to its source."

"You already know it was government money. What more could you possibly learn?"

"I need to understand which government department the funds were budgeted from. Frank Hayhurst had some friends and connections in high places, and I just want to know who I'm really working for. Since I was brought in, I've had too many questions about the whole project. Now, with Frank gone under mysterious circumstances, and with the CIA looking for me because I took an unannounced vacation, I need to know the truth behind the project. Your self-admission last night that you left

NASA because of some concerns about recruiting ethics and procedure has my brain working overtime. And my time travel machine seems to be the focus of all their attention, whether they admit it or not." Finn suspended his explanation and slowly sipped his hot coffee.

Maddy asked the unthinkable question. "You don't believe they had anything to do with Claire's death, do you, Finn?"

Finn thought before he spoke and then slowly, as if he had planned to answer this question someday, said, "Maddy, what I know is that Claire was unhappy with my staying on and pursuing my physics degree. It was the only reason we ever argued. Frank Hayhurst knew how she felt, and the influence she had over me, and he reported to someone up the money chain. I never bothered much with that part of the physics business. It's a long stretch, but I feel comfortable with making it. The police report said that Claire was shot at close range by a purse-snatcher who just happened to be dressed in a business suit. A purse snatcher in a business suit—does that even make sense? And one more thing. Frank Hayhurst had a peculiar method of choosing graduate students. He confided that to me in the beginning of my tenure as his vice chair. That's all I know about it—and probably all I ever will know. It may seem to be happenstance superficially. I just don't believe in coincidences!"

Dan reached for the coffeepot. "Assuming we don't break any laws, I think GIM can get your answer for you today. Most of what he does is related to financial transactions. What will you do if you learn that you are now working for the Pentagon or CIA, or even some deep cover government security agency?"

"Then," said Finn, "I shall finish my personal research agenda and turn the device off and hide it where it will be safe until I die with the secret."

Maddy furrowed her brow and stared intently at Finn while he continued. "I think it has far too much potential for abuse than anything in history devised by the hand of man. Dan, don't you agree? Maddy, don't you see my point?"

Maddy shook her head and looked at Dan.

Dan, always the wise sage, thought for a moment and then said, "When and if the secrets of time travel become available to mankind, I would hope that the use would be monitored and controlled by some authority. I can envision the day when time travel without that authority's consent could be a criminal act."

"So now I get it," Maddy responded. "With the ability to possess this secret, the government would be in a position to change outcomes of current political situations, for example, and then, in changing the outcome, obtain more and more power. The unintended consequences would most assuredly change history as we know it, leaving paradoxes that would lead to unimaginable events, all of which could have a negative effect on the population of the world, not just our nation and—"

"We are at the point in this discussion," Finn interrupted, "where the classical conundrum faces us. Do we keep the secret from those who bought and paid for its development, or do we give them their property? Said more mundanely, do the ends justify the means?"

Dan was quick to set aside Finn's last statement with another argument. "The secret to time travel is your intellectual property. You have a responsibility to use it well and share it only with those trustworthy enough to hold it. It is not at all clear to my Jesuit logic that the government has a right to your invention since you were unaware of their support for this development.

"The mere fact that the government seemed to manipulate you and perhaps push you through the developmental phase without your consent exonerates you from their claim to your invention."

There was no conflict to resolve when they finished their discussion. It was clear to all that the time machine must be kept a secret. They set about with the business of the day. Work needed to be done in preparation for the return of the payload Finn had sent to the moon. There were also plans needed to complete the second mission from One Fifth Avenue. Finn shared with Maddy and Dan that when he visited Syracuse and Archimedes, he hoped to observe the war machines the philosopher had devised. He believed there was more to learn than what he had accidentally discovered. To do this, he would have to go back to the island of modern-day Sicily, to the city of Syracuse, during the Second Punic War. Once there, he would witness history and perhaps discover a method of preventing war.

Though she couldn't help but fill resentful as she pulled needle through cloth—a task she'd once vowed never to return to—Maddy had been spending a good deal of time on the costume project. She stayed with it out of love and shared this plan with no one. Rather, she told the boys that she'd not yet had any luck finding the right place to purchase a costume for Finn's journey. Not only did she hope to surprise Finn when he insisted he must leave, but she hoped the lack of proper attire would perhaps delay his impulsiveness.

Dan tinkered with GIM for the rest of the day, doing financial research into the money trail as Finn had requested.

Finn was comfortable that he could honestly discuss his secret theories with Dan and Maddy. He was content as he plotted out his next time travel adventure. He mused about taking Dan and then discarded the thought. Dan was the steady hand here at home base to assist if

something went wrong and to neatly dispose of all paraphernalia should the worst happen and he did not get
back.

CHAPTER 19

Return from the Moon

Sunday morning, August 22, 2010:

Virtually everyone in Manhattan, save Finn, Dan, and Maddy, paid attention to approaching weather patterns on the news. Since Friday morning, a category-3 hurricane picked up wind speed and force from the clashing of two major storms over the warm Atlantic Ocean. Landfall predictions centered the storm in the general region of the Mid-Atlantic States. Meteorologists debated whether New Jersey coast or the city of New York would be the first contact point.

The fragrance of brewing coffee didn't awaken Finn this morning. The sounds of wind and rain battering the glass windows and skylight in the office suite held that honor. The majestic dawn with painted sky over the lower Manhattan skyline usually greeted him, finding him fully rested and ready for another New York day.

Today an ugly dark sky with ominous swirling black clouds and rumbling freight train blasts rattled the glass roof and walls, jolting him from sleepiness. Then, of course, the lightning display with bolts the size of skyscrapers flashing and exploding like bombs in the sky threatened impending disaster. They were too close and too fast for any sense of comfort, and Finn sought shelter, standing in the hallway. He expected that the force of the storm would shatter the glass wall and ceiling around him at any moment, abandoning him in the fury of the hurricane and leaving him helpless on the open top deck of One Fifth Avenue.

Landfall by the largest hurricane storm in ten years had occurred as predicted. As the storm came ashore in New York City, all citizens aware of the forecast were prepared. Finn, Dan, and Maddy had been taken by surprise.

Finn's first concern was a power outage possibly disrupting the return of the canister from the Sea of Tranquility. Dan assured him that electronics around GIM included ample battery power to run the office through any temporary interruption in electric utility service. Maddy made breakfast, prioritizing extra coffee-filled thermos bottles. They gathered near an inside wall and ate breakfast uneasily while the fierce winds pelted the roof and wall with bullets of water.

Discussion centered around the flashing *113 Minutes* signal on the computer screen. Dan speculated that the worst of the storm would pass by then, hopefully. Instantaneously, the room was rocked with vibrations of two more electrical explosions. Sounds of shattering glass and abrupt shifting wind pitch were deafening. Lightning bolts seemed to emanate from the room's center, and then a green crystal-shaped light materialized, filling the room. The temperature plummeted. Wind and water were forced through the shattered skylight to fill the vacuum.

Maddy found herself lying on the floor, holding onto a heavy couch as it slid slowly toward the center of the room. Finn and Dan clung to one another while Dan gripped a doorframe to avoid being upended and sucked into the central void. The green glow solidified and faded. Atmospheric pressure in the room stabilized to normal. The violent force sucking the contents of the room to the center subsided, and all three, frightened and disheveled, stared at the canister on the office floor. Ice crystals formed on its surface, and the glass portal was fogged at the same time. Gray powder covered the lower and middle regions of the canister, spewing onto the antique Persian rug.

Dan ran to move it, and Finn rapidly intervened. "Dan," he yelled, "don't touch it! Lunar surface temperatures can be as low as minus two hundred and sixty degrees. Give it time to equalize." Dan ran to a closet and donned leather gloves, bringing a towel, too. Focused on preserving his antique rug, he gently lifted the canister onto the towel. The gloves froze to the canister and Dan extricated his hands, leaving the gloves attached. As they watched, the ice crystals melted, and the water rolled down the sides of the canister, purging the gray dust away. The residue pooled as a gray mud, staining the towel.

Finn watched as the gloves adhering to the canister fell away as well. After a few minutes, he touched the canister. It was cool but able to be manipulated, and he released the pressure lock and freed his Nikon from its nest. Taking the flash drive from the camera, he placed it into one of GIM's control panel apertures.

The screen lit up with a slide show of lunar landscape, leaving the three adventurers in wonder—watching and waiting to see if the secret Dan had revealed had substance.

Finn announced that the crater that was the Sea of Tranquility was more than eight hundred kilometers in diameter. From their perspective, they saw only an endless lunar desert and could not be certain of the distant landscape. GIM was asked to calculate the position from the angle of the shadows on some of the photos. The confirmation from GIM that they, in fact, had a proper view of the landing site was approaching 93 percent accuracy.

Time flew by, as did each photo of the blank gray lunar landscape. The longer they watched, the surer they were that Dan's secret had been verified.

They held a collective breath as they watched the soundless touchdown of the lunar module. Clouds of gray dust flew up from the lunar surface and wrapped around it like angels wings, gently placing it on the surface. The dust reflected rainbow-like color as it reflected sunlight and floated in the lunar day. Slowly the lunar dust yielded to gravity, and perched on its landing gear was the LM, silent, motionless, and apparently, to the glee of the time adventurers, unmanned.

Nothing could yield more certain satisfaction that they had proven Dan's secret to be true. Timing was everything throughout history, and going public with this story seemed meaningless.

They were sure enough to broach the subject of the next adventure, but not until Dan and Finn had a heated exchange about risk. The time/space machine had proved unpredictable, and Dan demanded from Finn some further research into why the canister came back 113 minutes too early.

CHAPTER 20

Weather Report

Maddy was already commanding GIM to display an analysis of the weather and a summary of the weather reports available on network news and other professional sources. The screen switched to multiple views of the various weather agencies' reports.

"I sure hope you can explain to me what happened after you examined the equipment," Dan said to Finn,

Finn shook his head in concentration and remained silent as he investigated the time machine. Finally, he said, "My only judgment at this point is that it behaved as if the power were turned off prematurely, but I see no evidence of that, or even a power surge."

Reports from GIM's monitor indicated the following: "This is a category-four hurricane. It hit a bull's-eye on Manhattan. Reports of wind damage were already measured in the millions of dollars, and a death toll of twenty-four is still rising. The electrical activity of the storm was one of the most turbulent in recent history. The entire power grid was in danger of failing because of the damaged circuitry. There are reports of power company transformers that were suddenly overloaded with currents that exceeded the highest ratings. In all, the electrical instability caused by ionization of the atmosphere during the storm proved to push the network beyond its limits. A selected series of shutdowns is now being arranged."

With that, the lights dimmed, the screen blinked, and the backup power supply was accessed. GIM asked Dan which circuits could be closed in the office to conserve power.

Dan became increasingly alarmed as he watched the devastation that was reported. He mulled over with Finn possibilities regarding the unexpected malfunction and began to argue. "Finn, you must pause here to do proper analysis. Your plans for the next trip must wait."

"No, there is little time left for me. I'm sure General Gunter and his agents are hot on my trail and will find me here by the end of the week. I must stay on schedule."

"Let's perform what amounts to a debriefing of all our records and try to work in concert here. There must be a clue somewhere in GIM's memory, or even in the log sequence of lunar photos," Dan responded, trying to temper his fear for Finn's apparent willingness to jump into the time vortex again without understanding the malfunction fundamentals essential to avoiding another mishap.

Finn couldn't be swayed by any logic at this point. He continued to work, feverishly reviewing data. "I'm staying on schedule," he stated flatly. "I have nothing to lose by risk taking. Everything I have worked for is at risk, if they catch me before I finish my research."

Finn's facial grimace made clear his intention to proceed. Dan pressed his lips tightly and adjusted his glasses, indicating personal stress. Explosive tensions mounted between the men, who always were able to find neutral ground.

Maddy yelled, breaking the strain. "Boys, I think

I've found something here." She hurriedly hit the memory rewind and turned up the volume on a local news station. The commentator left the screen, backing up into a Ford commercial when she hit pause. She turned to Dan and Finn. "You are not going to believe this!"

"This is the Eyewitness News report: 'The Season of Hurricanes,'" the invisible announcer declared to a flourish of music and drumrolls.

There in the winds and rain of the hurricane stood a television reporter dressed in a clownish yellow slicker, wearing goggles to keep the driving rain out of his eyes. Flashing across the rolling border was the headline *STORM DAMAGES STATUE OF LIBERTY.*

The reporter leaned into the wind as the video cameras took inventory of Ms. Liberty. There she stood on her pedestal in New York Harbor, right arm out stretched as it had been since 1886. The torch that had welcomed teeming visitors and immigrants to America for more than a century was gone. Searchlights dueled in the stormy sky, like swords clashing, to reveal Liberty's empty hand. The flame of the torch seemed to have been torn violently from the statue's arm, and the jagged edges reflected in the beams were twisted and frayed. The reporter, who was barely audible above the wind, went with the story.

"Shock and dismay are the only words for this unseemly act of nature. The mayor's office has announced that there are no video surveillance tapes of the moment of destruction. The city plans to start a search for the missing pieces in the harbor when the storm passes. The federal government has announced a state of emergency for New York City, New Jersey, and Connecticut coastal communities. They have indicated that the safety of our citizens is a top priority in the aftermath of this storm.

They have also announced dispatch of Navy SEALs to search for missing parts of the Statue of Liberty."

The newscast continued with other storm-related videos. Dan and Finn looked at Maddy as if she had completely missed the point. Maddy got the message from their puzzled expressions. "Boys," she said, offering a broad, toothy smile, "I'm not just the sweet older sister here. I know just enough to think I have solved your puzzle."

The men enjoyed Maddy's teasing and listened dutifully. "Finn, your vortex requires a catalyst of precious metal to travel through it if I learned my science correctly, right?" she questioned, then volunteered the answer herself. "Yes." And she added, "I recently read that the Statue of Liberty was made of a copper skin applied to a steel frame." She paused. "What makes my theory interesting is the fact that the torch is also made of copper on a steel frame, but it's covered with a thin layer of gold leaf."

Finn nodded and broke into a grin of recognition. Then a flicker of a different thought crossed his mind, and his face dropped. "We may be responsible for this," he wondered aloud.

They looked at each other in silent despair, with the suggestion that their experiment may have somehow made the storm worse.

Finn staggered back on his feet and took the conversation over. "Maddy, the hurricane is not just a chaotic blast of wind and lightning that occurs without organization. It is a rather formal structure with revolving winds in a circular fashion that may even acquire a spiral shape to it now and then. Actually, I am betting on that! My experience tells me that that emerald-green light sometimes seen in violent storms may be similar to that generated by my time machine force field."

"So the implications are that the storm opened the vortex, and the canister came scooting back a little early?" Dan contributed.

"Yes, Dan that is my interpretation. I am tormented by another thought. If Maddy is correct, then I speculate that Ms. Liberty's torch is now anchored deeply in the gray lunar dust of Tranquility Base, ready to greet the next explorers fortunate enough to walk on the surface of the moon."

Dan smiled. "This seems like the world's most perfect irony."

Artist's Rendition of Archimedes' Claw

CHAPTER 21

The Search for Archimedes

August 22, 2010:

Finn sat at the console, working on the recent dilemma. He asked GIM to open the file on his computer to the *Rules of Time Travel*. Finn studied his rules to determine where revisions were necessary.

He began with an additional exception to rule three:

> 3. Turning off the power to the time travel field can result in the return of the experimental time traveler. Examples: the silver triangle, H's amalgam filling, diamond (with the addition of more catalyst). Exceptions: H's body (perhaps losing the filling at the wrong moment made his journey erratic).
>
> Additional exception: turbulent electromagnetic fields of natural occurrence concurrently operating with a time journey interferes with the fail-safe and may alter the travel of a subject or add an additional subject to the vortex.
>
> *Solution* – Not apparent. Take extreme cau-

tion in planning, including observing weather patterns.

Next he deleted the word "possible" from the fourth rule and revised the solution slightly:

> 4. Find a replacement for Kathryn in order to control the device's timing.
> *Solution* – Use a clock or GIM to control timing.

That done, he glanced at rule five and sighed. He typed the only possible solution:

> 5. There are moral consequences involved in changing history.
> *Solution* – Follow the rules and hope it's not too late already (e.g., torch from the Statue of Liberty may now be on the moon).

Finn scanned the page, his eyes coming to rest on rule twelve, and added a simple note:

> 13. The approximate vortex interval for thirty years is one hour.
> *Solution* – Not apparent.

When Finn was done with his review, he added three new rules:

> 14. Plan ahead. Food is a problem unless you have local currency, a wedding invitation, or skills at theft.
> 15. Dress for the location, date, and weather.

16. Have a backup plan in case your departure is prevented by unusual events in the time warp vortex. Traveling through time is like a needle pulling thread. If the thread is cut, it can be difficult to find the needle again.

He pressed save and enter. He asked GIM to display the rules on an adjacent small monitor as a reminder to himself, Dan, and Maddy.

With the rules updated, and ambition nagging at his reasoning skills, Finn pressed on to undertake his last planned mission. He gathered his dear friends around a library table in the office suite. On the table was a topographical map of Syracuse, the ancient city, with its borders superimposed, outlining the fortified wall. The legend's map scale indicated that the wall approached twenty-four kilometers in length. It was easily discernable that the wall was built to surround Syracuse and make it a fortress.

To the northeast of the city was a sort of plateau that formed part of the barrier wall, and to the southwest, the wall tapered into high hilly terrain. The city sat on a deep harbor with a natural rocky seawall separating it from the bay. The harbor road was wide enough for commerce. Finn laid out his strategy to Dan and Maddy, pinpointing how he hoped to approach the scene during the Roman siege.

"The Second Punic War was essentially an assault upon the Roman Empire by Hannibal," he said, offering a historical explanation. "Hannibal lived in a period of great stress in the Mediterranean world. It was when the Romans took dominance over some adjacent nations, such as Carthage." Before continuing, Finn paused to show a larger map of the Roman Empire. He placed a coin on it to mark the location of Carthage.

"Hannibal's ambition from his early years was to seek vengeance upon the Roman Empire. He rose in stature, to be the most skilled military commander in Carthage and traveled to Spain to raise an army to oppose Rome. With the help of Gaulish allies, he successfully crossed the Alps in wintertime, attacking the Roman Empire from the north." Finn again looked at his friends to be sure he had their attention. He took a marker pen and, with a wide sweep of his hand, demonstrated the path taken by Hannibal on the map.

"Hannibal had a superior cavalry to the Romans, and he triumphantly destroyed Roman forces in two decisive defeats: the Battle of Trebia and the massive ambush at Trasimene."

While Finn assumed the role of a professor giving a lecture, Dan sprawled in an armed chair at the table and Maddy poured fresh coffee for all.

"These two battles set the stage for a new Roman strategy of warfare named the 'Fabian Strategy,' after the dictator Fabius Maximus," Finn continued, ignoring his cup. "The strategy was simple. The Romans would avoid staging set battlefields. Instead, they would wage guerrilla style warfare against Hannibal with the intention of interrupting supply lines, inflicting annoying damage and destruction, demoralizing the enemy.

"This Fabian approach was very unpopular with proud Roman citizens, and they again turned to engage Hannibal's forces in an additional major battlefield. The result was another resounding defeat for the Roman army at Cannae. Political ramifications were that many Roman allies switched allegiance to the Carthaginian side, and that included the Kingdom of Syracuse.

"The impending fear: Carthage had persuaded them to switch allegiances. When diplomacy failed, the battle for Syracuse was begun. The siege lasted three years."

Almost finished with his lecture, Finn reached for his warm coffee and sipped it slowly before continuing.

"That's when Archimedes put his defensive weapons to use, and it's the time and location of my best chance to learn more," he said. "It's my goal to journey back to the Kingdom of Syracuse and observe firsthand the tools that Archimedes devised, and to further investigate what he knew about antigravity and the time vortex."

Dan reiterated his concerns, urging Finn to be sure he could justify the personal risk. Relying on Jesuit wisdom, he asked, "What more could you learn by going there?" Harping on the theme, Dan applied more pressure. "Finn, this trip is more dangerous than your others. You are going to a war zone unprotected. Be sure of your justification as to the personal risk."

There was a heated discussion between the men. Maddy interrupted with a compromise. She suggested that, with GIM's help, they could design a fail-safe into the device.

They all agreed on a trigger that had a singular purpose. It would activate the time machine to return the traveler to the present. She also suggested that the return location be different from the departure point as an added defense for the time traveler. Finn became reluctant when he considered the delay that might result.

Dan took the side of safety, and Maddy chimed in, supporting Dan. "Please think twice about this, Finn. I don't want to grieve for losing you too."

"I appreciate your concern for me," Finn said, agreeing to the additional work of engineering a fail-safe into the device. "But I must go to Syracuse. I have given this the most consideration of all my work. I feel this is my destiny. If there is more to learn, I am the one who can discover it. And when my work is done, dear friends, I have nothing left to lose."

Dan pointed out the price too many men had paid for the sin of pride.

Finn, unmoved by any argument, began to lay out his strategy on the map: conquer the Kingdom of Syracuse.

ℯ⌒ℰ⌒ℴ

August 23, 2010:

Up in the morning and back to work, Finn was hovering over the table, plotting a course with assistance from GIM, when Maddy, ever the mother, walked up to him with a hot cup of coffee and a blueberry muffin. Finn looked up with gratitude and love for his adopted sister and acknowledged her effort with a wink and a "thanks."

Dan put in an appearance after reading his usual morning prayers from his prayer book and saying a private Mass. Cup in hand, he remarked on Maddy's java and told Finn matter-of-factly, "I leave you in Maddy's competent hands today, my friend. I'm off to Fordham to organize the semester's curriculum in philosophy and to meet my senior students for the coming year. I also leave you in the hands of Divine Providence, should my dear sister fail us."

That said, Dan departed for the day.

Maddy shrugged her shoulders and looked powerlessly at Finn. "Please don't leave on a time trip today. Wait till Dan gets back?"

Finn smiled. "I love you too much to let you face Dan's wrath on that one, but I plan to leave tonight and to arrive in Syracuse this evening. Dan must be here as failsafe. He understands GIM well enough to make sure I get back.

"Let me tell you what I need," he added gently. "I know you haven't found the right costume yet. But,

Maddy, I need something to wear. Is there any way you could—"

Maddy cut him off. "I told you. I don't do costumes. I have not sewn one rag to another since we left the Michigan homestead. You aren't really giving me credit," she added, "or at least you're seriously underestimating my value."

Though the design phase of her costume was complete, she hoped her emphatic statement would delay Finn's plans further.

"Well." Finn sighed. "I've never used a needle and thread, except on my surgery rotation in medical school. Knots were my nemesis, and that's why I chose internal medicine. But I suppose I could give costume design a try."

Maddy relented. "You are in for a surprise, Finn. I hope you're not sorry."

An hour later, Maddy displayed the supplies she had been secretly hoarding for Finn's next adventure. Among these was a bolt of naturally dyed material to fashion an outfit suitable enough to help Finn pass as a Syracusan. Maddy played it cool, still offering resistance to the chore, and tried to let Finn feel as if he had to work hard to persuade her in the task. She would never let him know she had already done the lion's share of the work. Joyfully humming a tune to herself, Maddy feigned working long into the day.

Feeling victorious, Finn prepared for Syracuse. He selected coordinates that would guarantee a soft highlands landing, northeast of the city wall. He measured three times and was certain he would arrive at night, with the light of a full moon, under the protective shadows of olive trees. The time of the year would be late spring— the dry season, with warm nights, warm days, and no severe weather.

On arrival, he planned to make a small camp. Once secure, he'd gather firewood and behave as a shepherd living in the hills. Finn was determined to maintain a low profile. His camp would be easily concealed by the local terrain. With luck, he could find a rocky crevice to light a fire for warmth and to cook any hunted wildlife.

In case he found no food, he would bring beef jerky and chocolate bars, but he would spend the day rewrapping supplies in biodegradable paper containers. Hopefully almond trees had dropped enough of the previous year's harvest to enhance his diet. Rationing his time to two days, he feared General Gunter's agents would be on his trail. He counted on their being delayed by the extreme hurricane that New York and the New England states had just endured. The government was resourceful and pernicious in its pursuit of those it wished to control. Finn was close to the top of their wanted list. Fortunately, they wanted him alive.

When Dan arrived, Finn was standing in the middle of the office with bare feet and the bottoms of his trousers rolled, reminiscent of the image made famous by T. S. Eliot in *The Love Song of J. Alfred Prufrock*. The image was fleeting, for Maddy immediately draped the final set of clothes over Finn, transforming him into the epitome of Greek antiquity fashion.

Slipping his size tens into the leather sandals concluded the entire scene, and Dan belly laughed. Maddy smiled and Finn, realizing the statement he was making, grinned his traditional Gaelic grin. In the release of tension with uncontrolled laughter, Maddy joined in the hilarity of the moment.

When the laughter died down, it was clear that Finn was all about the business of his final mission. With reluctance, Dan accepted the inevitable and huddled with his dear friend over last-minute plan adjustments. Departure time: 8:00 p.m. eastern daylight time. GIM assumed the role of master computer for the time machine. Accepting the calculations, GIM double-checked them, flashing its ready message. The countdown warning was given by GIM, starting with a pause at two minutes. Then, at sixty seconds, announced in one-second intervals, the countdown was continued. Finn had programmed a two-hour cushion for vortex time. Loading his inside pockets with snacks to sustain him, he decided to wear jeans and a T-shirt under the disguise.

Acknowledging the countdown, Finn stepped into the center of the skyscraper office suite, bidding farewell to Dan and Maddy, promising to be careful as the green mist and lightning show engulfed him. Once again, he listened to the musical symphony of time and fell into the fiery whirlwind he now understood to be the tunnel to the past.

e⁓ɔe⁓ɔ

When Finn arrived, it was pitch-black night and pouring rain. Trees surrounding him could only be recognized by touch, not to mention a sudden bruise or two. He rested in the fork of two massive trees, sitting in a pool of water, rain pouring down his face. How much wetter might he be if he had landed in an open field? The wind howled, and for a few moments, he thought a transcription error had thrust him into Central Park the previous morning. If it weren't for the freshness of the air, in spite of the ozone layer from lightning flashes, he would have presumed an error and walked to the edge of the park. The air was far too clean for New York City, even with a hurricane. The smell of the recent garbage strike would have been pervasive.

Finn knew by analysis, his frequent ally, that he had

reached his destination, and surely a full moon was shining down brightly on the other side of storm clouds. *So
much for weather forecasting in time travel, even going
back in time, it's hard to get the weather right.*

After a brief rest, he chose a direction not by starlight
but by moving with the wind at his back. As he carefully
felt his route through the dark wilderness, he hoped the
storm was coming from the northeast. After some time
traveling by touch, he suddenly caught a glimpse of light
in the black fog and drizzle. With great care, he walked
toward the light, not able to see clearly, even fearing the
ground itself.

Guideless in an alien time and place, he wished he
had not forgotten a flashlight. As he drew nearer to the
light, he realized that it was a campfire. Wishing to dry
himself by the fire, he imagined different ways to wander
into the camp. Rejecting those, he found partial shelter
under a deadfall, which grabbed him as he fell right into
it. Crawling deep into it in the utter darkness, he suffered
many scrapes and abrasions. He felt a surge of relief
when, in its depth, he felt dry grass and leaves. There on
the crest of a small hill under a fallen tree, he nestled into
the one dry shelter available and rested, waiting for the
storm's end and the beginning of the day.

He considered the general effects of bad weather on
his time travel experiences and succumbed to new humility. Yes, the power of nature was still no match for
mere man.

෨෨෨

As dawn broke and the sky cleared, Finn crawled out
of his makeshift shelter and gazed upon the distant camp.
What he saw caused him to hold his breath.

In the distance, no more than the length of a football

field, was a flag. He recognized it immediately for what it was: the *vexillum* with *aquila*. Held high on a pole marking the ground location of one of history's fiercest killing machines, it was a legion of the Roman Republic.

Recognizable by the deep red banner, crowned by a gold eagle and with gold fringe adorning the foot of the banner, it spoke to all those who looked upon it the meaning of the four gold letters embroidered on its center surrounded by gold laurel. "SPQR" was an acronym for "Property of the Roman Republic."

Finn turned away from it and moved quickly but quietly in the opposite direction. Wind was now in his face and, breaking into a slight jog, he felt dampness on his body and palpitations in his chest. *That*, Finn thought, *was a close call.* He felt the results of sheer terror as his pace accelerated into a run, and the cold sweat of adrenaline produced by mortal fear was replaced by the warm perspiration of an all-out run. Finn kept up the pace for another ten minutes before he tired. All at once, he was filled with enough hope that he had placed safe distance between himself and the Roman legion. He stopped to rest.

Expeditions like this were no stroll in the woods. Finn soon learned this as he discovered the walls of the

Kingdom of Syracuse. Guards gathered on the bulwarks and turrets as bees did on spring flowers. Hope soon switched to fear of failure, but not apathy, as Finn sat in the shade of a grove of almond trees, pondering his predicament. He was not swayed by the weight of a new problem. He noted his appetite surging and swept the nearby undercover for intact almond shells. Finding the almonds, he removed his knife from the meager tool kit he packed, and opened about a dozen. He laid the fresh almonds, still moist and clearly edible, across his flowing robes as his legs held them in a crease folded in his lap. Finn reached into the pocket that contained the rewrapped Hershey's chocolate. Mixing the two delicacies together, he became the first man in history to eat a chocolate bar with almonds, if one considered the actual date.

After breakfast and realizing how much he missed Maddy's coffee, he began to search for a chink in the amour that was Syracuse's wall. He spied an opportunity in the branches of an olive tree, which the old tree suspended over a narrow sliver of the wall. If he were to shimmy up the tree and drop down without detection, he could pass for a Syracusan. He was never more thankful for the university gym pass he'd used daily before his adventures started.

He grabbed the tree trunk, sandals tied together and hanging from his neck, and began to inch his way up to the third tier of branches. He was so quiet that his own breath sounded like the wind of last night's storm to him. No guard noticed him, but he was startled when a flock of birds suddenly rushed to escape the tree, sensing he was near. He climbed out slowly on a limb and waited.

From his perch, he had an unexpected view of the other side of the rampart. From the safety of the olive tree, he saw all that he had ever hoped for was within his vision.

Men worked like ants in a hill, doing their part in the defense of Syracuse. The guards in turrets acknowledged advance scouting reports in Greek, echoing throughout the protected city on the secure side of fortress walls. Finn understood Greek words: a major battle was brewing. Syracusans hauled boulders in carts, led by asses or pulled by men, to the base of the wall. A wooden crane with many levers dominated the scene. Men handling the levers worked as a precision team.

By using the levers, numerous man-sized boulders could be moved to an elevator by only a few workers manning the carts. The elevator was a series of massive wood and iron buckets shaped like a V at the bases. Troughs connected by chains were attached to enormous wheels at the bottom and the top of a conveyor, with buckets separated by wooden rails and knotted chains. An aqueduct appeared to be powering the slow-moving conveyor system.

Water flowed into the grove hollowed out in the center cap on the wall and was directed to flow into the elevator buckets, moving the huge stones upward to a holding area, a large turret. As water weighed the buckets down to the base of the conveyor, the boulders rose to the top. The design was simply to have the V-shaped troughs dump their loads as they passed a critical point and began their downward movement to collect the next round of rock.

Finn recognized the fruits of Archimedes' famous "eureka moment" as the water displaced the weight of the stones carried up to the turret.

Searching for more information, Finn noted no mountain stream feeding the aqueduct. He climbed farther out on his limb, straining his neck enough to see men laboring to walk in a circle as they pushed spokes on a wheel. Noticing the pond from which the pipe drew water, he looked closer and confirmed that the inner works were none other than an Archimedes Screw.

As the sun rose in the southeast sky, Finn retreated closer to the trunk of the olive tree. His discovery had to be prevented. Suddenly, Roman legions marched up to the perimeter of the city, halting at a distance that Finn estimated as a bow's length from the wall. Smoke billowed up into the air from within their ranks. Black smoke could only mean one thing. Ground troops were signaling their position for the Roman navy.

He waited and kept watch while Syracusans continued their preparations. Fires were ignited in large basins of oil on top of the rampart. Soldiers kept oil fires burning by carefully pouring fuel into the flaming bowls. Siege conditions caused them to be conservative with fuel resources. Small measured amounts of clear oil were added to smokeless flames several times during the hour.

Looming up ahead, a spectacular array of sleek wooden ships coated the seascape horizon. Finn estimated fifty to sixty long, narrow ships with outriggers, equipped with sails and teams of oarsmen. The ships approached the bulwarks of Syracuse with military precision and unexpected speed.

Beak-like structures from the bows of the boats were reinforced with shining bronze to ram any obstacle in their paths. Bowmen lined the decks and stood ready. Doom radiated from the Roman navy as seamen appeared, borne up on waves of confidence. The battle waited.

A loud chorus of horns, signaling a call to arms, preceded the constant thunder of Syracusans drumrolls. A perfect distraction, all eyes turned to trumpets and drums. Finn departed his perch, settling neatly behind a rampart, looking very much like a patriotic subject of the Kingdom of Syracuse.

He immediately assumed an air of authority. He strode back and forth, surveying the balance of fortifications. From his vantage point, he had seen a vast number of Roman sailors and soldiers and estimated the naval force alone at twenty-five thousand. He assumed ground forces had been assembled slowly in equivalent numbers. He looked around at citizen soldiers on the wall. Against all reason, they did not appear to be afraid.

The sun rose higher, surprising him. Face-to-face with blinding light from within the city fortifications, he used the rampart as a screen to ease the intensity of the glare. He squinted and saw a series of large polished mirrors and lenses on a platform designed to change height and direction. Recalling the siege of Syracuse, Finn presumed that these mirrors were possibly the mythical heat rays that Archimedes had designed to capture and focus the light and heat of the sun. He watched in awe as fires ignited in the very sails of the amphibious assault ships, the pride of the Roman navy. Screams of joy arose within the turrets of the defensive walls. Shouts of soldiers and citizens proclaimed in Greek the success of the solar weapon. The cheers ceased, however, as the Roman navy, undaunted, continued to move to the shore.

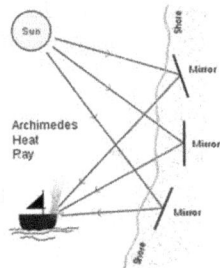

ARCHIMEDES HEAT RAY

Archimedes may have used mirrors acting collectively as a parabolic reflector to burn ships attacking Syracuse.
(New World Encyclopedia)

There was another flare of battle trumpets, and thousands of bowmen ascended the wall by ladders from within the city. Once on top, bowmen waited patiently as the long, narrow ships came within range, and they launched more than ten thousand arrows into the armada, some hitting fatal marks if not deflected away by raised shields.

The amphibious attack persisted, with Roman legionnaires returning arrows like rain upon the bulwark and the city. Finn ducked behind the rampart and observed with uncertain ease. Losing all track of time, he watched the battle unfold. His senses, sharpened by adrenaline, surged, his heart raced, and he breathed heavily with excitement and worry. With no decisive turn in the action, death and devastation triumphed.

He worried that he would spend all his time here, hunkered down behind a wall and dodging arrows, in fear for his life.

Finn began to sweat. *Dan was right again.*

Roman ships now appeared at the edge of the harbor. There was a series of pairs of boats. Single boats following them were designated to erect siege towers to be offloaded onto the partnered craft. Thunderous drumrolls resounded, shaking the very structure he stood upon. Gates to corrals of boulders yielded to the weight of the stone and opened when planks locking them were knocked away by the guards.

Rocks tumbled into the channel behind the rampart. Men with levers shaped like hockey sticks diverted rolling stones into large hinged wooden chutes. The chutes were aligned so that falling boulders would descend upon an elaborate sculpture built at the base of the bulwark. Finn recognized the metallic spirals, each the size of a small church, as the relic made of copper wires, which he had found in the ancient dig at Syracuse.

Each one was a perfect Archimedes spiral. Rocks descended like a roaring waterfall onto the apparatus. Finn watched in amazement as the falling rocks approached the force field, which was repelling the boulders. In a split second, with colossal speed, massive rocks arced over the forbidding wall, crushing and splintering Roman ships like giant hail from the heavens. Before any response, large cranes manipulated by a series of levers and ropes, lifted monstrous shiny metal grappling hooks over the coiled spiral machine.

The crane operator dropped these hooks individually into the antigravity field built by Archimedes.

Once launched, a tri-pronged claw bounced up from the force field of spirals, flying over the wall a great distance and landing like a fish hook on the end of a chain. The gaff-like claw at the end of each chain then snapped back, powered by a catapult device. Claws returned in succession toward the fortress wall, reminding Finn of fly-fishing. Each Archimedes' claw was pulled with great force by the catapult into the sides, sterns, or bows of Roman ships.

Once grasping a ship's hull, a crane operator could toss the boat up and over, into deep harbor water. Some ships were struck in the exterior bulwark. The claws whipped them airborne a considerable distance. They crashed into the city walls with enough force to reduce the ships to firewood.

As combat continued, the harbor turned blood-red. Unforeseen demise and obliteration became the Roman navy's destiny. Escaping ships positioned themselves at tenuous safe distances, only to be clutched and sunk by flying Archimedes' claws.

Finn noticed a difference in behavior between the boulders bouncing off the antigravity field in perfect predictable arcs as compared to the somewhat erratic and flight path of the claws. He recalled a similar irregular activity with metal objects used during the first lab antigravity experiments. He understood the need for Archimedes guidance system of catapults, levers, and chains to transform the claw into a usable weapon. His task tonight, if he made it through the night, was to disconnect a chain from one of the claws and hope to study its behavior without the retraction restraints.

Finn studied the propulsion system for the boulders and claws, carefully noting men with levers operating a platform securing the machine. These laborers adjusted the platform angle and the direction it faced. As the device was turned in the direction of the Roman soldiers, Finn watched devastation commence again as ground forces were pelted with a continuous spray of jagged rocks. Romans broke formation and ran in retreat.

Once the legionnaires were out of sight, boulders stopped flying. The battlefield was now the color of red. Syracusans began the tedious work of reloading their war machine. As the sun set in the western sky, the long first day of battle ended.

Finn descended a ladder, looking for a reasonable place to spend the night, hoping to access one of Archimedes' claws soon. Guards casually let him pass, as if he were a well-known citizen. He spied a well near a gate in the fortress wall and joined a group of Syracusans awaiting a turn to draw water from the common bucket. Quenching his thirst, he went into a public building and found a corner to rest until darkness allowed him to do his simple experiment.

He could see no paradox resulting from his mischief but gave little thought to the possibility of causing a convulsion in the logic of the time vortex.

His nap was short. Without realizing it, he had chosen a temple to some pagan deity in which to rest. Worshipers with oil lamps began to fill the space, and he made a sleepy but casual exit. Once outside, he headed for the cranes where the claw devices were stacked. Being stealthy was necessary as soldiers were posted up near the weapons. He searched his tool kit and found his Swiss Army Knife. The file blade had never been used. He shimmied up the outside strut of the tower securing the claws and spotted an Archimedes' claw in the shadows of the wall. Out of direct sight, Finn went about disconnecting it by filing through the chain link designed to retrieve it. Hours later, satisfied, he put the pocketknife away and separated the chain from the claw with a slight tug. Celebrating his deed with chocolate and a piece of beef jerky, he departed for safety on the path atop the city wall, seeking refuge and a nap behind the rampart.

ᘓᘓᘓ

The next day, the battle resumed just after sunup, and the rerun of the previous day's stalemate continued. This time the siege towers were brought in already erected from the far side of the harbor, across paired boats tied together by rope bound to their outriggers. Oarsmen pulled against the sea as the floating attack towers came closer to the fortifications. Showers of boulders and flaming barrels of oil pummeled the navy. Most warships retreated. The ship hauling siege towers remained a threat, and the Syracuse commanders appeared to signal the release of Archimedes' claws.

The first one dropped into the force field was repelled, and it vibrated and hooked sharply to the left. A strange flash of green light became visible as it disappeared. The crane operator scrambled to reload, discarding the broken chain, but before an effective shot with a second claw occurred, the siege tower abutted the fortress wall. A squadron of Roman soldiers was able to breach the city, slaying many citizens before the responding Syracusan defenders killed or captured the patrol. Before the second wave of Roman soldiers could mount the siege tower and the fortress wall, an Archimedes' claw ripped through the tower, pulling vessels up out of the sea and dropping them on other ships trying to retreat. Finn had seen what he needed.

The claw would not have disappeared if he had not severed the chain. He presumed that Archimedes recognized that it was pointless to send claws out into the harbor without the ability to control their direction. Luckily, no one present, except Finn himself, understood the significance of the lost claw.

Nighttime came and went. Finn was not called back as expected, and he began to analyze what may have gone wrong. He remained close to the spot behind the rampart where he had spent most of the last two days. As the sun moved across the sky, he worried that his fate might be tied to that of Syracuse at the hands of the Romans. Fortunately, there were buckets of drinking water on the parapets, and his face had become familiar to those seeking to quench their thirst.

Unfortunately, he had run out of chocolate and beef jerky. Nagging at his mind was the fear that someone would become suspicious of his lack of conversation. Thirst overcame him once more, and he went back for water. As the battle raged on both sides of the wall, he heard shouting and saw Syracuse guards running at him with weapons.

Getting up, he ran in the opposite direction. As his mind focused on the urgency of the moment, he realized his impulsive flight from his post revealed him as a spy. Fleeing from the Syracuse warriors, he ran directly into the hands of Roman foot soldiers that had scaled another part of the wall. He could only hope that Dan's computer would attempt to retrieve him before he was impaled by the swords coming at him from both sides. Resigned to a dismal fate, he thought about Claire and said a prayer. He shed his clothes, shocking his assailants, and stood for a moment in blue jeans and T-shirt, choosing a direction in which to leap.

The oncoming soldiers were slowed by the display of future fashion. As he propelled himself off the eighty-foot wall, he glanced at his gold wedding band, arms outstretched in front of him like the comic book hero Superman taking flight. His body arced in a downward path, hitting the force field exactly where the disconnected Archimedes' claw had struck it the day before.

CHAPTER 22

Archimedes' Claw

S cience and prayer seemed to have worked together this time. Finn flew through the time vortex, staring at the gold wedding band that Claire had placed on his left hand. The music he heard this time was that of a church organ.

Christmas carols, thought Finn.

❧❧❧

August 26, 2010, 2:00 p.m.:

Finn returned a little past midday on Thursday, August 26, almost a day later than expected. He arrived in the office at One Fifth Avenue humming the melody to "O Come, All Ye Faithful" and grinning his McGee smile at the joy of landing on his feet instead of his face. Somehow, he couldn't remember the moment he tucked and rolled.

Assuming it happened just before he reversed direction in the force field, he blamed memory distortion on time warp. Only recall of bracing for a fall on his face persisted. That afterthought and the organ music whirled in his mind like fire in time's tunnel. His emotions were raw. Anxiety magnified by thoughts of impending death numbed his extremities. Being captured in the fiery tornado of time travel and fearing facial injuries gave him little reason to grin.

He remembered his father telling him that a smile would prevent enemies from knowing when he was vulnerable. He had no enemies here, but emotions were spinning out of control.

Instantaneously, he stumbled across the room, confronting Maddy and Dan. Their faces mirrored expressions of relief as he flailed his arms awkwardly even after his sandaled feet had landed firmly on the Oriental carpet. Dust shed from his sandals accumulated on impact. Snagged by the Swiss Army Knife hung the garment thought to have been shed just before leaping from the parapet onto Archimedes' force field.

As an unexpected breeze blew through the office, the garment caught the slightest bit of that wind. It billowed up and out from his leg, suddenly giving Finn an insight into possible danger.

Without hesitation or warning, Finn leaped forward, tackling Dan and Maddy. With outstretched arms and using the full force of his body to protect Dan and Maddy, the impact sent them sprawling into the adjacent hallway beyond the arched door. He lay across them spread-eagle, trying to shield their bodies, when a multidirectional pulse wave exploded from the office.

Had a grand piano been dropped from the skylight into that space, the clamor would have been the same.

Finn got up first and helped Maddy to stand, while Dan, a bit dazed, arose carefully. The danger Finn had sensed appeared in the center of Dan's favorite Persian carpet, beneath it more dust than when Finn arrived. Everyone stared in disbelief at Archimedes' claw.

They all started speaking at once, until Dan took the lead in debriefing Finn. As Finn answered his friend's questions, GIM recorded precise descriptions of the Roman navy and legionnaires, fortifications at Syracuse, behavior of the force field, and loss of the claw. The supercomputer took notes and displayed them on its screen. The final analysis of the time tunnel's aberrant behavior was attributed to the lost claw.

Once it penetrated the time warp, it stayed locked in until Finn followed, with his gold wedding band acting as a catalyst. The linear function of time travel demanded that the claw be coughed out on the back edge of the organized pulse wave Finn rode home.

Scientific conclusions set, Dan moved quickly into the philosophical. He asked Finn if he had considered ramifications of the siege tower advancing close enough that Roman soldiers entered Syracuse and died in battle, not to forget the Syracusans who perished at the same time.

"Perhaps they weren't supposed to die then. What paradoxes has your interference created?" Dan scolded Finn. "What part of our world and future has been affected by the premature deaths of those men?"

Of course, the words were only rhetorical at this point, for in fact the world they knew already existed. Only in a parallel world where Finn had never released that claw from its chain would the difference be observable. Simply by accident, Dan had passed through a plateau in logic and reasoning about time travel, which was sure to give him a sleepless night.

"And look," he reprimanded further, "do you understand the danger you were in? What if you were unable to get back? What if you fell to your death or were pushed out over the harbor and drowned? Clearly you can now understand that you must desist from any further attempts at time travel until more is known about safety."

Finn remained unresponsive, still without his bearings in the present time. Then he felt sad, and he choked back tears. He had not experienced such melancholy since the death of Claire. *Uncertainty is a principle of quantum mechanics,* Finn thought, *not of my mind and emotions.* He felt cornered by Dan's logic—and shattered by it as well. Had he not planned to make the most recent trip his last? Had he not made that clear to Dan and Maddy? Why was Dan so adamant now? Tears formed in his eyes and flowed down his cheeks.

He felt restless and began to pace. His face reddened with his friend's onslaught of words. Head hanging, body shaking with sobs, he spoke to Dan of his sense of loss and sorrow.

His research had ended. Finn had finished his life's work and now felt so empty and transparent. He openly shared these emotions with his friends. His lot was to forever seek the grand design, the secret to the superglue that held the universe together. In accomplishing that, he came up short. Empty-handed, alone, on the verge of despair and uniquely restless, he sought more, not satisfied with the end game.

I have been more deeply wounded, he thought, *than if I were run through by a sword at the hands of the ancient soldiers. It would have been better than standing alone before the world with a secret I cannot share.* He pointed to Archimedes' claw, the relic of ancient war. "Is that all there is? I must even hide that from the world? I left Claire unprotected and helpless so that I could find this?" Sobbing and pacing gathered a frenetic rhythm.

Dan spoke softly and reached out to Finn. "Claire is happy, Finn, and you must understand that. She is in the presence of God and has peace from gazing at the face of

God. You must let her go. You can have peace and be happy, but you must let her go."

Dan witnessed the moment of insight on Finn's face as his eyes grew larger.

"That's it!" Finn declared. "I too will see the face of God!"

There on a table sat Finn's Nikon, reengineered for safety and containing a backup miniaturized time machine. The concept was Dan's idea, the alteration of the hardware running the microphysics was accomplished with GIM's assistance, and the device in development for the past week had been inserted into the camera while Finn was visiting the Kingdom of Syracuse.

Finn moved compulsively toward GIM and reached for the keyboard. He typed in a set of instructions while Dan watched. As he was furiously typing and pressing the enter key, Maddy was aghast when she realized he was programming GIM for immediate departure. In one motion, Finn slung the Nikon around his neck and swept the tattered costume he had worn from the floor, donning it like a cape. Facing Dan squarely, he said, "Wish me luck."

Impulse again ruled Finn, and he pressed enter and stepped into the center of the office.

Maddy pleaded, "Finn, that's not what he meant."

But the humming rose in crescendo as Dan and Maddy observed helplessly. The electrified air turned jade, and the molecules that were Finbar McGee dissolved from sight—while the clock on GIM's monitor began a seventy-two-hour countdown. Dan was relieved to see Archimedes' claw still resting on its side. He thanked God that it hadn't followed Finn into the warp.

The clock on the computer said 3:00 p.m. The destination: Jerusalem, 33 AD.

CHAPTER 23

Alpha and Omega

33 AD, Jerusalem:

The stench of death blew in Finn's face. The rematerialization of his physical body unexpectedly brought him to a place of rotting flesh and old blood. The ground was stained with it. Trampled into the earth and rocks were random patterns of maroon-brown dirt. Moist red earth spoke of recent violent death. Birds flew in unpredictable patterns, smashing into each other as they tried to flee hidden danger. No longer blue, but dark and blackish-green, the sky imitated the heart of a severe storm.

Lightning struck, and thunder shook the land repeatedly. No, that was a misperception. Wiping dirty rain from his eyes, he only saw one lightning bolt for certain. Air molecules collided and seemed to explode. The thunder jolted the earth, assaulting the very atmosphere with the fury of...nature?

Finn trembled and wrapped himself in the pre-first-century Greek-style cloak Maddy provided. The warmth gave little relief to the terrors unleashed upon him by nature. The earth continued to shake. Women wailed, crowds ran. Armored horsemen with spears fled in shock. Horses snorted with the thunder, their eyes seeming to bleed in response to a horrible vision. Was their Creator displeased?

Bolting to escape the hill, steeds catapulted their riders. Sweating profusely, they collapsed on each other. Finn was shoved to the ground. Wind crushed out of his lungs by running feet, he lay protectively over the camera hidden in his tunic. Rolled along by the frenzied mob, Finn tucked into the fetal position. He was pushed up against jagged rocks, abrading his skin. Walking sticks and horses' hooves chaotically buffeted his unprotected body. He attempted to control his reactions and not draw attention to himself.

The trembling continued. Fear was contagious. Finn, caught up in fright, was puzzled and cried out in despair. His howl joined the chorus of moans from the stampeding horde running down the hill. Falling upon each other, the injured lay motionless on the rocky path. Human flesh lay convulsing in anxiety, while others lay in death. As enormous crowds receded, the earth continued to rumble. There were violent spasms of what was possibly an earthquake, and then a blast escaped from the valley, like a giant wall collapsing.

Yes, it was a quake destroying parts of the nearby city. A moment later, the echo came evermore frightening—sounding like a massive curtain tearing. The shrill sound set off a volley of screams. Voices of desperation, horrid complaint, or serious repentance grew in crescendo from the valley.

Far from the hillside, in the pastures around the city, he watched as even the sheep bolted and ran from their shelters into the storm.

Shepherds too frightened to care about the retreating

sheep huddled together as if to shield themselves from the blackening sky.

Finn was lying in bloody mud, rain pouring on him, soaking him to the skin. Gooseflesh from anxiety covered his torso. He was confused, lost in time, perhaps. No human experience rivaled this present state—not in his life or in Claire's death. Nor had he ever read about such hellish places. Where had he gone? What impulse had carried him here? Could he survive the end of the world before his timer in Dan's office counted off seventy-two critical hours? In the moments of crisis, his crisis, he had forgotten the end point, the program he had so impulsively loaded and entered into the time machine. The omega of his time travel had arrived.

Face pressed to the dirt, he tasted bloody soil and spit it out, repulsed by the flavor of decay and evil. Pain in his ribs and back pinned him vice-like to the ground. His vantage point, facing down a long hill, confirmed throngs of people retreating rapidly. Sensing imminent danger, he was relieved when the earth stopped shaking. His torso felt the gallop of a frantic horse approaching, accompanied by the unintelligible wailing of its rider. Keenly aware he lay in the path of the runaway horse, he mustered all his strength and miraculously rolled out of harm's way. Suffocating pain persisted. Turning his head, he saw the three crucifixes on the crown of the hill. He spoke the word "Golgotha" as he passed out.

❧❧❧

Painful dreams of running endlessly through an unfamiliar ancient city emerged. Splinting muscles were wincing in agony. His joints throbbed with each dreadful pace. Racing past graveyards, his dreamlike vision perceived graves opening, the dead reawakening. Figures of men and women with burial dresses hanging from their bodies, soiled with dirt from their tombs, walked slowly past crumbling walls of the City of Peace, once called Salem, now Jerusalem. As the dead continued marching, living human beings looked at them and wailed.

His body writhed in pain and ached from injuries. Finn awakened from dreaming at night. Darkness blanketed everything. There were few city lights. The invisible new moon was expected at Passover in the Judean calendar. If the stars were not present, night blindness would have paralyzed Finn. Instinctively, he knew the cross would be vacant, but he painfully limped the way to the crown of Golgotha. Due to the darkness and rocky terrain, the trek took longer than expected. He bore the aches of his injured ribs and leg as he climbed to the summit. Clutching the camera case tightly under his cloak to protect it, he challenged himself to reach the summit without falling. Minutes passed, seeming endless. Was this an exaggeration of time travel or the sting of his contusions? Unable to check his Rolex in the blackout, he could almost feel it clicking off time. Curiosity about the duration of his journey in the vortex, if possible to assess, would have to wait until morning.

His thirst for knowledge peaked as he approached the cross. People carrying oil lamps were surrounding the crucifix. Some were Romans...or perhaps Greeks. No Jew would be there tonight, for the Sabbath began at sundown. He felt at ease some, believing he would be able to communicate in Latin or Greek. Aramaic and Hebrew were alien tongues. He felt grateful for his classical education. He would converse in Latin, for the Romans were the occupying power in Jerusalem. And if his questions left those to whom he spoke mute, he would fall back on Greek.

He approached the Cross in the dead of night, and

when he was within a meter's distance, he noticed two remarkable findings by the light of the oil lamps. The center portion of the Cross was about four meters higher than he thought possible, and the crossbar was now missing. A notch indicated its absence. If the cross were intact, it would have resembled a low "tau," the Greek letter resembling the small letter *t*. He smelled blood. The earth was soft with wetness.

He gazed upon the beam in quiet awe, trying to understand and absorb its presence. On the top of the vertical beam appeared to be a standard with a written inscription, unreadable from below in the darkness of night. One of the few loiterers by the Cross held a torch. Finn gestured to the man to come closer to the beam and hold the fire high. He was then able to make out the written words on the parchment fastened to the top of the vertical plank.

"Iesus Nazarenus—Rex Iudaeorum," he uttered aloud. Then he translated in a softer voice, "Jesus of Nazareth, King of the Jews." Had he not been convinced of his location in time and space before then, this confirmed it.

Looking around, he tried to assemble pieces of a simple puzzle. Where was the crossbar? Gesturing, he borrowed the torch from its bearer and searched the site for signs. While exploring the flat portion of the hill, he came upon several crossbars lying against a boulder. With effort, he moved the heavy timbers, finding the only one with nails covered with fresh blood. He put the beam aside gently.

Spotting ladders and rope behind the pile of wooden planks, he began to understand. The crucifixion victim would be attached to the crossbeam with ropes thrown over the top of the center post and then be pulled up until mounted. Men with ladders and tools would guide this process from either side, setting the crossbar with the victim in place to die. Upon death, removing the corpse reversed the procedure. When the crossbeam was unfastened and lowered to the ground, the executed body was removed. Surely, the crossbeam would be reused. As the remaining loiterers watched him with guarded interest, Finn sensed that they had a different plan for this particular crosspiece.

He gave the borrowed torch back to the man and said in Latin, "*Quis venio hic hodie?*" asking what happened there today.

"*A vir eram iuguolo,*" said the torchbearer, saying that a man was killed.

Finn again spoke in Latin, now comfortable that he could communicate. "*Quisnam eram ut vir?*" he said, asking who the man was.

"*Iesus Nazarenus,*" was the answer.

"*Qua est vir?*" Finn said, asking where the man was.

The man pointed. "*Tumbus per meridianus parietis!*" he said, explaining that the man was in the rock-hewn tomb by the wall.

Finn logged the parameters in his mind, judging a few landmarks that were mere shadows in the darkness. He indicated farewell by raising his hand over the stranger's as if in a blessing and turned on his throbbing leg. He proceeded slowly down the incline toward the wall of Jerusalem.

From his location, he headed northeast, searching the sky for familiar constellations to help him stay the course. He located the North Star and kept it in his peripheral vision as he limped toward Jerusalem. Fortunately, a downhill trek with his injuries was less difficult than an uphill climb.

As the walk progressed, the desperate stillness of the Jerusalem night weighed heavily. Sabbath observance kept the Jews occupied with tradition and law, but something else kept Roman occupiers and occasional Greek merchants quiescent. Even night animals and beasts were inaudible. The silence, save his aching march down the hillside, proved deafening.

Breaking through the quiet, jeering screams of crowds and wailing women arose from deep inside his head. Echoes of people in the frenzy of mass hysteria called out. Painful shrieks and moaning rolled invisibly off the hill.

Histories of crimes against the state—crimes of passion, greed, murder, and insurrection—assaulted his mind, seeping through the very rocks of the earth. Passionate mobs advancing relentlessly to the executioner's site whipped men into a boiling brew in the steaming cauldron of hell on earth.

Guards ruled the mobs with ruthlessness, flogging transgressors. Perched on their steeds and grinning with reckless abandon, soldiers wreaked terror. In this place, there existed a void. Peace was missing and unaccounted for in the darkened mist.

In his exodus from the very brink of the dark side, rats besieged him, running away from the city as if from a sinking ship. Enraged, they massed into herds, scampering away up the hill of death, confronting Finn. He dodged, skipped, and landed on aching limbs randomly to avoid vermin contact.

Inevitably, the creatures assaulted him, ripping his sandals, climbing up and inside his cloak.

Finn writhed and twisted in defense. Stinging from their claws and bites, he began to beat himself, scattering and chasing the swarms and preventing further gnawing injuries. *No nightmare could match this horror.* Seeing no relief or cessation to the rodent army torture attack, he yelled in desperation, "God save me!"

Unexpectedly, the rats ceased attacking and scrambled away quicker than their flight from the walls of Jerusalem.

Fatigue finally overcame him. Finding little shelter on the side of the hill, Finn lay down against a boulder in order to get some rest.

Suddenly, the gathering forces of nature alarmed Finn. A fierce wind surrounded him. Tornado-like winds circled him from darkened clouds in the night sky. Sounds of molecules of air colliding with ever-increasing intensity suddenly hurt his ears, forcing him to cover them. In an instant, the dark clouds flashed green light. It flickered as he watched and, without warning, rose in intensity.

The sky became a palate of whirling green glow—flashes of red lightning then orange as the tempo of the wind matched the intensity for the light in rapid crescendo. Wind song evolved into a roaring chorus of noise as if orchestras were playing competing symphonies.

He felt the lift of the field and rose with it, surrounded by the familiar patterns previously observed when traveling in the vortex. This time, the field was violent, clearly out of his control and perhaps any control. He was buffeted by opposing energies as the force consumed him. Trapped like a bottle floating in rough seas, he was at the mercy of chaos itself. It took but an instant for panic to rise inside of him.

Back in the time warp, he thought quickly of Hayhurst and how afraid he must have been to find himself locked in a similar unplanned, uncontrolled random time warp Finn was attempting to master.

Finn feared an eternity of anguish as a consequence of this unexpected maelstrom. He considered the rules of time travel he'd so carefully devised from his prior experience. Just before he was trapped in this unpredictable event, he was certain of the principle of linear time travel.

There was obviously more than one way to travel through time. He began to realize that he was witnessing the progression of time at a much slower pace than he had previously experienced when journeying in the vortex. He surmised quickly that the buffeting forces of gravitation he felt now were somehow related to the slower speed at which he was pummeling through time's tunnel.

Considering the present dilemma forced him to analyze the fail-safe device he had engineered into the Nikon. It was designed for him to deploy if he needed to escape to present time. He had built it at the urging of Maddy, with the engineering skills of GIM. It only had one function, to deliver him to a safe house in rural Illinois from anywhere he found himself in time. The conundrum was simple.

Would it work outside of time, in the tunnel of eternity in which he was now trapped? If he pushed the button now, could he safely exit to the present, or would he be stuck in the past or, worse yet, trapped in eternity, just outside the reality of time, and then be doomed to watch the eons pass by as the cosmos evolved? He would have to be desperate to press the fail-safe button on the device.

All he could do now was observe and learn for as long as he could hold out. Dan and Maddy had been right about the risk. If he ever got another chance, would he listen to reason? Would he tread carefully into the unknown, or would he be doomed to repeat his impetuous behavior. Could he learn from this if the whirlwind gave up its deathlike grip on him? Could he find redemption?

The vortex spun, and he was lifted to the stratosphere instantly.

From Finn's perspective, he could now see the earth's rotation. He witnessed the spin and the rapidly changing surface of the planet. Countless sunrises and sunsets came and went, yet he remained in the tight grip of the time warp. Suddenly, he dipped down in a rush, back toward Jerusalem. The sense of motion was like the descent of a roller coaster from the highest peak. Trapped in the unyielding force that surrounded him, history unfolded and gave him a glimpse of another time.

Unexpectedly, Finn was riding alongside Saul on the road to Damascus, encountering his anger and deadly rage at the new heretics of Judaism. Saul fell from his horse, segueing into vivid glimpses of this man now called Paul, beheaded in defending persecuted beliefs. History sped up like the roller-coaster ride he was on.

Finn was whipped again to a sudden stop and saw with his own eyes the ancient city of Rome burning. Emperor Nero, persecutor of Christians, bathed in extravagant decadence, playing his lyre at the Antium. The fury of the music matched the frenzy of the fire. Then visions of civil war, Jews against occupying Romans, and sustaining slaughter, invaded Finn's consciousness from his prison outside of time. Herod's temple was devastated in violent reaction to resistance, spurring the pagan Romans' retaliation.

He witnessed the prophecy of destruction of the temple. No stone was seen upon another. More horrifying sightings surrounded him. Pompeii erupted. The boiling lava and glowing crimson ash buried the dwellings and the inhabitants living on the mountain's perimeter. Asphyxiated by the deadly gas cloud, humans crawled in poses of death.

Finn cried out in mortal fear, believing he too would choke on the poisonous cloud. He was uncertain now that the vortex would keep him safe.

Then, in whip-like fashion, he was pulled about and soared through the ages from the edge of space, sometimes close enough to the earth to feel the friction of its spinning on its axis. Madness, not sanity, seemed to be at the throttle and brake, with split-second reversals in height and speed, acceleration and braking. Despair came quickly as he surmised that he was only along for a random excursion.

Finn faced endless images of war and demise. The ages danced and paraded before him. They assaulted him in never-ending headlines, from what he slowly understood was the safety of his time warp cruise through history. Thoughts of how to stop this ride did battle in his head. Science had never betrayed him before. There had always been an answer. It was not time to push the button. Yet without that, he had no tools to stop the process. He pined for the luxury of a control panel like in the H. G. Wells novel *The Time Machine*.

He was abruptly carried down in a thrilling rush from the stratosphere to Europe. As he was gently transported close to the surface of a congested medieval town, he saw the alarming conditions of human civilization, which he knew he could not endure. Bodies were being carried from houses and loaded into wagons. He followed the wagons from his airy perch, watching the same bodies being dumped onto a pyre. Moments later, flames engulfed the human remains. As he watched, he knew the Plague was annihilating half of Europe. The warp shuddered, and he screamed in fear, "Not here!"

It continued to vibrate, and loud quakes of sound overcame him, causing him to tremble. His worst fear might be happening. There was nothing left but the strength of his hope and a prayer that he would not wash up on these terrible shores from his involuntary time voyage. He sensed the impending end of the time warp and watched the whirling fires that surrounded him slow to a stall. He reached for the fail-safe, ready to deploy it if he landed here. Then, in the last instant, he was thrown back by the field, accelerating laterally and then upward. With it, he rose, but he felt the G-forces of the transition and then abruptly was hovering weightless again, waiting for the next event.

Below him, continuing sunrises and changing seasons loomed with the ever-menacing progression of history. He knew he was lost in time. He understood that a darkness of the human mind covered the known world. He wondered if he would come to a halt in the Eastern Mediterranean territories as the first wave of Islamic aggression absorbed the masses of humanity that lived there. Would he experience the destruction of human knowledge and witness the destruction of the Library of Alexandria? He could not bear the thought of seeing the burning of the only repository of Archimedes' written works.

Could he be set down by time's machinery in Africa and watch the slaughter and separation wrought by the Arabs at the beginning of Negro slave trade? His fears overcame him, and he lost control of himself with a rage of indignation.

Again, he descended into the cumulative geography of history to England, where rioting crowds were rampaging. The vortex hovered to a halt, tenuously holding Finn within. He watched an angry mob. They carried torches and guns, corralling women and some men into sites of public execution.

"They are guilty!" a cry arose from among the horde of people.

"Burn them alive!" another woman demanded.

"Heretics," Finn said aloud and then, correcting himself, uttered the word, "Witches."

The vortex brought him closer to the horrifying scene. He saw the terror in one woman's dark eyes as she pleaded with her captors. She began to scream as they bound her to a stake atop a bale of hay. Her shrieks echoed over the crowd even before her executioner threw his torch at the hay, and then she was engulfed in flames. The fire roared, and her agony was announced by the bloodcurdling cry from within the fire. Finn felt panic as the scent of burning flesh and hay penetrated the vortex.

His emotions ran wilder than the vicious crowds, and he began to weep for humanity. If he stopped and materialized here, the danger of being burned alive was too real. He held the trigger on the fail-safe gently, ready to squeeze down.

Another whiplash trip occurred to the edge of outer space. Finn was astonished with the vista. Remarkable forces tethered him between reality and infinity, and the march of time progressed below him. The process continued at an unbearable pace. Whipping back and forth from the edge of space to the surface of the planet, he witnessed Columbus discovering the Americas, the invention of the printing press, Martin Luther acting at Wittenberg, the industrial revolution...

As he watched, he thought, *Poor become poorer, rich become richer.* He observed the knife of war being sharpened by greed, civil war in France and America, World War I, the rise of Adolph Hitler, World War II, the Holocaust, hundreds of thousands dying or enslaved by Lenin and Marx and Mao Tse-tung, death becoming the culture in Cambodia and Vietnam, and darkness and villainy chaining themselves to North Korea.

Another jolt sent him out into space and pulled him back like a bungee cord. History sped by, and the pace increased. He saw mushroom clouds on the earth's horizon and then instantly saw atomic explosions on the surface of unknown planets. He had been flung far into his own future, past the moment of interstellar travel. He realized imminent doom with the explosion of a massive strange star that glowed blue-white and then surrounded him with green serenity. His last thought was that he had reached the final cataclysm of the cosmos and would be swept into oblivion. G-forces pressed upon him and then stopped after an eternity.

Snapping back was a shock to his body and mind. Cold wind blew, and small rocks rolled by the wind pummeled his body, as did branches broken from nearby trees, striking his flesh like missiles. The rules of time travel worked. He was in the void felt by the forces of the cosmos. He lay on the ground sore and battered by his journey. Looking around, he saw the darkness of the night and the small group with lanterns on the hill he had run from. Only then did he realize that he was back in Jerusalem in 33AD. Crawling back to the rock where he had just sought shelter, he dozed off. Some of the splintered sticks pierced his flesh as he slept. Drawn blood oozed through the borrowed garments and dripped to the ground.

His pulse climbed to dangerous heights, as did his blood pressure. An observer would have seen a man in the grip of constant convulsions as his muscles rhythmically contracted and relaxed. In this state of unresponsiveness, he could not feel the pain of the spasms but would certainly realize their result when he regained consciousness.

ᘒᘒᘒ

2010:

Almost at the same time, Dan was too uncomfortable with the chill in his guest quarters. He got up restless and for one of many times that night reset the thermostat. Worry agitated him and sleep would not come to him. He tried to get his mind around something important.

A thought had passed briefly through that same mind earlier. The harder he worked, the more elusive the thought. He got back to the edge of sleep and, again, there it was, tugging at him to remember. Then it blossomed like a flower, and he was wide-awake, contemplating the siege tower massacre that Finn had referred to in their debriefing discussion.

"What part of our world and future has been affected by the premature death of those men? Only in a parallel world where Finn had never released that claw from its chain would the difference be observable."

That was true. Nothing had changed in the world that they knew. Could it be true? There was no effect on history as Dan knew it. What about history he did not know?

Dan sprang up and out of bed, groping his way through a darkened hallway to his library. These books he had owned for years.

He opened a Rand McNally map book that had accurate maps of all the countries in the world. He randomly searched for variations in their borders. Borders he had memorized were unchanged. History books were next. After an hour of plowing through random text, he was sure of his hypothesis. So sure that he picked up after himself in the dim light, ignored his basic impulse to include GIM in his research, and dragged his weary body back to the comfort of his bed, where this time he dreamed peacefully.

ᘒᕲᘒ

33 AD:

Finn woke up with a start.

He rested for a while and let his racing heart slow down. He was unrefreshed. With new aches, he hobbled to his feet. He attempted running downhill, pain from his injured leg reminding him of consciousness and real time. Adrenaline surged, and his heart raced. He could feel his blood pressure push the limits of safety. Almost at the base, he tripped and fell. Lying in the gravel path with a fresh set of abrasions, peace prevailed.

The eastern sky became green-gray with the first edge of daylight. Remaining conscious, Finn's sighed. His pain hadn't let him rest. Looking around, he saw that the light gradually intensified. He saw a body—bloody and trampled. He reached for the man's carotid artery. The flesh felt cold with no pulse. The man was dead.

Fine considered the coming daylight and the day ahead. Using residual strength and ignoring his painful leg, he grabbed hold of the dead man's arms and drew him behind a rocky crevice.

Studying the man's headdress and noting that there were tassels and blue cords on his robe, he concluded that he was a Jew. Stripping away his clothes, Finn stole them and dressed the corpse in the tattered costume Maddy had fashioned. Finn briefly prayed over the dead man's body, abandoned the comfort of the rocky shelter, and limped out into the light of the dawn of the Jewish Sabbath. Not sure if he could pass as a Jew even with his new outfit, he maintained a slow pace toward the temple, wearing the head cover from the dead Jewish man.

He deliberately displayed the tassels attached to the four corners of the stolen garment. He gazed upon the great ancient city of Jerusalem's sand-colored stone walls and devotedly walked toward its nearest gate with his head bowed.

In the spirit of Roman conquest, King Herod, a prideful leader, compromised his ruling hand with temperance designed to appease the conquered. Herod's architects had designed many pagan temples and monuments, appeasing both Romans and Greeks. His clever concern promoted the rebuilding of the Temple of Jerusalem, a symbolic gesture to the most devout of his subjects. Temple Mount's massive creation required reshaping the top of the mountain with concrete structures to make a platform.

Although unable to tear down the temple of Solomon until all the stone for the new temple was quarried and delivered, nothing was spared in constructing this iconic building meant to reflect the ideals of Judaism and the splendor of King Herod. Herod's architects had created an elevation revealing the temple as the focal point of the traveler or pilgrim.

Views of Jerusalem rose from the horizon as a specter, transfixing observers who approached it from the foundation base of the hill upon which it was built.

After the assassination of Julius Caesar, Mark Antony appointed Herod, born of an Arab mother to govern. As most politicians did, he made sure that taxes paid by his mostly Jewish subjects were used to support construction of all temples and monuments in the city, regardless of the ultimate purpose.

In negotiations, he adopted rules of Jewish law and hired a thousand Jewish carpenters and masons to complete the inner sanctum, the Holy of Holies.

The major portion, the "temple proper," as constructed by Herod, followed the same dimensions as the Temple of Solomon. The measurements, in modern terms, were ninety feet long, thirty feet wide, and sixty feet high. In this space was the Holy of Holies—thirty feet by thirty feet in size—and the remaining space was a part of the tabernacle called the Hekal. Access to both was restricted to Jewish men.

If one entered the outer temple, an embroidered veil hung as a visible marker to the tabernacle. The veil itself was blue, white, scarlet, and purple in color. It contained two curtains. One folded back on the south side and one on the north side, enclosing the Holy of Holies. Legend stated that two teams of oxen were required to move the veil due to its massive weight and size. Priests entering the temple into the Holy of Holies were obliged to enter on a diagonal. The Holy of Holies was an empty space containing an altar of incense. The Hekal contained a seven-branched candlestick to the south and a showbread table to the north. Above the gate to the temple were golden vines and grape clusters as large as a man.

Finn trudged slowly to a gate on the wall of the city. He planned to survey the devastation wrought by the Sabbath's earthquake and storm and verify the historical authenticity of the rent in the temple veil. It was understood that if he entered the holiest parts of temple and was discovered to be a Gentile, it meant certain death.

The sun rose rapidly in the morning desert. Perspiration soaked through Finn's clothing. Parched, he craved water. Surveying the gardens and the topography outside the south wall, he made a mental note of sites that might possibly be the burial place of Jesus. Most the inhabitants of Jerusalem were inside the walls except for Greeks, Romans, and pagan slaves not observing Sabbath rituals.

Outside the gate, he hesitated, spotting a well and a cistern where he could draw water. With little understanding of how strictly Jewish law had to be followed, he proceeded cautiously. Work on the Sabbath was forbidden for Jews, and should he draw water from the well, he might be discovered as an imposter. Finn passed the well, choosing to remain thirsty.

He considered the historical conundrums of this period. There existed sharp division between the devout Jews and remaining occupants of Jerusalem. Ironically, King Herod publicly acknowledged himself as Jewish, but most historians reported his behavior as Hellenistic. Most certainly, the king could get away with drawing water on the Sabbath, but not the average Jewish man.

Finn felt uncomfortable in the deception. His moral compass was rebelling at violating rules of his Jewish brothers observing the strict code of the First Covenant. Whatsoever, he was here now, having survived the darkest of nights, motivated once again by impulse and passion. While commencing his own personal tour of ancient Jerusalem, he reflected on his last argument with Dan. He knew now that Dan was right after all about these trips being more dangerous than he himself realized. He recalled the discovery that he may have actually been chosen, groomed, and manipulated into a specific career so he would be able to invent exactly what his handlers envisioned. He could not blame Dan. Treachery was not in his heart when he planned with NASA and government agents to proceed on a course of research that would ensnare his friend in a life-altering pursuit.

He had to blame himself. Ambition, power, prestige, and the reluctance to live in the usual suburban home with the white picket fence and two and a half children were indeed his unworthy masters. Was his obsession going to lead to his own destruction? It almost had in Syracuse—and now in Jerusalem. He still had to get back from this voyage, and it was likely to be his last. By his return, if he did return, he was sure to face General Gunter's rage and his army of agents, who would doubtless treat him as their prisoner henceforth. He would never be free again once they caught up to him.

They knew about his time machine, he was sure, and they would enslave him for its technology until their other more loyal scientists had learned enough. Then what?

Would they dispose of him without a guilty thought, as if he were just a loose end that they were trying to cut off? Yes, surely that would be the consequence. It would not be a new identity and a secret oath to keep. Just as they disposed of Claire when she got in their way, it would be a bullet in the head in some isolated parking lot when he was running out to a 7-Eleven for a six-pack or something else so mundane or trivial.

He must have a plan. He would take this time to work on it and hope he would survive this last trip in order to hit the ground running when the vortex returned him to 2010.

He breached the city walls without as much as a hiccup. No one stirred or even bothered to notice his presence. He looked up at the enormous city walls, the stone buildings, and the ornate decorations of the temple as he drew closer to Temple Mount.

Once inside, the saw-toothed crowns on the city walls cast geometric shadows of dark squares elongated by the sun. The visual effect was an ever-present reminder that the ancient walls were a barrier against the less-civilized barren regions. The walls separated enclaves of humanity from the wilderness.

Houses were typically one level and were quiet, with clay roofs baking in the midday sun. Larger homes and palaces were clearly visible on crests of hills and along mighty walls. During his walk, he thought he spied David's tomb with its familiar pyramidal shape. Nearby was a palace that was consistent with Jewish tradition and architecture, and he was certain it belonged to Ciaphas.

He toured the byways of the city, in no hurry to arrive anywhere. He felt the driving thirst rising in his throat again and occupied his mind with sightseeing, occasionally stopping to rest.

Near one of his rest stops, he saw what appeared to be a Roman slave drawing water for his master. He boldly stood up and approached the slave. Speaking to the

Roman in Latin, he begged the slave to draw for him a drink from the well. The response was instant and neighborly. Finn greedily drank from the bucket handed him by the slave, indicating his appreciation. He continued to walk slowly toward the temple.

It was a steep climb, certainly not the kind he could have endured when he was dizzy from thirst. He sought the entrance to the temple and found a great number of men there. All were there for the Sabbath and the remaining days of Passover. There was evidence of structural damage to the courts, and some walls had cracked and tumbled apart. None of the men were working on repairs, only praying, either quietly or aloud, as if they did not see the damage.

Finn worked his way closer to the temple proper. The architectural accoutrements were stunning. Marble verandas and columns crowned with even more fabulous marble arches marked the temple into sections. He only wished he had had the chance to study more in preparation for this adventure. He knew there were various courts, one for Gentiles, one for women, and many others with even more refined purposes.

It was easy to spot the entrance to the temple proper. There was a passage at the great entrance. The well-known sculpted vines above the entrance shined, reflecting bright sunlight from their golden surface. Finn became cautious as he approached, for he noticed many priests assembled in the entrance. They were in deep argumentative conversation, and it was clear from their very attitude and posture that they were discussing something within the temple. One man, pointing, was leading a discussion among the rest. Beyond this group, Finn could see the famous temple veil. The colors red, white, blue, and purple were brighter than he had expected. The veil indeed appeared heavy, and on close inspection, it was clear that it was rent from the top down, almost to the bottom. The view into the inner chamber, only seen by one priest every year, was now open for any intruding eye.

Did Finn dare approach even closer? He'd come here with discovery in mind. He was satisfied that the scriptural references to the tearing of the temple veil were indeed accurate. Now was the time for self-control. Any wrong move or even overtly suspicious behavior could be destructive to his entire mission and put him in imminent jeopardy. There was nothing more important for him to learn.

Slowly and deliberately, Finn turned away from the assembly at the temple gate and withdrew into the crowd. He gauged the angle of the sun in the western sky and knew that within several hours, the Sabbath would be over. *Preparations for a place to keep watch should begin,* Finn thought. Hunger also pulled at him. He was thankful he'd had water. He would endure a long fast unless he was offered food. He had no way to purchase it.

He mused with himself at the paradox that could have been created by an errant Hershey bar wrapper in the ancient city of Jerusalem—or indeed the seeds from an apple core tossed aside. He made a mental note about adding to the rules of time travel. If he were to do it again, he would have to carefully research the potential sources of food and how to acquire it.

Finn proceeded to the garden outside the gate. Appreciating the clean desert air and the evening chill blowing gently from the west, he sat on a boulder and watched as the sun gradually set. He heard birdsong and felt comfortable in his clothes for the first time since borrowing them from the dead man.

Then suddenly he flinched as most modern men do when they think they have lost their wallets. Grabbing at his bulky clothing, he felt it, and the tension in his muscles eased. Slowly he worked it free from the depth of his garments. He took out the camera and examined it.

Opening the back, he saw the clever insert he'd spent half a week designing with GIM's instructions. He mentally thanked Dan for the idea and for installing the insert. On the back was the escape trigger, and next to it was a small warning light. He pressed the button to check the capacitor. "Full charge" was the reading. Finn examined the entire device carefully.

It was now a complete digital camera with four gigs of computer memory, an adjustable fifty-millimeter lens, and a miniaturized version of his time machine. Dan, Maddy, and GIM had applied their logic to Finn's need for secrecy. Finn had allowed GIM to copy and store the plans for the complete time/antigravity machine, and to save bulk, they'd imbedded a small flash drive in the outer case that he could use to install and load the entire ephemeris. Finn had hours left to go on this journey.

GIM's artificial intelligence had assisted with the design for cloning and miniaturizing his device in order to provide a fail-safe for his return to 2010. The interference by the rogue Archimedes' claw had disrupted his departure plans by closing the warp in time and failing to allow him access to the vortex when the power shut down in 2010. He realized that the failure of the homing function on his trip to Syracuse had almost led to his being captured and likely killed.

Even before that, a safe return on future journeys had been an obsession of his home base team at One Fifth Avenue in 2010. He imagined it would intensify and knew his friends would consider every possible option for improving the mechanism for returning him safely.

For now, he was happy with the mechanism they'd agreed on. Maddy was the one who'd insisted on programming the emergency return option to take him to a safe house location. It was a property she inherited from her grandfather in Marengo, Illinois. It had special meaning to her, and she made it part of the plan for Finn's fail-safe return.

Finn became hungrier as time grew short. He thought of contemporaries in this time and place from scripture, like John the Baptist. He ate locusts to survive in poverty and seemed to turn out all right. If Finn had a locust now, he would consider its value in appeasing his appetite. He marveled at the losses of modern man in not being able to fast as long as ancient Jerusalem men once did.

Endurance like that could form a firm commitment to the law of God. Then men were real men, none of them wimps.

He found the tomb of the Christ. It was the only tomb with guards and the fresh sent of myrrh. There were two Roman foot soldiers and a centurion, who had just arrived with a white Arabian horse, which he tied to a nearby tree.

Finn spied the tomb—a rock-hewn cave with a stone in the opening, which only three men with a horse could move. The guards made a fire to keep warm and took turns napping.

The night sky was not as black as it had been Friday night. The edge of a crescent moon and millions of stars lit up the night. There was a glow of color on the northern sky. Finn had seen photos of the northern lights and was surprised they were visible from Jerusalem. For hours, the nighttime birdsong entertained him. He dared not sleep for fear of missing something.

A piece of leather he found became his shelter. He wrapped himself in it against the dropping temperatures. Inside the makeshift covering, the odors of old sweat and tannin invaded his nostrils. He gave up cocooning and, for relief from the smell, poked his face out of the leather tent to breathe clean desert air.

Watching the stars, Finn imagined life in the future from where he was. It was already a world he knew well, filled with pain and joy in opposing poles. He was tempted to use his knowledge to reconstruct his shattered life. Dan's comments that Claire was at peace tempered his will. Dan had assured him that there was peace and happiness in just seeing the face of God. He'd assured Finn that Claire was in heaven, seeing God's face and finding eternal joy in that.

Finn waited patiently for the dawn. He had not foreseen this trip. He had jumped into the vortex of time, to this very place and date, on passion and impulse. Passion had caused him to wish to somehow share with Claire a last equivalence. He lay and waited in the shadows of the desert night, watching a tomb in a garden by the wall of ancient Jerusalem.

Waiting to see if all that he was taught, all he believed, all that he hoped for, could at last be verified. He thought of the words of Jesus chastising Thomas, telling him that those who believed without probing His wounds were blessed. Finn knew that he was an exceptional but flawed man. He was in awe of those who could accept things on faith alone. *Thomas the doubter*, Finn thought, *shared a certain kinship with me*. At least, after the fact, people referred to Thomas as "Saint." Would it be that Finn could achieve such parity? With a chill, Finn shook his head. He doubted it.

Then he noticed something: all at once, the guards fell asleep as if given some potion. No one was left standing to keep the grave secure. The very air seemed to glow white gold and warm.

Two beautifully handsome men appeared at the cover to the tomb. The stone wheel that sealed the tomb was

enormous and weighed more than was manageable by
three men with a lever and blocks. One of these "men"
rolled it back as if it were weightless. The other went inside with fresh garments. The inside of the cave glowed
at once with a magnificent light. Finn edged nearer. He
worked his Nikon loose from his clothes. It hung loosely
and like a beacon of alien status from his neck.

He held it tightly in order to remain quiet while he
approached. Realizing the foolishness of his behavior, he
berated himself. Thinking that being quiet could result in
hiding his presence from what he expected to be a spiritual encounter of the first kind seemed absurd.

He noticed the faint glow of daylight in the eastern
sky. Dawn was approaching, and with it would come the
realization of his ambitious journey. He wondered how
his presence might affect the miracle he sought to witness. Perhaps he might fall asleep like the guards as he
drew closer to the tomb, subject to the spiritual decision
made by the Highest Power. If he would just swoon into a
deep sleep and miss it all, he would understand that he
was not meant to witness what he had come to see. But
hope was rising, and he was close enough to where the
soldier slumbered—so he remained alert.

He pulled a thread from clothes he wore—done easily from the frayed edges. The clothes were well worn,
and their owner had been poor. He recalled a definition
observed in the East about the definition of dawn. It has
been defined somewhere in an ancient book he read that
the moment of dawn coincides with the human eye's ability to see the color of a thread as the sun rises in the sky.
The thread was neutral.

Finn noticed the aching in his leg. It was the beginning of the third day since the injury. He always told his
patients that the worst part of an injury was the third day.
As he was preoccupied with the tomb, the pain had acted

contrary to nature—it was subsiding. He attributed this truly unexpected benefit to his very location in time and space.

Watching, as if for an eternity, he finally noted that the light in the tomb had brightened. He stood almost by the entrance now, being careful not to block it. Anticipating the moment, Finn crouched in a balanced stance, Nikon at the ready. He thought to himself how so many scientists and tourists were compelled to see the world through the lens of a camera. He found humor in the solemn moment that he knew was unfolding and swore that he would not use the entire time gazing through the works of his single-lens reflex camera.

The luminescence grew, and the intensity was fierce but not blinding. Colors, unimaginable for a brief moment, filled his visual field. Then he saw…the Man.

His beauty was stunning in its universal appeal, yet he was ethnic. He seemed to glow in the light before dawn, but there was no other light. Finn gazed upon His face. He gazed back, tossing his long hair away from his brow to reveal wounds from the crown. His eyes were so peaceful and so deep that they drew Finn into their depth with one glance. He smiled at Finn as if to say, *I knew you would be here.*

Finn's trembling stopped. He felt warm, and the pain in his wounds disappeared. The Man was dressed in white that was brighter than the sun but cool and soothing to gaze upon. The garment He wore was draped over one shoulder, and half of His chest was bare. Finn saw the wound under his heart. Finn held up his camera and snapped a picture as the Man held out a hand to show a wound near his wrist. Dropping to his knees, Finn put the camera down and gazed upon his Lord, speechless as the dawn broke. "My Lord and my God," he shouted.

Christ turned to him and stared but said nothing.

Finn's eyes filled with tears, blurring and then blocking his vision. The heavy chains that bound his heart broke away. The pain and misery of lost love melted into a new hope, a purer love that could never die. Claire was happy. He understood it now, and the knowledge of her happiness emancipated him from the depths of captivity that were in the well of his sadness at her death. He even forgave her killer in the same moment, and an ocean of tears mixed on a cresting wave of peace overcame him. When the tears cleared, He was gone from Finn's vision, but not from his knowledge or his soul.

There was another "man." Finn assumed he was an angel. Indicating to Finn that he could go inside the tomb and see for himself, the angel exhibited patience. Finn looked at the camera and the lens. In stunning surprise, he saw what was present.

Burned into the glass lens was an image of the Lord, arms held out as in blessing, revealing the wounds on both hands and standing barefoot in the sand with wounds on His feet. Finn took the lens and placed it into his clothes.

Then he saw a clay urn, which contained myrrh used for embalming.

Taking the Nikon and its backup time travel core, he placed it into that urn and laid the urn in a rocky crevice out of the sunshine and the sight of anyone who might come by.

Hesitating, Finn entered the tomb and sat on a rock slab to gather himself, trying to understand why he was given the privilege to witness the Resurrection. Moments later, he noticed that the angel was gone without a word spoken.

He heard voices of women and looked for escape, but it was too late. They were upon the tomb. Finn hid himself in a dark corner.

They were screaming. Finn did not recognize their words but knew what they were asking.

Then the angel reappeared and spoke: "The one you seek is not here. He is risen."

The words spoken were understood immediately by all. The women turned and ran. Alarmed and not wanting to be found, knowing they would be back soon, Finn made a quick decision.

He hastily bolted for a distant grove of trees. In their thick foliage, he hid himself. From the shade of an olive tree, he watched the unfolding of a familiar history. For hours, His friends and followers exhausted themselves searching for some answers. Finally, they left the tomb unguarded.

Finn realized that time had gotten away from him once more and began to run. Furiously and fast he ran, without the limp recently acquired, but not fast enough. In a sprinter's stride, only meters from the jar of myrrh that encased his Nikon and the time machine, he reached out desperately to capture the device. Failing, he found himself engulfed by the whirling firelight of the vortex, listening to all the echoes of time.

The empty tomb of Jesus Christ

CHAPTER 24

*The Time Synapse and
the Principle of Fixed Reality*

Sunday, August 29, 2010, New York City:

Dan stood chest-to-chest with General Gunter in the foyer of the office suite at One Fifth Avenue. Flanked by two unidentified men in suits, Gunter argued with the Jesuit, demanding the current whereabouts of Finbar McGee. Dan, close to his tolerance level for this encounter, felt his blood pressure rising. He stood his ground.

Spit flying as he vociferated his tantrum inches from Dan's face, Gunter, ignored crossing the line from proper military demeanor to verbal assault on a taxpaying citizen. He launched several four-letter words and then a racial epithet.

Beads of sweat formed on his brow. His bulging veins stretched his skin, while his face turned crimson from the tempo of his assault on the priest. The men in suits stiffened, as if horrified at the violation of Dan's space and person.

Dan shifted his feet slightly, thrust his jaw forward

defiantly, and turned away from the general in a cool display of personal power. "General, we are done with this conversation if that is all you have to say," he said quietly.

Ever the Jesuit, tough to the core from youth in the Detroit ghetto, skilled in application of intellect, Dan pivoted on his heel and entered his office triumphantly. Pausing, he casually wiped the rimless glasses, part of his scholarly image, clear again. The general's party of three hesitated at the door, collecting the ruins of their pride and cooling their heels.

෴

Kathryn was inside, sitting in one of the leather chairs. Recounting recent events precipitating her trip to warn Finn, she dabbed tears from her eyes and denied culpability for leading the general to office headquarters. Kathryn went on to explain that she had gone through Finn's computer files and discovered Dan's address. Maddy, listening patiently, reacted to the shouting in the hallway with only a furrowed brow and a mild frown. She resisted her instincts and remained seated with Kathryn, assured her younger brother would handle the rabble. The frown turned to a smile when the door closed gently and Dan walked victoriously into the office. "Save that pride for when they really go, Dan. It's too early to be such a rooster."

"Sister, you're injuring my self-esteem now—and in front of company, to boot," came Dan's teasing retort. "Of course, they'll stay out there waiting for Kathryn to come out, even if Finn doesn't. I will cross their paths again by morning when I leave for my lecture at Keating Hall. They haven't arrested me yet, and I don't expect that they can. However, I do worry for Finn."

Kathryn described how the past ten-day timeline had unfolded in Syracuse. August nineteenth seemed like an eternity ago. She held out the silver triangle Finn left on his desk and offered it to Dan. She held it with tenderness but quickly understood that it represented Finn and wistfully released it to Dan's grasp.

Something in the way she gazed at it revealed the honesty in her story. Truly, she wouldn't have betrayed Professor McGee.

In revealing the history of her life since Finn's departure, Kathryn spoke initially of the general's brutality, then of her conflict of interest as a member of the CIA on sabbatical. Agents monitoring the professor bullied their way into the office moments after his car was taken for repair service. She told Dan she had expected their response, having spent the better part of the day scripting her reaction. Within hours of discovering McGee AWOL, room 0045 became temporary headquarters for Gunter's thugs in suits.

Her interrogation lasted most of the evening and the next day. Their belief that she withheld his location was unrelenting. Attached to McGee on special mission, she was supposed to be their agent on the inside. Stalemated by separate goals, the interrogation concluded with a warning that Kathryn should inform them of her daily whereabouts.

In spite of having taken control of the physics building, the authoritarian guards insisted that she continue her research in spite of intruding eyes.

Dan winced at Kathryn's recanted episode as she revealed the consequences resulting from the Internet background check following GIM's meeting with Finn. The IP address led the search locale to New York City. Then again, referencing Finn's communication with her and the transfer of files from the physics department, he just shook his head. Of course, he expected this trace, inevitable as gravity. Sleuths from the CIA under Gunter's expert command had found their man.

Dan knew Gunter would soon be knocking down the door with a warrant to search the premises, and he advised Kathryn and Maddy of this. Dan quickly updated Kathryn as to Finn's impetuous choice to jump back into the vortex. Perspiration rolled off his brow as the clock on GIM's monitor descended toward zero. He wanted to disarm Gunter with his own plea toward logic before Finn came tumbling back into the present.

With the chance of delay visibly shrinking on the clock, Dan turned off the monitor timepiece and ordered GIM to display stock market reports.

The knock on the door was authoritative. Dan walked to the front parlor and opened the lock. Still red-faced, General Gunter crossed the threshold waving a warrant. Flanked by his same two men in suits, he spoke apologetically.

Clearly understanding that his prior verbal assault required atonement, he nevertheless firmly demanded answers—with the dignity of his rank and position.

Dan had not been rattled earlier and was sticking close to his plan of defense. "General," he declared, "Dr. McGee is not here. However, his assistant, Ms. Dobbs-Moore arrived earlier. Of course, I suspect that you're well aware of that fact. We all presume that you followed her here in quest of Dr. McGee's whereabouts."

"Reverend Gilmore, your sense of my mission is a bit more sinister than its true purpose. Finn McGee is—how should I put it?—absent without leave. He is carrying government property and secrets that I am charged with keeping safe. I have no intent to harm or interfere with the good doctor. I just want to secure his protection and the safety of our government's secrets."

"Perhaps, General, your tactics and purpose are at odds with one another. I would define secret as something that no one knows, were I to be logical about it. The facts being what they are, your 'secret' is no longer a private matter. All the people present in this suite are party to it and the working supporting principles. Do you therefore plan to arrest us all and keep us prisoners? And by the way, if you did, would that guarantee that your minions of scientists could successfully reproduce Finn McGee's results without our cooperation?"

The general grunted. Frustrated, he stepped back a pace from Dan's space and shifted his weight uneasily, beginning to contract and relax his hand in rhythmic fashion—perhaps a telltale sign of his conflict.

Dan pressed on. "General, the facts are clear in this relentless pursuit of Dr. McGee that the real danger he must be protected from is our government. They have observed his career, pushing him along to the very brink of success, and now desire to use his invention as an arsenal addition. Apparently, you'll stop at nothing to achieve your goal of weaponizing his intellectual property. To me, the evidence is compelling that Finn McGee's only danger is from his own government."

Dan never lost his focus or his quiet, determined demeanor. Gunter still fidgeted and increased repeated opening and closing fist movements. Eye contact was nonexistent. Dan took it to mean that his summary outlined the truth.

Suddenly, the general gazed into Dan's eyes and spoke honestly. "Finn McGee has been our longtime project. We discovered his talents early, choosing him from a larger group of young men who, with our efforts, would blossom into the kind of genius he, in fact, is. We knew how to pull strings, push buttons, and spend money so he would simply follow the path we had chosen for him, believing it his choice. The molding process worked. Unfortunately, our prized master inventor of technology became the target of enemy interests as well. His wife, Claire, recognized this danger when she got caught up in its web. She reported being followed to Professor Hayhurst. We arranged protection for her, even provided her with a nine-millimeter pistol for self-defense.

"Fortune uncertain, an enemy agent was part of a hostage attempt to nab Claire to get to Finn. He botched it. And while struggling, he ended up shooting her dead. Finn McGee courts this same danger. My mission remains to protect him and his knowledge from falling into enemy hands."

Dan thought Gunter's accounting plausible, accepting the story as an olive branch of peace. Knowing Finn would not be dissuaded from long-held paranoia about the government's intrusion into his life, Dan offered additional information as a method of applying balm to wounds yet to be reopened.

"I know you believe in your purpose as much as Finn McGee believes in his. Understand, General, my plan is to protect Finn, too. We are as brothers in spirit. I will not destroy his faith in me. Knowing my motive, I will acknowledge that Finbar McGee is not currently here."

The general looked at his watch, asking casually if Dr. Gilmore expected him back soon. Gunter mused about Kathryn's presence and the time of her arrival, mentioning that he had been hot on her trail the minute she'd left Syracuse since she was the most likely person to lead them to Finn if their information was faulty.

CIA officers had sent him intelligence that Finn was here with Father Gilmore. Furthermore, no officer had seen him depart this famous address. The building had been under surveillance even through the peak of the hurricane.

Dan held out his hand like a good host and directed them down the regal hallway and into the large office that he and Finn had set up as their lab and staging area. The general seemed quite impressed with the understated elegance of the private offices, even with glass wall and skylight ceiling still showing the jagged crack.

Gunter assessed the view and damages. "Tsk-tsk," he uttered in empathy, assuming the cracks were caused by hurricane forces. GIM's monitor silently rolled data on the latest trades, concealing its own personality silently.

"I don't exactly know where McGee is, or when he will return, but I believe it will be soon. You can see, General, that we have collected a rather large artifact in my office."

Dan was pointing to Archimedes' claw, which the general had noticed but thought was an attempt at sculpture. Clustered about the claw were odd collections of dust, splinters of wood, and seaweed-like vegetation. A Persian carpet of tremendous value displayed all as if on a jeweler's velvet tray.

Gunter and his men, intrigued by the claw's size, studied it closely.

Even before they asked, Dan informed them that this war device had been fashioned under the direct supervision of the Greek scientist Archimedes in 212 BC. With his special gift for teaching, he gave them the complete travelogue version, as a docent would at a museum of history. Punctuating the presentation with the lunar origins of the gray dust incited group giddiness.

After adding the irony of the probable location of Ms. Liberty's torch, the group exploded with questions, which Dan patiently answered, content with the effects of his oration.

The articulations and the superfluid flux drive of the time machine were also present, but he avoided technical questions about the complex inner workings of the equipment, at least for the time being.

Dan divulged Finn's time travel exploits to date. Never at a loss for words or audience, he played professor, feeling buoyant by the collective awe. The general appeared quite pleased at the developing facts—face less red, teeth protruding from an uncontrollable grin. However, lust and greed for power were obvious. Ambition filled his eyes.

Dan, a keen observer, waited for the right moment. "General Gunter, you are struck by what I have told you—that is clear. Horizons opened by this technology are more than just a shift of paradigms. Brilliant days lie ahead for this nation and the world if this technology becomes widespread. Certainly a military asset, antigravity propulsion preempts world shattering. That science, if used properly, consistent with our country's history, should be a tremendous force for peace and vital to economic recovery from the current financial crises. Beware that the prideful use of this technology will destroy us.

"More important than use of any antigravity engine is the possibility that you see time travel in your own heart and mind. I am simply a doctor of philosophy. My interests are logic as well as moral theology. Without input from Finbar McGee, I have used reasoning and scientific method to come to an inevitable conclusion. You may remember, from exposure to physics, a principle stated by Heisenberg. The fact arrived at mathematically is that one cannot simultaneously know the location and velocity of a particle. This theory is part of a revolutionary science called quantum mechanics in its day."

Dan paused to collect his thoughts and continued. As he did, he brought his listeners close to the glass wall in the office. He was silhouetted by the panoramic views of Manhattan. Daylight to his back, he felt an advantage as they stood watching him speak with the light of day on their faces. "In preparing for this encounter with you today, I tried to read your mind. I know what you want from time travel. Sorry to disappoint you, but you cannot have it."

General Gunter stiffened and grimaced. The agents stood at ease beside him and did not react.

"Beyond my power or Dr. McGee's is ultimate truth. Bluntly and simply stated, the time traveler can go back in time to observe and learn. If he chooses, he may take action to affect the future. In opting for such a course, he will never be able to appreciate the effects of his decision, because his life experiences are fixed in time. Already familiar with the resulting history, in essence, time travel can never be used to change a political, historical, or strategic outcome, at least in the observer's eyes. I've named my hypothesis 'The Time Synapse and the Principle of Fixed Reality.'"

Shifting his gaze to the skyline of the city and cocking his head in thought, Gunter's face distorted with a frown, as if longing for a deeper explanation. He seemed perplexed indeed, as if trying to absorb the scientific principle. "But what—"

The beginning of the question was interrupted. Humming was heralding the time traveler's return. A jade mist prism appeared, followed by molecular reassembly of Dr. McGee. He appeared full stride, continuing to run through the amazed onlookers. Slowing briefly to snatch the silver triangle resting on the coffee table, he disappeared through the service exit without a word.

Gunter calmly reached for his communicator to dispatch an alert and pursuit order to forces on the street.

CHAPTER 25

The Last Train to...

August 29, 2010, New York City:

Finn had given no thought to stopping for a chat. He'd recognized General Gunter and Agents Finch and Becker and still considered them an unholy trinity. As the mist in the time field cleared, he witnessed the strain of his pursuers and Kathryn and Maddy. Finn considered the opportunity for escape when he realized that Dan held them captive by his rhetoric. In the blink of an eye, he saw the silver triangle, his last memento of family. He grabbed the triangle and took it with him.

Leaping down flights of stairs from the penthouse to the street punished his legs. Breathless, muscles throbbing, he pushed the pace, clinging to the handrail three and sometimes four steps at a stride.

While descending, almost hitting free fall speed, he formulated his plan. Still dressed in clothes of a first-century Jew, he'd fit right in with Manhattan's eclectic crowds.

Agents parked below in shiny black government-issued SUVs, would probably be looking for Professor

McGee dressed in a suit and tie or, at worst, smart casual for a hot August New York City afternoon.

The concept came to him at just the right moment. Finn halted his descent to the ground floor, approaching the entrance to the second. The door was unlocked. He tiptoed silently into the marble inlaid corridor, past variegated arches fitted with oak doors. Stained a rich brown, they granted uniformity to the lowest residential level of One Fifth Avenue. Outside of one door, a brass umbrella stand held two umbrellas. Borrowing them, he rode the elevator down to the lower level parlor.

Once in the brass compartment, he mused about being incarcerated. The lift stopped automatically, opening at the lobby.

Finn hunched his shoulders to appear smaller and attempted to sell the umbrellas to the concierge. The bronze sign over the desk announcing no solicitors didn't deter the pretend panhandler.

The burly man rose from his stool behind the counter, grabbed Finn by the shirt collar and sash on his garment, and escorted him out forcefully. Finn's old sweat smell and body odor branded him a homeless person. He reeked. In fact, the concierge handled him quickly in order to run back inside to wash his hands.

Finn surveyed the sidewalk, counting the government vehicles neatly lined in a row and walked boldly past them. His malodorous scent scattered agents out of the way. After getting his bearings, he started the forty-four-block walk to Grand Central Station. His plan: board a train out of town.

Money was his only problem now. In the SoHo District, he spotted David's Pawnshop, a Jewish Star in the window complementing the typical display of used artifacts brokered. Now past their due date for redemption, displays were offered for purchase.

Finn took off his Rolex, placed it on the counter, and asked the owner the terms for a loan. David spoke in a heavy Yiddish accent. "I will give you five hundred for the watch and fifty dollars for that outfit."

Finn, realizing an opportunity to alter his looks, made the deal and purchased an eight-dollar canvas fanny pack that could hold his precious belongings: camera lens, Swiss knife, and remaining chocolate bar. Making a comment to the broker about not needing to worry about time anymore, he departed the store and headed toward Grand Central Station at Forty-Second and Park Avenue. In the light of day, he looked exactly like everyone else, wearing his jeans and T-shirt, blending with the pedestrian crowd heading north.

Herds moved in unison once they adopted rhythm and direction. For some, the migration appeared to have purpose. In Manhattan, survival instinct, urgency of schedules, and random shoppers entering and leaving stores produced the herding illusion. People on sidewalks moved from one intersection to the next.

Crowds with grouped individuals pouring out into traffic and waiting for the all-too-brief flashing walk lights intensified the suggestion of migration. The flock's shepherds were traffic cops and electronic signals on every block.

Finn felt safe and slowed his pace, jostled by another pedestrian now and then, while zigzagging through the mass of people. An "excuse me" was rare. Most pedestrians acted as if they couldn't see him. The noise of the city reverberated from tall buildings through canyon-like streets. These skyscrapers directed the hot summer winds swirling about, randomly changing directions.

The August afternoon was bright and hot. Dripping sweat punctuated the ambient humidity. A T-shirt clinging to wet skin and the odor of a week without a shower were unusual trappings but highlighted his sense of caution as he proceeded.

Pausing at Fifth Avenue and Thirty-Second Street, Finn had to make a decision: go west to Penn Station, to leave the city in any direction, or go twelve blocks north to Grand Central Station, limiting him to one direction but providing more opportunity and more commuter trains. Grand Central it was. Walk lights never synchronized with the urgency of pedestrians as Finn edged his way into slow-moving foot traffic against the light.

Auto traffic zoomed from the left as he darted between cars. Horns blared and honked amid the growl of cars with broken mufflers. Traffic cops frantically blowing whistles and the screeching brakes were enough bedlam to cause Finn some paranoia, and he often looked over his shoulder, searching for signs of his pursuers.

The scent of diesel fuel fumes from delivery trucks was most annoying in the heat of the summer sun as it plumed up from the exhausts of the vehicles in gray clouds.

However, he tried to stay in the smoke and congestion as a defense while he pressed on. He looked through the haze and thought he spotted a government car. Taking evasive action, he darted out against a red light and into an intersection.

Suddenly, a black SUV with darkly tinted windows screeched to a halt, blocking Finn's progress. General Gunter and Agent Becker exited from the right side of the vehicle. Becker's pistol was drawn but not pointed at Finn.

Gunter ran up to Finn, grabbed his left arm, and ordered, "Come with me."

In the grasp of his captor, and almost at a run through heavy traffic, Finn kept a sharp eye on Becker's pistol. A child darted out of the crowd, away from her mother, who began screaming for someone to help catch the girl. Finn lurched out of Gunter's grip with a lateral roll and reached for the girl, catching her instantly as brakes screeched. Dividing his attention between saving the girl and eluding his captors, Finn became disoriented.

Behaving as if danger lurked everywhere, the general pulled Finn down again as he released the girl to the thankful mother. Finn was unable to free himself from the forced crouch. General Gunter's face showed real fear as he paused as if to speak to Finn. The noise in the street drowned out his words. He pulled Finn up and, with him in tow, began moving.

The general's grasp on his arm firm, Finn found himself running with Gunter toward the SUV. One, two, and then a third loud explosion came from the south. Gunter released his grip, stumbling helplessly to the pavement. The back of his uniform jacket leaked maroon, exiting a small hole. Finn bent down and turned him face-up. Gunter was gray and sweaty. More of the warm and sticky maroon fluid soaked his uniform blouse.

The general's face contorted in agony. Getting control of pain briefly, spending the last of his strength, he looked Finn in the eye and uttered, "Get lost."

After that final order, he stopped breathing.

Becker, pistol ready, searched for the source of the shots, saw his mark, and returned fire from his automatic pistol.

Rounds exploding out of the gun barrel drowned the screams of terror from the scattering pack of humanity running away from the scene. Finn ran, too—only this time toward the government vehicle. Finch behind the wheel and Finn strapped into the shotgun seat, the SUV peeled out due east on Thirty-Second Street to Park Avenue, where Finch veered left, sirens blowing, as they headed into rush hour traffic.

"You know, Professor," Finch remarked, shaking his head, "you're a difficult man to protect."

Piloting through heavy traffic, horns blowing and lights flashing, Finch focused on aggressive driving and less on conversation. Finn held onto the armrests, white-knuckled. Amid lurching and weaving, Becker brought Finn up to date on General Gunter's and the CIA's efforts to protect him. Not a word was lost on Finn, reeling with the unexpected for what seemed a lifetime. Finch explained the general's obsessions—watching over Finn and his family, concerns raised by Hayhurst, and increased security efforts after Claire became a target. He had taken Hayhurst's advice and consented to the plan not to inform Finn about the incident. Claire had been a willing participant, feeling reassured by her security detail that she would be protected. Claire herself had wanted to protect Finn from the details, as she feared his reaction would result in further confrontation. He deplored the catastrophic failure leading to Claire's death and Gunter's fatal wound while trying to rescue Finn.

Apparently, a well-trained double agent mercenary had been commissioned to gain to access to the new technology. A modern man hunter, Finn was his prey. The payer and prime mover was a known worldwide terrorist organization with deep intelligence entrenched in American colleges and postgraduate educational systems. Because of his scientific knowledge, Finn was their primary target.

Perplexed, Finn's mind whirled as truth came into focus. Gunter, perceived archenemy, was in fact his martyred protector. Finn had forgiven the general for Claire's death. Now, as erratically shifting g-forces of Finch's evasive maneuvering shook his limbs savagely, Finn forgave himself.

Whiplash was demoted to just a word after this trauma. Language was faltered at this point. Simultaneously, mind and body came to an abrupt halt—and then zoomed off in another direction at a faster clip. The light of truth and the reality of the cosmos collided in that instant and became a parable. His destiny, fostered by determination, would be to deny his pursuers their prize.

Craning his neck, Finn looked for his assailant. Luckily, a harness secured him in the passenger seat of the careening truck. He sensed the shooter was tailing in congested traffic. Weaving buses, trucks, taxis, and exhaust fumes, mingling with rising heat from the pavement, limited vision to a blur. Out of nowhere, doing an erratic dance in the jam-packed road, a motorcycle snaked its way recklessly in their direction. The rider wore black jeans and T-shirt, matching his helmet. Strapped to his chest was a holster, presumably holding a large-caliber pistol. In no position to hold anything but the handlebars, he bore down on them quickly.

Finch swerved the government-issued SUV up onto the curb with a jolt, aggressively driving on the sidewalk, pedestrians scattering out of the way. Finn feared for the lives of the frenzied people avoiding the oncoming truck by leaping into traffic lanes and open storefronts. An elderly man in a wheelchair collided with the front of the SUV. Finn looked back and saw the man sitting on the sidewalk next to the crumpled wheelchair, seeming relatively unscathed.

The victim was alive and well enough to hurl a series of curses at them, waving his arms about in wild anger. Their chaotic exodus terrorized the sidewalks of New York as Finch drove off-road for several more blocks. Flying off the walkway, they found a free lane. Two blocks short of Forty-Second Street, the SUV braked, skidding its back end into an intersection, right into the motorcycle's path.

Finn released his seat belt and opened the right front door, spilling into the street. He tumbled and his feet gained purchase as he sprinted toward Grand Central Station. Darting in and out of shop entrances, he ducked behind display shelves and kept an eye out for the man in black.

Before crashing into the SUV, the pursuer had fallen off the motorcycle. Rolling behind a parked UPS truck, he pulled out his weapon and began to rain bullets at Finch's position from behind the shiny black vehicle. Finch held his ground, but his attacker began to circle wide to the north, toward Finn. An exhausted Finn bolted though the shop door, running serpentine, advancing closer to Grand Central Station. Even with massive rush hour crowds, he weaved and dodged his way toward the terminal entrance.

The milling crowd's echoing conversation reverberated through the vast terminal lobby. Finn was within sight of his hunter. If he tripped or hesitated, he would become instant prey. Surveying the clock looming above the central information booth, indicating the next departing train, Finn spied his assailant's weapon drawn. The escape to track 110 on the lower level was blocked.

Desperate, Finn pulled himself up and over the information booth counters, shocking the attendants. Shouting at Finn, one man leaped at him, forcing a withdrawal behind a half wall to escape tackle. Serendipity played out its part with the discovery of a spiral staircase hidden from public view, connecting the main concourse with the lower level booth.

He hurried down and around the corkscrew staircase, relishing the delicious irony of another escape by spiral. Liberated from the lower information booth, he darted to track 110.

Seconds before gate closure, Finn boarded a local

toward Mount Vernon. The railcar passenger seats smelled new, in sharp contrast to Finn's one-week-shower-free state. Other travelers wisely moved away, leaving him isolated on a new leather bench. The darkness of the station tunnel gave way to the brightness of the hot August sun. As the train picked up speed, Finn peered out the window, keeping an uneasy eye out for the man in black.

"Mount Vernon Station," a voice hissed through the loudspeaker as the train slowed to a stop. Finn climbed out of his seat while the commuter car was still braking. Managing a broad gait to keep his balance, he ducked into the exit stairwell. The automatic doors snapped open, and the hot, humid air hit him in the face. Scaling all three exit stairs at once, he hit the platform at a brisk pace.

Paranoia forced a lookout for a quick exit and a chance for obfuscation. At the rear of the stopped train, on the same platform, stood his stalker. Recognizing him instantly, Finn picked up his pace to an all-out run toward the front of the commuter train. His assailant spotted him and gave chase.

The train lurched slowly forward. Finn longed for running shoes instead of sandals, but managed to be ahead of the train near the end of the ramp. Frantic for one last evasive maneuver, he shifted gears and flew into a sprint. His muscles strained. His hair flew uncontrollably. Sweat poured from his body and soaked an already foul T-shirt. Heart pounding, arms reaching, he looked back at the train and believed he could make it.

A pistol shot rang out, pinging off a metal barricade yards from his spot. Launching himself with one last effort across the tracks and into the accelerating train's path, he remembered the exhilaration of similar feats as a youth. Unfortunately, he was no longer young.

The pure desire to conquer this ultimate test of reflexes long gone dormant propelled Finn to touch track
number two's safe ground, a railroad tie.

ᏜᏜᏜ

Later, Dan and Maddy, aware of the developments,
watched a live *Eyewitness News* commentary. A reporter
was interviewing a witness. She was in her sixties and
had clearly been extremely attractive at one time. Identified as a local real estate broker named Maryann, she was
firm in her opinion of recent local events.

"The attacker was dressed in a black T-shirt and
jeans. He ran up those stairs to the exit. Yes," she confirmed, "the man with the pistol shot one time in the direction of the southbound tracks. I thought I saw a man
fall in front of the train, but when it passed, he was nowhere to be found."

CHAPTER 26

Marengo

Exhaustion overcame Finn as he assumed the identity of a homeless hitchhiker. Dirty, unshaven,
smelly, and outcast, he trusted no one as he
hitched rides from truckers at diners and truck stops, periodically begging for work and for food. He slept in coffee shops when he had the chance. Westward travel along
truck routes with small towns and villages became his life
as he gradually put distance and anonymity between himself and the assassins.

No near misses or shots had been fired since Mount
Vernon, and he found himself on his way to Maddy's
land. He stared at the map he'd borrowed from a trucker.
Marengo was about fifty miles west of Chicago. He
hoped he would be safe there.

It was the fail-safe point, was it not? No one but
Maddy and Dan would know, and they were as close to
siblings as he had.

Betrayal was not their way. *Dan would die first*, Finn
thought as he rode along in a pickup truck. "But then—
what if he did?" he babbled to himself.

"Huh? You say something?" the driver asked.

Finn turned, fatigue making him punchy. "Sorry. I was just drifting off."

The driver, dressed in old gray jeans and a white T-shirt, had more hair on his face than his head, and Finn looked at him with hope.

"How far now?" he asked, his voice trailing off again.

As the driver turned to him with a response, Finn was asleep.

"That's good, fella. You look like you could use a good nap. We still got more'n two hundred miles to Marengo."

As he was dozing off, Finn recalled his narrow escape…

❡❡❡

A sandal had flown off of his foot, tossed aside by the trailing train. So one sandal off and one on, he continued to the next platform. Hurdling into milling crowds cleared his path onto another train. Fear motivated him, and he moved like the wind through the throng. He grabbed the steel handle by the entrance to the passenger car and pulled himself up off the platform with the last of his strength. Muscles burned in his arms and back from the taxing effort.

Gaining purchase and then his balance, he watched the entrance to the car until it was well in motion. Seeing no threat, he found a seat near a window.

Inside the train leaving Mount Vernon station, he had a wide-angle view of people standing on the northbound side. He saw his relentless enemy running up a double flight of concrete stairs to a station exit. Men and women huddled and pointed at the escaping man. One woman, a well-dressed senior citizen, looked directly at Finn.

Grinning at his good fortune, he rested his head against the window. There was little doubt that he would find safety in anonymity. Secure in believing he was well on his way to a less stressful place, he closed his eyes in brief contemplation. He knew his destination now. He hoped it would remain secret.

EPILOGUE

2020, Marengo, Illinois:

In the cool silence of his private cell, Finn knelt in contemplation. At the Friary of the Franciscans of Strict Observance, spring crops had been planted and ravages of Midwestern winter repaired. Breezes brought rural scents of livestock, tended by traditional Franciscan labor, mixed with the scents of wildflowers. While June's sun descended low in the western sky, its orange horizons haunted Finn. He concentrated deeply in prayer. Footsteps breaking the peace of the moment echoed though the granite hallway.

Finn felt the approach of the guardian as his stride's cadence grew louder. The moment froze, responding to the cool of the evening. Beads of perspiration erupted on Finn's face as knocking on his door commenced. He opened the door, allowing Brother Peter into the sanctuary of his private cell.

"The time has come, Finn," whispered the guardian. "Here is the article in the journal you have been awaiting." He handed Friar McGee, now a Franciscan friar, a copy of the *American Journal of Archaeology*. The lead story announced the beginning of excavation below the tomb of the Resurrection in Jerusalem. The guardian spoke again. "I will prepare your departure immediately." Turning silently, he left Finn alone in his quarters, contemplating his new journey's urgency.

Finn, who had been ordained into the Franciscans of Strict Observance just before his sixth decade, finished the Mass he began at dawn. The guardian led him by the arm into his private office, closing the door after him. Hewn from barn board, the room was simple. Heated by a woodstove, book-lined shelves and an oak desk signified the only evidence of contemporary life. Removing a large brick from the base of a wall, Peter withdrew a wooden box from a cavity functioning as a safe and displayed the contents on the desktop.

A black velvet sack held the fifty-millimeter lens that once fit his Nikon camera. The guardian held the optics carefully, inspecting the lens and one final time cherishing the permanently sealed image of the risen Christ. Returning it to the bag's soft caress, he transferred the contents into a plain canvas carry pouch, reminding Finn of its priceless value.

A brown sealed envelope and a passport remained on the desk. The guardian revealed the gift from Dan Gilmore's charity trust.

Five thousand dollars remained after building the friary, and it was earmarked for Friar McGee's final mission. A notation on the corner of the envelope in Dan's handwriting confirmed verification. Finn's passport was up to date, held by the guardian in constant anticipation.

Friar McGee took the pouch and knelt before the guardian, receiving a final blessing. Preparing to leave, he stood, reaching under his shirt to remove what had become a personal symbol of the Trinity.

Handing the silver triangle, tarnished by time, to Peter, he asked him to forward it to Father Gilmore with blessings and prayers. Grabbing his roller suitcase, Finn turned away, walking out of the friary gates and up an endless dirt road to the Route 20 bus stop.

☙☙☙

July 2020, Jerusalem:

The Israeli bus surprised Finn. Air-conditioned against desert heat, fresh, modern seats complimented the efficient use of space as well as provided reliable service. Somehow he'd expected old European engineering, not the most advanced mass transit system in the modern world. The contrasts drawn from memory of visiting the ancient city of Jerusalem proved greater than anticipated. The city was bustling with commerce and tourists. Ever present were the soldiers and police, still in 2020 remaining vigilant, protecting inhabitants from random acts of insanity.

Terror remained a lucrative business in the Middle East. The bus came to rest in a parking lot fenced off for transportation of students and archeologists working in the dig. After waiting in a long line, everyone go ID badges distributed by the Bureau of Antiquities to hang from everyone's neck.

The most ambitious project allowed by Israelis in years was well under way. Finn, no stranger to history or archaeology, knew the rules. The excavation site just outside the Holy Sepulcher bore remnants of the pulverized road, down to the natural rock formations carved out by burial workers two thousand or so years prior. The Israeli Department of Antiquities now controlled this site. English, French, and Hebrew signage and armed guards were posted at the sole entrance and exit.

Finn unbuttoned his Roman collar signaling his

priesthood. Being dressed in a khaki T-shirt and jeans permitted carrying out his share of the dig labor.

He carried the canvas pouch, which contained Christ's lens image carefully concealed in the bottom. Tools, camera batteries, and meager rations filled the rest of the pouch. He snapped a full canteen on his belt.

By the end of the first week, working daily from dawn to sundown, Finn rested at the bottom of an open pit, once a road. Thirst from heat became his constant companion. Each worker used fine tools and brushes to remove layers of dust and rock hiding the once-lush garden with olive trees shading the hand-hewn tomb of Christ. The dig, organized to find period-specific relics, bordered the side of the tomb itself. Finn began to recognize rock formations previously visited. He made a point of working in areas most familiar, hoping to find the 2010 relic left behind.

Required by law to stop labor for the Hebrew Sabbath and his own law of Sunday rest, he arrived at the cavernous pit on a bright and early Monday morning. Myrrh jars unfamiliar to modern men caught Finn's trained, experienced eyes. He froze, transfixed on one with a still-intact lid. The pot was breaching a familiar rocky crevice. The amber clay had hardened and dried to match the color of desert sand.

He was certain it was the one he had touched in the past. Finn approached it carefully and attempted to work it loose. Under watchful eyes of guards and the master archeologist, he brushed the dust away and toiled for hours, trying to preserve the trophy's exterior. No assistance required, he clearly demonstrated the skill and professionalism of a seasoned archeologist. For the moment, traditions worked in his favor.

Dusk marked the end of the workday, the precise moment he was able to free the jar and remove its cap.

The fragrance of myrrh still lingered, escaping when the lid came off. Lengthy shadows helped Finn covertly remove a well-preserved, almost-petrified leather camera case.

Palpating the Nikon in the shadows, he confirmed the intactness of the camera and miniaturized time machine. Next, slipping the velvet bag out of his pouch, he fumbled for a new lithium battery. Like a Wizards' Club honoree, he deftly manipulated the old battery out and the new in place, without an audible click. He leaned into the camera strap loop, lifting the assembly with his neck. He replaced the velvet bag in his pouch. Seconds later, he stood in the queue of fellow workers checking out for the day. The sign-out routine was usually brief, just a signature and then a walk to the bus.

Without warning, two armed Israeli police seized him and ushered him to a waiting van. Alarmed and trying to avoid personal injury, he didn't resist as they took his pouch. The self-locking steel door slid shut, trapping him inside. Sirens wailed as he rocked back and forth in captivity. Without a doubt, his destination was police headquarters lockup. He regained composure, regretting his loss of freedom.

They'd surely examine the contents of the velvet bag and lens, and hopefully they would see it as a modern Christian symbol, not a relic from the dig. But then what? Would they search him? Would they examine the myrrh-scented leather case and strap?

The camera was surely at risk. Analyzing it, could they decipher its secret purpose? He had spent ten years in a friary, in prayer as a priest, planning for the chance to regain the time machine. He could not let a relic of modern man disturb the holy gravesite of the redeemer of man. How would that corrupt the future?

He had interfered with the past on impulse and had

repented for his behavior. Nothing left to lose but life, he feared death the least. His confidence in faith prevailed.

Intentionally, without fear and with conviction, he reached into the camera case and set a predetermined program in motion with the press of a button. The switch yielded with a scraping sound, courtesy of two thousand years of waiting. Music started, and green fog filled the van with its prism shape, expanding through the steel roof.

Something he had never witnessed before, the prism-shaped field could not be held in an enclosure and exhibited no limitations. He stood tall as the familiar symphony of time filled space, and a whirling dervish of fire enveloped him once more.

The police officer driving the van saw the field melt through its walls. He slammed his brakes to stop and turned to watch through the window. The officer's jaw dropped. Finn waved at him, grinning, and then disappearing.

The last sound he heard before he disassembled was the *Ting* of an orchestral triangle fading into nothing.

అంఅ

Dan returned from a desperate summer. Maddy's funeral had taken its toll. He'd loved his sister. Depression followed dark moments. He needed space, time, and a friend, but Finn was not there to provide the needed solace. Then the guardian sent Finn's triangle.

His black night yielded to sun as joy sprang forth in his soul, prompting prayers for Finn's success and thanksgiving.

Dan prepared his syllabus for the Logic 201 class he taught at Fordham College.

The silver triangle weighed down his papers at the

podium as he stood before the assembly at Keating Hall. "Ladies and gentlemen, logic, like math, has rules. Last year you learned the fundamentals. Today we will start applying those principles to scripture as history." He posed the question, "What do we know about Melchizedek? Genesis tells us he was king of Salem and a priest who offered bread and wine to the 'Most High' God. Hebrews tells us that he was a man without a father, without a mother, without descent, having neither beginning of days, nor end of life—"

Dan paused, giving the students a stern look. "Let us begin with that information and see what logic may tell us about this prophet."

ᏋᏒᏋᏒᏋ

Kathryn studied the box from UPS, on which the return address noted John Smith, Gettysburg, Pennsylvania. She opened the package to discover two Civil War uniforms wrapped in tissue paper. Included with them was a photo of two young wounded men in bloodied shirts, appearing strangely familiar.

One was wearing the uniform of the Union Army—and the other the Confederacy. They both wore blood-stained military caps. In the box, in familiar handwriting, a note proclaimed, *These boys were brothers.* It was signed by Professor McGee.

ᏋᏒᏋᏒᏋ

On a brisk autumn day, the diplomat arrived at the Vatican. His papers represented an emissary from the government of Israel. He was immediately ushered into a grand hallway and down marble floors into the papal office.

"Your Excellency, my government wishes you to have this. It was taken from an archaeologist suspected of removing a relic of antiquity from a dig outside the tomb of Jesus. We arrested the man, but somehow he escaped. We cannot explain this and prefer that you have it."

The image of the risen Christ emblazoned into the glass caused the pope to make the sign of the Cross as he personally sealed the lens in a parchment envelope and locked the door to the papal vault.

RULES OF TIME TRAVEL

1. Find a navigational tool that will define and identify ways to adjust the time machine in order to travel to a specific time and place.

Solution – Kathryn's ephemeris for space and time.

2. Time traveler must be accompanied with precious metal catalyst, such as silver and presumably gold and platinum, for both departure and return.

Solution – Send out digital Nikon camera retrofitted with sterling silver mirror on exploratory missions. Travel with camera or other precious metal.

3. Turning off the power to the time travel field can result in the return of the experimental time traveler. Examples: the silver triangle, H's amalgam filling, diamond (with the addition of more catalyst). Exceptions: H's body (perhaps losing the filling at the wrong moment made his journey erratic). Additional exception: turbulent electromagnetic fields of natural occurrence concurrently operating with a time journey interferes with the fail-safe and may alter the travel of a subject or add an additional subject to the vortex.

Solution – Not apparent; take extreme caution in planning, including observing weather patterns.

4. Find a replacement for Kathryn in order to control the device's timing.

Possible Solution – Use a clock or GIM to control the timing.

5. There are moral consequences involved in changing history.

Solution – Follow the rules and hope it's not too late already (e.g., torch from the Statue of Liberty may now be on the moon).

6. Secrecy is paramount.

7.All trips must have a valid purpose.

8. Travel light!

9. Time travel is linear.

10. The time spent traveling in time is real from the perspective of an uninvolved observer.

11. Real time cannot be measured from within the vortex because, by definition, the vortex is outside of time.

12. The approximate vortex interval for thirty years is one hour.

13. *Solution* – Not apparent.

14. *Postulation* – The transition of an individual to a different time, although possible, is not permanent. If one attempts to go to a destination in time and remain there, an imbalance may occur, which, like a vacuum, nature abhors!

15 Plan ahead. Food is a problem unless you have local currency, a wedding invitation, or skills at theft.

16. Dress for the location, date, and weather.

17. Have a backup plan in case your departure is prevented by unusual events in the time warp vortex. Traveling through time is like a needle pulling thread. If the thread is cut, it can be difficult to find the needle again.

About the Author

Born in Cincinnati, Ohio, raised in Hartsdale New York, Dr. Theodore Homa is a physician, seasoned history buff, and an avid science fiction enthusiast. Among his favorite themes are time travel, the unknown and places of unique historical interest. Travels throughout Europe and Asia have provided the opportunity to compliment his particular theological and philosophical areas of interest. After a long medical career devoted to his practice and consecutive weeks without free weekends, a health related calamity struck leaving him unable to work for an extended period. Utilizing the serendipitous time on his hands, he turned to inner creative talents and began to explore the world of writing fiction. Writing has always been an ultimate background career goal. After a year at the word processor in his suburban Chicago area penthouse and his summer home on Cape Cod, and with the continual support of his wife and dedicated friends, he completed his first literary work, *Archimedes' Claw*. Currently Dr. Homa continues the writer's journey, busily embarking on his follow up novel.

www.ingramcontent.com/pod-product-compliance
Lightning Source LLC
Chambersburg PA
CBHW062116170626
46813CB00002B/474